"Thank you for coming out tonight, Holt," Tory murmured.

His name felt intimate on her lips, and she wasn't sure if she liked the feeling or not. "Especially since you weren't on duty."

His eyes darkened as he watched her. "It wasn't strictly a business call, Tory." The words sounded almost reluctant, as if he'd spoken them against his better judgment.

"You know nothing about me," she whispered, her heart pounding. "And I know nothing about you. How could it be more than business?"

Slowly, almost unwillingly, he reached out and touched her cheek. His caress was feather light, stroking down her face and feathering across her lips, but she felt as if she'd been struck by lightning.

Holt dropped his hand as if the searing electricity had flashed through him, as well. *"That's* why."

Dear Reader,

By now you've undoubtedly come to realize how special our Intimate Moments Extra titles are, and Maura Seger's *The Perfect Couple* is no exception. The unique narrative structure of this book only highlights the fact that this is indeed a perfect couple—if only they can find their way back together again.

Alicia Scott begins a new miniseries, MAXIMILLIAN'S CHILDREN, with *Maggie's Man*, a genuine page-turner. Beverly Bird's *Compromising Positions* is a twisty story of love and danger. And welcome Carla Cassidy back after a too-long absence, with *Behind Closed Doors*, a book as steamy as its title implies. Margaret Watson offers *The Dark Side of the Moon*, while new author Karen Anders checks in with *Jennifer's Outlaw*.

You won't want to miss a single one. And don't forget to come back next month for more of the best romantic reading around—only from Silhouette Intimate Moments.

Leslie Wainger
Senior Editor and Editorial Coordinator

Please address questions and book requests to:
Silhouette Reader Service
U.S.: 3010 Walden Ave., P.O. Box 1325, Buffalo, NY 14269
Canadian: P.O. Box 609, Fort Erie, Ont. L2A 5X3

THE DARK SIDE OF THE MOON

MARGARET WATSON

Silhouette®
INTIMATE™MOMENTS®

Published by Silhouette Books

America's Publisher of Contemporary Romance

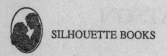 SILHOUETTE BOOKS

ISBN 0-373-07779-3

THE DARK SIDE OF THE MOON

Copyright © 1997 by Margaret Watson

Books by Margaret Watson

Silhouette Intimate Moments

An Innocent Man #636
An Honorable Man #708
To Save His Child #750
The Dark Side of the Moon #779

MARGARET WATSON

From the time she learned to read, Margaret could usually be found with her nose in a book. Her lifelong passion for reading led to her interest in writing, and now she's happily writing exactly the kind of stories she likes to read. Margaret is a veterinarian who lives in the Chicago suburbs with her husband and their three daughters. In her spare time she enjoys in-line skating, birding and spending time with her family. Readers can write to Margaret at P.O. Box 2333, Naperville, IL 60567-2333.

For Myrna, who has always been there when I've needed her. Thank you for your friendship, and for everything you've given me.

Chapter 1

She tasted the blood again, sharp and metallic. Its salty tang flooded her mouth as grinding terror enveloped her like a dark cloud, seeping through her pores and settling deep inside her. She tried to call for help, but blood gurgled in her throat.

The policeman stood over her, his knuckles clenched white around the baton poised for another blow, his dark eyes glittering with rage. Her blood was smeared on his face. His other hand hovered over the gun holstered at his waist as he waited for her to move.

Roadside gravel dug into her palms as she pushed to her knees. "Say it again," the policeman demanded. "Tell me it wasn't you." The words echoed in her head, growing louder and louder until they drowned out the hum of cars from the road, drowned out the frantic fluttering of her heart, drowned out everything but her fear and his rage.

Tory woke with a start and opened her eyes, looking around the dark room with an unfocused, disoriented gaze. There was no traffic. It wasn't dusk on a Chicago expressway. She was alone, the only sound in the room the pounding of her heart. She struggled to sit up, the residue of fear filling her mouth with a bitter taste. Her left hand automatically reached for her face, but she felt nothing except a small, thin scar high over her cheekbone. There was no blood and no pain.

"You were dreaming again," she whispered as she slowly laid down in the bed. "Only a dream."

She smoothed her hand over her face one more time and told herself to go back to sleep as she lay tense and rigid under the down comforter. Taking a deep, trembling breath, she inhaled the faint aroma of cleaning solution overlaying the old, musty smell of the house and the more distant scent of pine. She tried to ignore the frantic thudding of her heart, but she finally sighed and slid out of bed. She knew from experience that she wouldn't get to sleep easily after the dream.

Padding to the window, she looked out at the surrounding woods. The moon was a thin sliver in the clear, dark sky, its weak light barely illuminating the endless forest surrounding her. The dense, dark north woods seemed to go on forever here in Michigan's Upper Peninsula.

Everything looked different at night, she thought, resting her fingers against the cool glass as she stared into the darkness. But instead of the tranquillity she expected to feel from the silent forest, a sense of unease slowly stirred. The tall pines felt closer than they had this afternoon when she'd moved into the house. Swaying gently in the slight night breeze, their dark green branches almost seemed to be reaching out for her, beckoning her to come closer. Urging her to hurry to something waiting for her there. Fear twisted in her stomach as she stood at the window, unable to move.

Energy hummed from just beyond the edge of the woods, thick and dark and coiled like a rope. Waiting for her. Calling her name with its pulsating waves.

Hypnotized, she watched until a night bird screeched somewhere in the trees and broke the spell. Stumbling backward, she shook her head and reached for her robe.

"Honestly, Tory," she chided herself. "What's the matter with you, anyway? You should be grateful there are trees outside your window instead of gangbangers and knife fights." Her voice echoed against the bare walls, its faint tremor mocking her.

It was the stress of moving and all the problems associated with opening the clinic that had triggered the dreaded dream, she told herself as she walked down the wooden staircase in the old house. That's all. There was nothing outside her window besides trees.

The third stair from the bottom squeaked, the noise unnaturally loud in the dark, quiet house. She froze. Looking into the still living room, she searched the shadows for a moment then forced herself to continue.

Flicking on the light, she glanced at the woods again and pulled the curtain firmly closed. She hated the shiver that shot up her spine, hated the fear she couldn't seem to control. Hated knowing that everything in her life had been out of control for the past several months.

They were only trees, she told herself again. There was nothing menacing about them. It was all because of the dream. The dream had dredged up memories she'd tried hard to suppress, and it wasn't surprising that the fear had transferred itself to the first thing she'd seen.

She went into the kitchen and brewed herself a cup of tea, carefully avoiding looking out the bare window. Carrying her tea out into the living room, she sat on the couch and picked up a veterinary medical journal she hadn't had time to read because of the move. If that couldn't put her to sleep, nothing would.

She jumped when she heard the pounding on her front door, dropping her magazine onto the floor. She must have fallen asleep, she thought blearily, looking around for a clock.

It was four in the morning. Slowly she looked at the door, wondering if the knocking had been her imagination. Hoping it had. Bending, she picked up the magazine and clutched it to her chest, never taking her eyes off the door. When it reverberated with another knock, she stared at it for a moment then slowly stood. Panic washed over her.

She'd taken three steps away from the couch when she bumped into a stack of her textbooks sitting in a haphazard pile on the floor. Without taking her eyes from the door, she bent and picked one up. Her hands, slippery with sweat, could barely hold onto the thick volume. As a weapon it was a pitiful choice, but she hugged it to her as she forced herself to take one more step toward the door.

"Who is it?" she asked, barely managing to push the sound past the lump of dread in her throat.

"Eagle Ridge police. Are you all right in there?"

The deep male voice penetrated the heavy door, surrounding her with its authoritative tones. Curling her fingers more tightly around the book, hating the instinctive terror that made her shake, she stood rooted to the floor. "I'm fine," she said.

There was a pause, then the man standing on her porch spoke with a touch of impatience. "Would you mind stepping closer to the window so I can see for myself?"

"It's four o'clock in the morning. Why are you here?"

"I saw your lights and wanted to make sure nothing was wrong."

Tory edged toward the kitchen and the telephone, catching a glimpse of a shadowy figure through the lace curtain at the window. The faint moonlight glinted off the star on his chest, and the sight made her stomach clench with fear.

"Nothing was wrong until you showed up. Go away!"

A loose board on the porch squeaked, then his face appeared in the window as he peered into her living room. Terrified, she ran into the kitchen and picked up the phone. Her hand shook so badly she barely managed to punch 911. As she stood in the kitchen, trembling, waiting for someone to answer the phone, she heard a recorded voice telling her to hang up and try her call again.

The receiver slipped from her hand and crashed to the floor as she tried to replace it in its cradle. Before she could dial again, the man on her porch spoke, his voice louder and edgy. "If you don't want to come closer to the window, at least turn on your porch lights."

"I told you, I'm fine. Please leave!" She heard the desperate fright in her voice and despised her weakness, but the nightmare was replaying itself in her head, and this time she knew she was wide awake.

"I'm not going to leave until I see your porch lights go on." He sounded implacable and much too close. Closing her eyes and taking a deep breath, she eased across the room to the front door and flicked the switch that controlled the lights outside.

"Thank you." His low voice reverberated around her, and she wrapped her arms around herself, trying to ease the chill. After a moment she heard his footsteps on the porch stairs, retreating. From a long way off, he said, "Leave them on for the rest of the night."

A car door slammed and gravel crunched as he drove slowly away. Forcing herself to the window, she saw a large black four-wheel-drive vehicle on the driveway. On the side door was the insignia of the Eagle Ridge police department. Tory stood at the window, watching, until it turned onto the road and vanished into the shadows of the trees.

The breeze riffling through the pines surrounding her house sounded like a whisper of laughter.

Tory's eyes burned and her head throbbed as she stood in the door of her veterinary clinic several hours later, watching her first client leave. "Goodbye, Mrs. Taylor. Give me a call if Frisky doesn't feel better in a few days," she said, forcing a smile onto her face.

The bright sun made her head ache even more and she turned and walked into the building, glad her next client wasn't due for a little while. A mostly sleepless night wasn't the way she'd planned to prepare for her first day back in Eagle Ridge.

She was cleaning her exam room when she heard a car

outside the building. Assuming that her next appointment was early, she tried to gather her composure as she walked into the reception area. The busier she was, she told herself as the front door opened, the less time she'd have to brood about the night before.

Tory's hand tightened on the counter and her welcoming smile froze in place. She fought her instinctive flinch of fear at the sight of the police officer's uniform and forced herself to look at the man's face instead.

His dark hair was too long and carelessly combed. His face was all angles and planes, his cheeks scored with deep clefts. Eyes the color of pewter watched her, their expression carefully controlled.

"Can I help you?" she forced herself to ask, licking dry lips.

"Dr. Falcon?" His voice was deep and slightly husky and sent a shiver down her spine. She gripped the counter more tightly.

"Yes, I'm Tory Falcon. What can I do for you?" She glanced around for his pet, carefully avoiding looking at his uniform.

He waited silently until she was forced to look at his face. Holding her gaze, he stepped forward and extended his hand. "I'm Holt Adams, the police chief here in Eagle Ridge. I need to talk to you."

Reluctantly she offered her hand. His palm was unexpectedly warm as it slid against hers, and she practically jerked away from him, startled at the strength of his grip.

Wanting to take a step backward, to put some distance between them, she forced herself to stand still. "What can I do for you, Chief Adams? Is there a problem with the clinic?"

He looked startled for a moment, then he smiled. It was only a small curving of his lips, but Tory felt as if someone had knocked the wind out of her. His smile transformed his face, softening its harsh lines and turning his eyes into burnished silver. Her pulse quickened as she stared at him, fascinated by the change and unable to look away.

"This isn't about your clinic," he answered, his gaze flicking over the bare walls of her reception room before returning to her. "And I don't have a pet."

"Then why are you here?" Tory asked. Her words sounded rude, but she didn't care. After the previous night, she didn't want to have anything to do with a police officer. Especially one who looked and sounded like this man in front of her.

"I need to apologize, first of all."

"Apologize? For what?" Tory asked in a cautious voice.

"I scared you last night."

Remembered terror swept over her at his words. "That was you at my door last night?" she whispered, staring at him.

"Yes, it was." The cool look he gave her didn't have much regret in it. "I was patrolling the area and saw your lights on, and I wanted to make sure you were all right. I didn't mean to scare you."

"You terrified me," she said, welcoming the rush of anger that temporarily banished her fear. "Don't ever do anything like that again."

"I won't have to." His gray eyes held her gaze steadily. "The next time you'll know who I am."

"There better not be a next time, Chief Adams," she warned. "I don't like anyone coming to my door at four o'clock in the morning. I don't care who they are."

"I'll do whatever I think is necessary to protect the people who live in this town. That's my job and I take it seriously."

"I'm sure the city council will be pleased to hear that, but why did you single me out? Or do you check on everyone in town?"

"You're new to Eagle Ridge, and you're isolated out here." His voice was even, and his gaze didn't waver. "Not many people are up at four o'clock in the morning."

"I guess city habits die hard." Her cool tone matched his. "Now that you've apologized, I'll have to ask you to excuse me. I have work to do."

When she tried to step away from him, he put out his hand and touched her arm. His fingers barely brushed her skin, but the crackle of electricity that shot up her arm stunned her into immobility. Slowly she looked at him, seeing his uniform again, and her sudden sensual awareness of him faded as the fear rushed back. She jerked away from his touch.

"That wasn't the only reason I came out here today." His low voice strummed some chord hidden deep within her. "I wanted to make sure you knew about what's been happening in Eagle Ridge."

As she stared at him, waiting for him to continue, he seemed to move closer to her. Her heart twisted, a tiny balloon of fear swelling in her chest at the sight of his guarded eyes. "What's been happening here?" she whispered.

His eyes changed, hardened. "There have been two murders in Eagle Ridge in the past month and a half." His voice was blunt and without expression. "One was a tourist, a young woman named Carrie Stevens who stayed here for a couple of days. The other was Sally Phillips, the postmaster."

Tory could feel the blood pooling in her chest, expanding and hardening into a lump of horror. "Murdered? Two people?" She stared at the man in front of her, desperate to hear that she'd misunderstood. "Are you sure it was murder and not an accident? I don't think there's ever been a murder in Eagle Ridge."

"There has now," he said, his voice grim. "No one gets their throat cut accidentally."

"What—" Stopping herself before she could ask for more details, she bit her lip, took a deep breath and started again. "I appreciate your telling me about this. I can assure you I'll be very careful to lock my doors and windows at night."

"I think you should do more than that." He leaned toward her, and again she fought the urge to back away. "Get a dog, get a roommate or leave town, at least until we've caught the person responsible for the murders.''

His words were so unexpected that she stared at him. "Leave? I can't do that. I bought this business, and I can't just pick up and leave it.''

"Is this business worth your life?'' His silver eyes blazed at her, holding her motionless. "I don't think you understand, Dr. Falcon. No one in Eagle Ridge is safe, as far as I'm concerned. I couldn't find any connection between the tourist who was killed and Sally Phillips. Both murders appeared to be completely random. If I were a single woman of your age, I'd put as much distance as I could between myself and Eagle Ridge.''

Passionate intensity seemed to flow from him in waves. It surrounded her with hot energy, making her pulse race. When she found herself swaying toward him she jerked backward, horrified. She deliberately looked away from him, letting her gaze wander around the reception area. *Her* reception area.

She welcomed the anger that stirred at his presumption. "But you're not me, are you?'' she pointed out coolly. "I have no intention of abandoning my business. Are you telling everyone who lives here to leave Eagle Ridge?''

"Of course not. But I'm telling them all to take precautions. Can you at least move into town until whoever killed those two women is caught?''

"No, I can't. This is my home now, and I'm sure I'll be perfectly safe. After all, the murders can't have anything to do with me. They happened before I was even living here.''

Hearing her own words, she relaxed slightly. The two women were killed before she'd bought Dr. Westbrook's practice. And what she'd told this cop was true. She wasn't going to leave. She couldn't. She had come home to Eagle Ridge to exorcise her demons, because that was where they had started haunting her. She'd be damned if she would run away again.

"The murders don't have anything to do with me, and I'll be sure to be careful,'' she said with more confidence than she felt. "So you see, you don't have anything to worry about."

He stared at her. She was five feet eight inches tall, but he seemed to tower over her. "You're wrong, Dr. Falcon," he said, his voice quiet and grim. "I have a lot to worry about. And if you won't take some precautions, you're one more thing to add to the list."

"I'm not leaving."

"Are you living out here by yourself?" The look in his eyes changed, the color deepening until the silver became smoke.

Tory felt a faint heat creeping up her neck at the intensity in his gaze, and told herself fiercely that it didn't matter. "Not that it's any of your business, but yes, I'm living here alone."

Something flickered in his eyes, and she felt herself warming again. "These buildings are very isolated. There's no one within a mile of you."

"That's one of the reasons I wanted to live here." She forced a cool tone into her voice. "I used to live in Chicago, Chief Adams. After a life filled with traffic, sirens and crowds of people, I'm looking forward to the solitude."

"I used to live in Detroit, Dr. Falcon, so I know exactly what you mean. Just remember, sometimes solitude isn't all it's cracked up to be." Pain shimmered in his eyes for a moment, then was gone so quickly she wondered if she'd imagined it.

She was unable to look away from him. The top of her head only came to his chin, and his broad shoulders blocked out the light from the window behind him. His tension seemed to wind around her, drawing her closer to him. Like bottomless pools, his silver eyes hid all sorts of secrets.

Suddenly she wanted to know what those secrets were. She wanted to know why a policeman from Detroit would come to a small town in Michigan's Upper Peninsula, a world completely different from the urban jungle he was used to. What was he running away from? And what was he looking for here?

"You must have known I wouldn't leave. Why did you even bother to ask?" she asked him, watching his eyes.

He stared at her for a long moment before looking away. "I don't want anyone else to get hurt. This type of murderer picks on women who are alone, and you certainly fit that description."

"What do you mean by this type of murderer?" she asked, a new chill rippling up her spine.

He was silent for so long that she didn't think he was going to answer. Finally he turned to her with an intensity that disturbed her. "I was a homicide detective in Detroit and I've seen more than my share of murders. Enough to have learned a few things. After seeing the victims of these murders and looking at the crime scenes, I don't think this guy is finished. And I'm worried about you."

"Why me?" she whispered. "There are several hundred other people living in this town."

"None of them are young women living by themselves, away from other people. And none of them are new to the area, without friends and family here."

"I'm not new to the area. I grew up here."

"I know that. I also know that you haven't been back since you left town when you were eighteen. That was thirteen years ago."

"I was back this summer when I decided to buy this practice." She heard the defiant tone in her voice and struggled to subdue it. She didn't have to prove anything to Eagle Ridge's police chief.

"I know that, too." His voice was steady. "But you kept to yourself and didn't talk to many people. Don't try to convince me you have a lot of close personal friends here in Eagle Ridge, Doctor, because you won't succeed. You're essentially alone out here, and as the person charged with public safety in Eagle Ridge, that worries the hell out of me." His hand fisted in his pocket.

"How do you know so much about me?" she asked,

watching him with another burst of fear. It sounded like he'd done a lot of checking on her. He'd been prying into her life.

"I make it my business to find out about things before they become a problem."

"And you think I'm going to be a problem?"

He looked at her, the expression on his face frightening. "I hope not, Dr. Falcon. I damn well hope not."

Gravel spit against a car in the parking lot, the popping noise unnaturally loud in the silence. Tory drew in a deep breath and stepped away from him. "It sounds like my next appointment is here," she said, glad for the excuse to busy herself behind the reception desk.

Before he could answer, the front door opened and an older woman walked in, clutching a small dog. "Tory Falcon, I swear I would have recognized you anywhere," she cried. "Do you remember me?"

The woman was the mother of one of her high school classmates. Tory's smile was strained. "Of course I do, Mrs. Brooks. Why don't you go on into the exam room and I'll be with you in a minute."

Once she'd closed the door to the exam room, Tory turned to Holt. "I'm afraid I'll have to say goodbye, Chief Adams." She drew in a deep, steadying breath. "As you can see, I have a patient waiting, but thank you for coming out to talk to me. I appreciate your thoughtfulness."

He ignored her formal words and opened the front door, waiting for her to precede him. His other hand curled around his belt, close to his baton. Tory swallowed hard, looked at the closed door of her exam room, then followed him outside. She stood with one hand on the doorknob.

"Agatha Brooks is the town gossip," he said, once the door was shut behind them. "I don't want to be overheard." Turning slowly, he looked at her house, surrounded by trees. As she followed his gaze, an eerie feeling stole over her, the same feeling she'd gotten the night before when she woke from the dream in the darkness. Even now, in the daylight, she shivered as she looked at the trees.

"Remember what I said." Holt spoke abruptly. "And if anything bothers you, anything at all, call me. I'll be here in minutes."

Tory thought again of the dream and shuddered as cold fingers of fear traveled up her spine. Somehow she didn't think he'd meant her nightmares. And a policeman was the last person she'd turn to for comfort from that particular horror.

"Don't worry, Chief Adams," she managed to say in a level voice. "I'm no hero. If I hear anything, I'll be on the phone to the police."

Holt turned to look at her. His gaze seemed to examine her, to peer into her soul. She felt exposed, as if he was probing for all her secrets, and she looked away abruptly.

"Call me Holt," he said, surprising her. "I have a feeling we'll be seeing a lot of one another."

She spun around to look at him again, but he'd turned away and was climbing into his truck. As she watched him drive slowly from the clinic, his car seemed to slow down and almost come to a stop as he passed her house. Almost as if he was memorizing the details of it. Her stomach gave a funny lurch as she watched him. Then, with a spurt of gravel, he sped up, turned onto the highway and was swallowed by the endless trees.

Tory stood for a long time, staring at the place where he'd disappeared. It wasn't until the door of the clinic opened and Mrs. Brooks stuck her head out, calling, "Yoohoo, Tory, is everything all right?" that she turned and walked toward the low building.

Forcing Holt Adams out of her mind, she plastered a smile on her face. "Everything's fine, Mrs. Brooks. What can I do for Bosco today?"

Holt eased his foot off the accelerator and loosened his grip on the steering wheel as he sped toward the town of Eagle Ridge. Tory Falcon had surprised him. He hadn't expected her to have so much steel in her backbone. From everything the people in Eagle Ridge had told him about the girl they remembered, he'd expected the new veterinarian to be a meek, mousy woman. Instead, she hadn't backed down once. Not even when she'd wanted to.

He hadn't missed the fear in her eyes when she looked at him. A fear that had grown, not diminished, when he'd introduced himself as the new police chief. And he hadn't missed the way she'd straightened her spine and looked him in the eye as she battled that fear.

Why was Dr. Tory Falcon afraid of him? He gripped the steering wheel more tightly as he sped down the two-lane road shadowed by the towering trees. And why was it suddenly so important for him to find out?

He hadn't given any woman a second thought for more than two years. A simple evening of pleasantries had been too painful to contemplate, let alone anything resembling intimacy. The last thing he'd expected this morning as he drove out to her clinic was to be attracted to the new veterinarian in Eagle Ridge. It was the last thing he wanted.

But he remembered the way she'd held her tall, willowy body all too well, could recall with painful intensity the way his fingers had itched to free her dark red hair from the braid that hung halfway down her back. His immediate, visceral response to the woman had shocked him. A woman, if her deep green eyes were any indication, with her own share of ghosts haunting her.

Thinking about her house and her clinic, standing alone and isolated among the trees, made him press down a little harder on the accelerator. It was happening all over again. The ugliness he'd thought he'd left far behind in Detroit had followed him to this town, and now other women were threatened. He had hoped to banish those memories forever, washing them away in the peaceful, uncomplicated life of a small, rural community.

He slowed down when he spotted the figure trudging along the side of the road. Even from a distance he recognized Bobby Duvall.

Bobby, the son of the former police chief of Eagle Ridge, had been determined to follow in his father's footsteps.

When the city council hired Holt instead, Bobby had quit the police force and turned his rage on his rival. Even though there hadn't been any outright confrontations, Holt knew it was only a matter of time.

By the time he reached Bobby, the car was moving at a crawl. When the other man looked at the car, Holt let his gaze travel over him. Bobby was tall and meaty, his golden blond hair gleaming in the mottled sunlight.

Holt held his gaze and slowly tipped his hat. Bobby stared at him for a moment, his eyes even smaller than usual as they glittered with rage. Then he spit on the ground and looked away.

Holt watched him for another minute, then pressed the accelerator and drove away.

When he saw the first two houses on the fringes of town he slowed down again. Their old frame sidings were gray and weathered, but they clung to the rocky soil as if they'd sunk roots far below the surface. They reminded him of the rest of Eagle Ridge. Barely holding on by its fingernails, it prayed every year for a lot of snow and the accompanying skiers. In the economically depressed Upper Peninsula, tourism was the difference between starvation and barely scraping by.

As he drove slowly past the shops in the downtown area, with their desperately cute signs and names, he wondered again why he'd chosen to come to this particular place. With his record in Detroit he could have gone almost anywhere. He'd been interviewed in more prosperous small towns in lower Michigan, in areas with thriving industries and healthy economies. But once he'd come here, to Eagle Ridge, all the other places had faded away like they'd never even existed.

Maybe it was because this town reminded him too much of himself. Its faith was gone, and hope was nothing more than a flicker in the distance. The only difference was that in Eagle Ridge hope was renewed every year, hinging on the snowfall predictions for the winter. For Holt hope was only the remote possibility that time would dull the pain and guilt.

He pulled up in front of the small building that housed the Eagle Ridge police station, strode into his office and tossed his hat on the desk, then reached for the coffeepot. As he took a long drink of the thick, muddy liquid, the dispatcher stuck her head in the doorway.

"Don't get too comfortable, Chief. I just got a call from the veterinary clinic. Sounds like they've had some trouble out there."

Holt set the mug of coffee on his desk very carefully, trying to ignore the rush of fear that swept over him. Pulling out his gun he checked it thoroughly before sliding it into the holster. Then, reaching for his hat, he strode out the door to his truck. He was doing fifty miles an hour before he hit the edge of town.

Chapter 2

"I didn't think we needed to bother you," Tory said stiffly, watching as Holt Adams examined the rear door to her clinic. He glanced at her, his expression unreadable, before pulling out a container of powder and dusting it over the door frame.

"Who would have touched this door?" he asked.

"No one besides Teddy and me, today." Tory watched him work. "Before that, I have no idea."

"The door and the frame have been wiped clean of prints. There's only one set, and I assume they'll turn out to belong to your employee." His voice was devoid of expression, but when he turned to look at her his face was set in rigid lines. "Who discovered that the lock had been broken?"

"Teddy did. He's the young man who's working for me. He didn't notice it when he got to work, because he assumed I'd opened the back door." Tory swallowed again, trying to dislodge the swelling clot of fear coagulating in her throat as she watched the police chief. "But when he tried to lock the door after he cleaned the kennel area, he realized the lock was broken. I told him Dr. Westbrook had probably left it that way, but he insisted that I call you."

"Damn good thing, too," Holt muttered as he measured the door. "The lock is broken because the door was forced open." He turned to look at her, his eyes blazing with intensity. "Someone wanted to get in here pretty badly."

"I don't think it's that significant." Tory hoped desperately that she was speaking the truth. "This clinic has been vacant for a couple of weeks. Anyone could have tried to get inside before I got here." She swallowed and looked at the broken lock. "We had a break-in like this in the clinic I worked at in Chicago. It was just kids, looking for drugs. That's probably what happened here."

Holt slowly straightened and looked at her. "Maybe so. But the marks in this wood are fresh. Did you hear anything last night?"

"Last night?" she heard herself ask, her voice faint. "Why do you think it was last night?"

He snapped closed the toolbox he'd brought. "A hunch. We had a couple of storms last week, but the gashes in this wood look too new and raw to have been exposed to a lot of water. And until yesterday, there would have been no reason to break into this clinic."

"You must be wrong." Crossing her arms in front of her, holding on to herself, she stared at the door. "The clinic has been sitting empty for two weeks. If someone was going to break in, they would have done it before I got here. Why would a thief wait until I moved in?"

"Unless it wasn't a thief."

Tory felt the cold lump of fear expanding. "What other reason could there be for breaking into a veterinary clinic? There weren't even any animals in the kennel yet."

"I don't know, Tory," he said slowly. "I don't know why someone would try to break into an empty building. But I'm damned glad you called me." He stepped away from the door and turned to face her. "You still haven't answered my question, though. Did you hear anything last night?"

She knew she had to look away before he saw the expression in her eyes, but before she could react he'd seen it. Grabbing her arms, he pulled her around to face him.

"What did you hear?"

She tried to back away, to step out of his grasp. His hands were gentle on her arms, but she could feel his strength in their grip. For just a moment panic threatened to overwhelm her, then she jerked away from him.

As she stood in front of him, her hands hovering over the places he had touched her, she caught a glimpse of his eyes. They didn't look like policeman's eyes. The shadows that hid behind their silver depths made her think he would understand about private hells all too well. For one insane moment they beckoned her to step forward, to lower her barriers enough to tell him about her dream and her foolish fear of the trees.

Gathering her strength, she looked away from his eyes, forcing herself to focus on his uniform. Her fingers lingered almost unconsciously over the place on her arms where he had held her as she said, "I didn't hear anything last night."

"Something happened last night, Tory." His low voice rippled over her, dark and seductive. "I can tell. What was it?"

"Nothing happened," she cried. Jamming her hands into the pockets of her lab coat, she looked again at the broken lock.

Holt didn't speak, didn't move. He stood behind her, waiting. And watching her. She could feel his gaze on her, making her skin tingle. Finally she spun around to face him.

"It was my first night in a new house. I was restless, all right? I had a dream, and it woke me up." She spoke too quickly, her voice high and tight. "That's all that happened. I didn't hear anything and I didn't see anything." Nothing except the trees, and a sense of something waiting for her out there in the darkness. She drew a deep, trembling breath. "I certainly didn't hear anyone breaking into the clinic."

There was a long silence. She avoided his eyes, but she knew he still watched her. After what seemed like forever, he said softly, "I'm not trying to intrude on your privacy, but sometimes our dreams reflect something that's going on around us. Can you tell me about the dream that woke you?"

"No, I can't," she answered baldly. "It had nothing to do with the clinic, and it's not something I care to discuss."

His silence hung heavily in the crisp autumn air, and almost unwillingly she raised her eyes. When she met his gaze, a flicker of something that could be understanding passed over his face. It was gone before she was even sure it had been there.

"Can you at least tell me what time it was when you woke up?" His voice was carefully neutral.

She started to shake her head, then remembered looking at the clock when she'd gone to the kitchen to make her tea. "It was around three o'clock this morning. I was..." She swallowed once, then continued, "I was awake for a while afterward, and I didn't hear anything then, either." Trying to pull herself together, she added, "Until you began pounding on my door."

He watched her with hooded eyes. "I didn't see or hear anything when I was out here. You're probably right. Most likely it was a kid looking for a thrill or looking for something to steal. But since two people have been killed here recently, I can't afford to take any chances. Anything that's out of the ordinary could be important."

A breath of fear washed over her, followed by a rush of welcome anger. "You're trying to frighten me into leaving, aren't you?" She stared at Holt, trying to read his face. "You want to scare me into thinking I'm not safe in this house or this clinic, so I'll pack up and run. Well, I can tell you right now, Chief Adams, it isn't going to work. I didn't come back to Eagle Ridge to be scared off by some punk looking for drugs in my clinic."

He took a step closer to her. "Why *did* you come back here?" he asked softly, his gaze intense.

"I grew up in this town. What's wrong with wanting to come home?" She balled her hands in her pockets, resisting the impulse to back away. "You're the outsider here. Why did you come to Eagle Ridge, Chief Adams?"

"I don't know."

His answer startled her, but as she looked at him she realized he was telling the truth. For just a moment, raw pain burned in his eyes. As she took an instinctive step toward him, he shuttered his gaze again and looked away.

The radio on his belt crackled, and he reached for it with what looked like relief. The voice on the other end sputtered with static, and she had no idea what it was saying. Apparently Holt had no problems understanding it, because he slid the radio into his belt and faced her again.

"I have to go." His gaze drifted from her to the clinic, then to her house and back to her again. "I'm not finished here, though. I'd like to check the rest of the locks on both your buildings. When would it be convenient for me to come back?"

"I'll be busy for the rest of the day," she answered. She didn't want him to return. He made her jittery, and she was far too aware of him. "Teddy and I will check all the locks."

"I'll stop by this evening," he said as if he hadn't heard her. "I go off duty around seven o'clock. I'll be here then."

Without waiting for her to answer, he turned and left. She started after him, to tell him not to bother, but stopped when he got into his car. She didn't want to confront him. When the locksmith came to fix the clinic door she'd have him look at all the other locks. Then she'd call the police station and leave a message that it had been taken care of.

Pleased with herself, she turned and found Teddy waiting inside the back door of the clinic. Wondering how long he'd been there, she pushed open the door and walked inside. The familiar smell of a kennel enveloped her, surrounding her with the scent of dogs and cats. There were no animals in the cages at the moment, but the smell could never be completely cleaned away. The faint animal odor calmed her, reminding her that here, at least, she was in control.

"What did Chief Adams say, Doc?" the boy asked anxiously.

Tory forced herself to smile. Teddy wanted to be a vet and had begged her for the chance to work at the clinic. He was taking a year to earn some money before going to college, and she'd been grateful to get such an enthusiastic employee.

"He said you did the right thing by having me call him," she assured him. "We're still not sure what happened, but I'll get someone out here to fix the door this afternoon."

"I didn't notice anything missing," the boy continued, his eyes searching the room. "I checked the kennel, but since this is the first day we've been open I wasn't really sure what to look for."

"Thank you, Teddy," Tory said, wondering why he was so anxious about the incident. "I haven't found anything missing, either. I'm sure it was nothing."

"I hope so, Doc." He shifted from one foot to the other and wouldn't meet her eyes. "I guess I'll go mop the floor up front."

"Thanks, Teddy." She frowned as she watched him hurry out of the room. Why was he acting so peculiar? If she didn't know better, she'd think it was guilt she'd seen in his eyes. But that made no sense at all. Teddy desperately wanted to go to veterinary school, and he didn't seem stupid. He would certainly know that breaking into a vet clinic was the quickest way to insure he would never get into vet school.

Telling herself that an attempted break-in was enough to make anyone nervous, she walked to her office and reached for the files on the patients she'd seen that morning. She wouldn't think about Holt Adams and the possibility that he would return to her house this evening. She especially wouldn't think about the fact that Teddy would be gone by then, and she'd be alone with the police chief. This was *her* clinic and *her* house, and she wouldn't let anyone intimidate her here.

Except she wasn't sure that what she felt around Holt was intimidation. Pushing away from her desk, she stared at her trembling hands. After a moment she shoved them into the pockets of her lab coat.

No, what she felt was something far more powerful and frightening. The tension between them hummed like a live wire, crackling with both attraction and repulsion. The sight of his uniform made her stomach instinctively clench with terror, even though she knew rationally that Holt was not the policeman in her dreams.

But something in his eyes and his face, something about the too-quiet way he held himself, made her want to take a step closer to him. It made her want to discover his secrets. God help her, it almost made her want to tell him hers.

She couldn't do that. Gripping her desk, she stared out the window but didn't see the trees and the blue sky. Only the fear swirling around inside her was real.

She didn't need anyone in her life, especially not a cop.

Tory didn't know how long she'd been sitting, staring out the window, when a car pulled into the parking lot. She roused herself with an effort when a man removed a cat carrier from the back seat of the car. She had patients to see this afternoon, and if she wanted to make a success of this clinic, she'd better snap out of it. Pulling herself to her feet, she walked into the reception area.

"Hi, I'm Dr. Falcon. Can I help you?"

Tory looked out her kitchen window at the rapidly darkening night. Her hands stilled over the sink as she watched the vivid pinks and purples fade from the sky, replaced by the faint light of stars. It was a sight that never failed to awe her. The years of living in Chicago had made her forget how many stars there were in the sky.

Her gaze stole to the clock above the stove before she could catch herself, and she forced her attention to the dishes in the sink. Would he come anyway? a tiny voice inside her wondered. Would he ignore the message she'd left for him?

It didn't matter, she told herself. She was an adult. She could tell him politely that she didn't need his help, and thank him for coming out. She didn't have to spend any time with him. And she wouldn't. Being around the new police chief made her feel raw and exposed, as though he had the power to ferret out her secrets merely by looking in her eyes.

The crunching of gravel on the other side of the house made her tighten her grip on the dish towel. She stared out the window at the darkening sky for another moment, then carefully smoothed the towel onto its hook. Taking a deep breath, she headed toward the door.

She opened it before he knocked to find him poised on her porch with his hand raised. He lowered it slowly.

"Don't open the door unless you know who's on the other side of it." He spoke sharply, and she took a step backward.

"I heard your car." She glanced past him to the black Blazer parked in front of the house.

"You heard a car," he corrected. "You didn't know it was my car. Look out your window before you open your door."

"I knew it was you." She heard the conviction in her voice and felt a wave of red sweeping up her neck. She hoped the dim light of dusk would hide it from Holt. "Who else could it have been?" she added hurriedly.

"A lot of people." He didn't elaborate. Instead, he took a step forward. "Should I begin with your house?"

"Didn't you get my message? The locksmith is coming by tomorrow, and he can check all the locks for me."

He watched her steadily. "And what would you have done about tonight?"

"There's a dog in the clinic tonight. If he heard anyone trying to get in, he would bark and scare them off."

"What about your house? Do you have a dog here, too?"

"I checked all the locks when I moved in yesterday." Her hand tightened on the doorjamb. "They were all fine."

He stood watching her for a minute, and she shifted uneasily beneath his gaze. Finally he said, "I'm not trying to scare you, but you don't seem to understand the seriousness of this. Two women have been killed. Why won't you let me check your locks? Do you want to be the third?"

Her stomach fluttered as she looked at him. If she kept resisting, he'd wonder why she was acting so strangely. Slowly she stepped outside and pulled the door shut behind her. "Why don't we start at the clinic, since that's where the lock was broken?"

Her nerves hummed when she brushed past him. It was easier to feel in control when they were dealing with the professional part of her life. And right now she desperately needed to hold on to that little bit of control.

His footsteps slowed as they walked toward the darkened building. When she glanced at him, she realized he wasn't wearing his uniform. She tore her gaze away, not sure if that was good or bad. His faded jeans hung low on his hips, hugging him in all the right places. The sleeves of his worn plaid flannel shirt were rolled up to his elbows, revealing sleekly muscled forearms with a sprinkling of dark hairs covering them. His masculine appeal was far more potent without the uniform to hide it, and as they walked toward the clinic she almost imagined she could feel an energy coiled inside him, barely held in check.

"Any good hiking paths through these woods?" The sound of his voice flowed around her, soft on the still evening air, but when she realized what he'd asked she shuddered as she looked at the silent trees that surrounded her.

"I don't know." Her words were too abrupt, she realized, and she tried to soften them. She wasn't in the mood for questions about the woods. "I haven't had time to explore them."

"Maybe we can go for a hike together sometime."

His words were casual, an offer made on the spur of the moment, and she deliberately looked away from the trees before answering. "Maybe so," she said lightly. As she fumbled with the key in the pocket of her sweater, she felt as if the trees beckoned to her again, their voice a whisper on the faint breeze. Jamming the key in the lock, she pushed the door open and hurried inside.

Her hand was trembling as she reached for the light switch on the wall. "That door seems fine," she said brightly, hoping Holt didn't notice the way her voice quavered.

He looked at her but didn't say anything. Pulling a flashlight from the bag he'd brought, he trained it on the front door and played with the lock. From the kennel area she heard the barking of the dog she'd admitted that afternoon.

"While you're checking the door, I'm going to check on my patient," she said, moving toward the back of the building. "He needs more fluids."

Holt nodded absently as he continued to review the lock.

Pushing through the door to the kennel, Tory took a deep breath as she looked at the German shepherd lying in a cage. "Hi, fella," she crooned, opening the cage door. "Let's get a look at you."

Moving around in the treatment area, she forced both Holt and her silly reaction to the trees to the back of her mind. She had a patient to take care of, and that's all she wanted to think about.

She was just settling the dog in his cage when Holt walked through the kennel door. "The front door is fine. I don't think anyone's tampered with it. What have you done to the back door?"

"Since we couldn't get the locksmith out here until tomorrow, Teddy nailed up a hook and eye that we found in one of the drawers. I know it isn't enough, but it's the best we could do."

Holt scowled. "Let me see." He strode to the back door, and after a few minutes turned to her. "This wouldn't keep out a determined raccoon, let alone a person who wanted to get in. You can't leave the door like this."

"What do you suggest I do?" Tory gestured around the

room. "I didn't have a lot of choice. Putting a chair under the doorknob seemed a bit melodramatic."

To her surprise, Holt smiled. It made his eyes soften, turning them to liquid silver that drew her like a magnet. "You're right," he said, his voice reflecting the smile on his face. "A chair wouldn't be much good. Now one of those—" he gestured to a pile of two-by-fours in one corner "—would do the trick."

As she watched him, stunned at the way her heart raced in reaction to his smile, he found a hammer and nails and pounded one of the boards into place across the door. "That should take care of the problem until you can get the lock fixed."

Seeing the sturdy board holding the door closed, Tory did feel better. "Thank you," she said, finding herself wishing Holt would smile again.

"You're welcome." He studied her for a moment, and she busied herself with adjusting the bag of intravenous fluids that hung on the dog's cage. "Are you ready to go?"

"Yes." Reluctantly she waited for Holt to walk out of the kennel ahead of her. Switching off the lights, she moved slowly to the front door. He would want to check the doors in her house next. That meant he would have to go into her home. Rationally, she knew she should be grateful that he could make sure everything was all right. But the idea of inviting him into her home had her shaking inside. And she wasn't sure it was entirely from fear.

The last vestiges of daylight had disappeared by the time they left the clinic. The sky was smeared with stars, a million glittering points of light above them. As she glanced up, she saw the dark trees out of the corner of her eye. They seemed to press closer, reaching for her as they thrummed with an ominous energy. Involuntarily she looked at Holt. The vibrations were so strong that she was sure he could hear them, too.

"Is something wrong, Tory?" Holt asked quietly.

She shook her head, clutching her keys tightly in her hand as she hurried up the steps to the front door. "Nothing." She swallowed hard. Suddenly she was fervently glad that Holt would be in the house with her. "I'm just a little chilly," she continued weakly. "Would you like a cup of tea?"

"How about instant coffee instead?" he said, closing the door behind them.

Tory hurried over and closed the curtains, shutting out the sight of the trees. But before she could escape into the kitchen, Holt put one hand on her arm.

"What's the matter?" he asked again.

His hand was warm and hard, and she almost imagined she could feel his strength flowing into her. She took a deep, trembling breath and tried to smile.

"I guess I've been a city girl too long. I'm not used to being surrounded by woods and silence. I'm going to have to get some recordings of sirens and cars to make me feel at home." Instead of sounding flippant, she just sounded scared, and she tried to pull away from him.

He held her for a moment longer, and when he finally let her go his words surprised her. "Maybe you should listen to your instincts and get away for a while."

His words only increased her sense of uneasiness, so she tried to dismiss them. "I didn't think you could go an entire visit without trying to convince me to leave." She headed into the kitchen, determined to regain her composure. "How do you take your coffee?" she called.

"Black is fine."

He sounded preoccupied, so she risked a look into the other room. To her relief, he was engrossed with his examination of the lock on the front door and didn't look at her. She watched him for a moment before retreating.

Her heart pounded and her mouth was dry as dust. Even though he wasn't wearing his uniform, everything about Holt screamed *cop*, from the way he held himself to the quick confidence in his hands as he worked on her lock. His self-assurance and calm assumption of the authority role were disturbing and uncomfortable. But she was glad that he was here, and that disturbed her more than anything else.

Pouring tea and coffee into mugs and putting some packaged cookies on a plate, she walked into the living room and set the tray on a table. "Here's your coffee."

He looked at her and straightened. "This lock is fine. No signs of tampering." Picking up the coffee, he watched her, his eyes guarded once more. "You should have a dead bolt installed, though."

Thinking about the minuscule balance in her bank account, she cringed inside but nodded with resignation. "That's probably a good idea."

Setting his coffee down, he said, "Is there a back door into your house?"

Thankful that he was concentrating on business, Tory nodded. "And one into the basement. I'll show you where they are."

Holt pronounced the back door fine also, then they headed for the basement. Tory hadn't been down there since she'd moved in, but she remembered how dark and dusty it had been when she'd looked at the house last summer. She grabbed an extra flashlight, and they headed down the stairs.

"Cheerful place," Holt said as they looked around the open space. The basement had one light bulb that dangled from the ceiling. It barely managed to illuminate the corners of the room, and its slow movement threw grotesque shadows on the walls.

"It's a typical basement for this kind of house." The basement was part of her home, and it held no terrors for her. Whatever had been making her uncomfortable had been coming from outside, not down here.

Holt cast her a curious look and headed for the door. It had a dead bolt on it, and after a few minutes he looked up at her. "This lock is sturdier than the door. You shouldn't have to worry about it. And no one's been fiddling with it, either."

"Great," she said lightly. Heading up the stairs toward

the welcoming pool of light that spilled onto the floor, she heard him right behind her. He was close enough that she could feel his heat and energy surrounding her, just as she had as they'd walked to the clinic.

When they reached the living room she paused, uncertain. She hadn't wanted him to come into her house, but when he left she would be alone with the trees. Taking a deep breath, she said, "Would you like more coffee?"

He watched her for a while. Finally he said, "I'd love another cup."

She reached for his cup, and his fingers brushed hers when he handed it to her. The sensation that shot through her made her fingers close tightly around the cup. She cursed herself for asking him to stay as she hurried into the kitchen.

"So," she asked a few minutes later, safely seated on a chair opposite the couch. "How do you like Eagle Ridge so far?" That was an innocuous enough topic of conversation.

"I like it just fine, with one rather glaring exception."

Swallowing a gulp of her too-hot tea, she realized the question hadn't been so innocuous after all. "Do you, ah, have any idea who might be involved in the murders?"

Something flickered in his eyes before he shuttered them. Something hot and blazing, hinting at the emotions boiling below his calm surface. "Now that would be telling, wouldn't it?" His voice was deceptively mild. "Actually, I was telling you the truth earlier today. There are no leads and not a lot of evidence."

"I thought there was always evidence at a crime," she said, raising her eyebrows.

"Damn little in this case."

"Why is that?"

"The guy who did it is either smart or lucky. Personally, I hope he's lucky. Luck won't hold forever. Sooner or later, it turns."

"What if he's smart?"

His lips tightened. "Then I have to hope that he makes

a mistake." He gulped his coffee, set his mug on the table and looked at her. "And that's all I can say about the case. I shouldn't even have said that much."

Tory looked away, wondering if one of the people she'd grown up with had managed to hide a twisted sickness. She'd never been close to the people of Eagle Ridge, but the thought that someone she knew could be responsible for two murders made her feel ill.

"Think about what I said earlier." His voice was unexpectedly gentle. "You don't have to leave permanently, but you should think about moving into town until I catch the murderer."

"I can't, Holt." His name felt intimate on her lips, and she wasn't sure she liked the feeling. "Besides the fact that I couldn't afford to, I can't run away." This was the place she'd run *to*, trying to get away from her problems. "I'm here to stay."

His eyes seemed to soften as he watched her. Their silvery depths beckoned her, urging her to get lost in them. As she stared back, he murmured, "As much as I would like you to leave, I think I understand. I couldn't run away either, Tory." He sighed and closed his eyes. "I just hope the evil in Eagle Ridge hasn't noticed you yet."

"I just got here, remember?" Her voice echoed with bravado, and she knew it. "It couldn't possibly have anything to do with me."

He stood and looked at her. "I hope to God that's true."

She stood, too, watching him reach for his keys. "Thank you for coming out tonight to check my locks. Especially since you weren't on duty."

His eyes darkened as he watched her. "I didn't think of it as strictly a business call, Tory." The words sounded almost reluctant, as if he'd spoken them against his better judgment.

"You know nothing about me," she whispered, her heart pounding. "And I know nothing about you. How could it be more than business?"

Slowly, almost as if unwillingly, he reached out and

touched her cheek. His caress was featherlight, stroking down her face and across her lips, but she felt as if she'd been struck by lightning. Holt dropped his hand as if the searing electricity had flashed through him, as well.

"That's how."

She stood in the middle of the floor and watched as he let himself out the door. After a moment, she heard the rumble of his engine as he drove away.

Staring at the door, she touched her face. It still tingled where Holt's finger had traced a path down her cheek and across her lips. She didn't want this, a panicked inner voice cried. She didn't want to get involved with anyone right now, especially not a policeman. She feared and mistrusted all of them. And Holt Adams, for all his hidden secrets, was a policeman.

She wasn't sure how long she stood in the middle of the room, staring at the door. When she finally moved away, looking at the clock, she realized it was time to head to the clinic to turn off her patient's intravenous fluids for the night.

Grabbing her keys from the kitchen counter, she let herself into the night and carefully locked her house behind her. As she hurried toward the other building, she tried to ignore the trees around her, but the sense of being watched was almost overwhelming. Finally, slowing down, she glanced over her shoulder.

A dark car sat in the entrance to her property, its lights out. Watching her.

Chapter 3

For a moment Tory was too frightened to move, trapped between the clinic and the house. Finally, though, as she stared at the car, she realized it was a Blazer. A black Blazer with the Eagle Ridge police insignia on the door.

Closing her eyes, she let both relief and anger flood through her. She held tightly to her keys as she stalked toward the car.

Holt stepped onto the driveway as she approached. "What's wrong?"

"What's wrong?" she echoed, her voice rising in disbelief. "What are you doing here? You scared me half to death when I saw your car."

He started toward her, but stopped before he reached her. "I just wanted to make sure everything was all right. I knew you had to go back to the clinic, and I didn't want you to be alone."

She struggled to keep her anger at bay. Finally she said, "Thank you, I suppose, but you didn't have to do this. I've been going back to vet clinics in the evening for years." She took a deep breath and exhaled. "You just checked the doors, and you nailed a two-by-four over the broken one. What could possibly happen?''

He studied her for a moment, then shoved his hands into his pockets. "I don't know, but I don't want to find out. You're alone out here, with no one around for miles, and you're walking into a dark, empty building. Why shouldn't I worry?" He looked at her again, but in the darkness she couldn't read his expression. "And I don't think you enjoy going back there alone, do you?"

She bit her lip, thinking of all the times she'd walked into an empty clinic at night and how she had always hated it. There was always that brief moment in the dark, before she turned the lights on, when she wondered if she was really alone, that instant of holding her breath and listening to the silence. No, checking on her patients at night had never been one of her favorite parts of her job.

She looked at Holt. How had he known? Where did he get the kind of perception that allowed him to see that? "How did you know that bothered me?" she asked in a low voice.

He shrugged. "It doesn't take a rocket scientist to figure it out. No one likes walking into dark, empty buildings." His gaze found hers in the darkness, wrapping them both in a cloak of intimacy. Something twined around them, drawing them together.

Fighting the pull of him, she shook her head and looked away. "It's all right. The dog would bark if anyone was there. I always have a built-in warning system when I go to a clinic at night."

"I still don't like it." His words sounded ominous in the darkness, and she fought against her fear.

"It's not my favorite part of the job, either, but it has to be done. Thank you for being concerned, but you can't sit out here every night while I go to the clinic." Her voice softened. "Go home, Holt. You've been working for at least twelve hours. You must be exhausted."

The light from the stars gave his silver eyes a bleak, desolate look. "I'll stay until you're finished."

"It may take me a while. It's all right," she insisted. "I'll be fine."

"I'll at least wait until you're in the door safely. Once you're inside and sure everything is in order, blink the lights two times. If I know everything's all right in the clinic, I'll leave."

"All right." She didn't want to tell him how relieved she was that he'd be there until she was safely inside. She started to turn away, then paused. "Thank you again, Holt." Brushing his arm with the lightest of touches, she felt his heat and tension pulsing through her fingers and she pulled quickly away. After one more look, she turned and walked toward the clinic.

She knew Holt stood outside his truck, watching her. She could feel his gaze on her back as she walked toward the low building. When she reached the door she turned and looked at him. He stood there, still and watchful. Raising one hand, she waved, then slipped inside without waiting for a response.

It was just like any other veterinary clinic at night. The furniture cast odd shadows on the walls, and there was the sense of life beyond the next door. It was just her patient, she knew, but it never failed to unnerve her. Switching on the light, she walked into the kennel area and glanced around. Everything was secure, and it only took a minute to check the rest of the building.

She walked to the front door and flicked the light switch two times. Almost immediately she heard Holt's truck start, and she listened to the growl of his engine fade into the distance.

He was gone. She was alone out here, with no one but a sick dog for company. Shaking off the sense of unease that settled over her, she made sure the front door was locked and walked to her patient.

Fifteen minutes later, she switched off all the lights and stepped into the crisp evening air. It was a beautiful night, with not a cloud in the sky to obscure her view of the stars. She stared up for a moment, unwilling to face the trees.

Then, telling herself firmly that she was going to have to get over this ridiculous fear, she looked at her house and began walking toward it.

The trees whispered to her, calling her. The pull was stronger this time, as if they sent out invisible threads to wind around her and draw her closer. She was almost at her front door when something made her glance over her shoulder at the black forest.

A dark form stood at the edge of the trees, silent and still. Watching her. For a moment, as she stared at it, the shape didn't move. Then, without a sound, it disappeared into the trees and was gone.

Her hands shook so badly that it took long agonizing moments to unlock her front door. Once she was inside, she turned the lock then looked around frantically for something to barricade the door. She started to pull a table in front of the door, then stopped herself.

"It was probably just an animal, you ninny," she said aloud. She walked into the dark kitchen and forced herself to stand at the window and look at the woods. Nothing moved except the gentle swaying of the pines in the evening breeze. In spite of what she'd seen there just minutes ago, the sense of evil she'd felt from the forest was retreating. For the first time that day, the trees in front of her looked like just that, trees. Not the personification of evil or some mysterious power that was trying to draw her closer.

She stood at the kitchen sink for a long time, watching out the window, waiting for another glimpse of whatever she'd seen. But nothing moved beyond her window, and nothing threatened. Finally she moved away and sank down on her couch.

It was probably just a deer, she told herself. It had been dark and hard to see. It couldn't have been a person. Her closest neighbor was a mile away. Besides, no one would be in the woods at that time of night.

Maybe it was Holt, a small voice inside her head said.

She thought about that for a moment, then shook her

head. "No, it wasn't." Her voice sounded wobbly, and she tried to push that thought out of her head. It couldn't have been Holt. He'd know how much that would frighten her. He wouldn't do that.

But how well do you really know him? the same small, insidious voice continued. *You just met him today. These murders started after he came to Eagle Ridge.*

She jumped up from the couch, horrified at the thought. Who said whatever was in the woods had anything to do with the two murders in Eagle Ridge?

Walking into the kitchen, she flipped on the lights and began heating water for tea. Her imagination had really started operating in overdrive since she'd moved here. First the trees threatened her, and now she suspected the new police chief was involved in murder. That dream she had last night must have really thrown her brain out of whack.

"This is ridiculous," she said. Picking up the phone, she dialed the number for the Eagle Ridge police station.

"Eagle Ridge police. Officer Williams speaking," a young man answered. It wasn't Holt. She wasn't sure if she was disappointed or frightened.

"This is Tory Falcon. I live at the veterinary clinic about three miles out of town. I think I might have seen a prowler in the trees a little while ago."

"I'll be right there to check on it, ma'am," he answered. "I know where you are. Stay inside and don't open the door."

He hung up the phone, and she slowly replaced the receiver into its cradle. As if anything less than an act of God would get her to open her door now, she thought as she fought down a bubble of hysteria. Somehow, calling the police station seemed to give more credence to all her dark fears. "It was probably just an animal," she told herself again.

"It was probably just an animal, ma'am." Officer Williams, young and earnest, had checked the entire perimeter of the woods surrounding her house and clinic and spent a long time at the place where she'd seen the figure. "I couldn't find anything. Not even any footprints." He shifted from one foot to the other and looked at a spot behind her ear. "But I'm glad you called. We've had a bit of trouble, and you can't be too careful."

She supposed she'd call two murders a bit of trouble, Tory thought, irritated that he was trying to hide the seriousness of the problem from her. "Did you call Chief Adams?" she asked casually.

The young man looked surprised. "How did you know? We have standing orders to call him with reports of prowlers."

Tory clenched her hands in her pockets. Her heart pounded as she said, "Just wondering. What did he say?"

"He wasn't there." Williams shrugged. "It's his night off. I'll make sure he hears about it in the morning, though."

She barely heard the rest of the young police officer's instructions. She guessed she must have made the appropriate responses, because he eventually left her alone. Waiting until she heard his car leaving the driveway, she walked to the kitchen and poured the tea she'd forgotten about earlier. It was lukewarm, but she carried it with her as she turned out the lights and walked up to her bedroom.

What she needed was a good dose of fiction to make her forget what had happened. She got ready for bed and slipped underneath the down comforter, picking up the book she'd left on the nightstand. It was a romance novel by one of her favorite authors. Opening the book, she tried to lose herself in another world.

Even in the darkness, she knew she was in the forest. The thick trees, dense and close together, strangled any moonlight before it reached the forest floor. But she could feel the wind.

It called to her, murmuring her name. Begging her to go farther, drawing her deeper into the woods. To something that waited for her there, something that knew her name.

Tree branches creaked, swaying in the wind. Tiny night creatures scampered away, as if even they sensed the evil there. The smell of pine and decay was overwhelming.

She wanted to stop and turn around, to run away, but she was powerless against the force that called her deeper into the woods. Whatever was there drew her inexorably into the nightmare.

Tory opened her eyes to the darkness in her room, her heart drumming in her chest. The bed was warm, but she shivered uncontrollably, and wrapped her arms around herself. The aroma of pine slowly faded, replaced by the scent of the lavender sachets in her closet.

She stared at the white walls surrounding her and struggled to banish the memory of the dream, but it refused to fade. The trees had been so vivid, whatever beckoned her so compelling, that she was afraid to look out her window.

At least she hadn't dreamed about the policeman again, she told herself as she curled into a tight ball on her bed. Nothing had happened, she insisted as she tried to go back to sleep.

But it was no use. When she closed her eyes the voice called to her again, and she lay in bed shaking with terror. Finally pushing back the bedclothes, she pulled on her robe and walked down the stairs.

As it had the night before, the third step from the bottom creaked. By the time she got into the kitchen, her heart had slowed down to near its normal speed. She fixed another cup of tea, then walked into the living room and sat on the couch, not even bothering to turn on the lights. Staring at the curtained windows, she sipped the hot tea in the darkness.

"Dammit, Jack, why didn't you call me?" Holt glared at the young police officer, who looked at him, bewildered.

"I did call you, but you weren't home. I checked it out and everything was fine. It was probably just her imagination. After I got back to the office, I didn't think there was any reason to bother you until this morning."

"No reason to bother me?" Holt heard his voice rising and struggled to maintain his hold on his temper. "What about the little matter of two unsolved murders?"

Officer Williams flushed. "I didn't see any footprints where she claimed she saw the prowler. There were no cigarette butts, no candy wrappers, nothing. There wasn't anything there, Chief. I figured this morning would be soon enough."

"You figured wrong. From now on, if you get a report of a prowler, I want to know about it if you have to call me every fifteen minutes all night."

"Sure, Chief." The young man looked at him and shrugged. "You're the boss."

"Someone has to take this seriously," Holt said grimly. "I don't want another murder in Eagle Ridge."

"The guy is probably a thousand miles away from here by now." Williams spouted the popular line around town. Holt just looked at him.

"Whose life are you willing to bet on that?"

Williams flushed again. "I'll be more careful next time," he muttered.

"Damn right you will." Holt stared out the window. As soon as he could, he'd get out to talk to Tory about what she'd seen the night before and check out the area himself. Williams's glib assurances about not finding anything made him uneasy. Even if Tory had only seen an animal, there should be some evidence.

As if by thinking about her he had conjured her up, he saw Tory walk into the small post office across the street from the police station. Ignoring the rush of heat he felt, he stood casually and reached for his jacket. By the time he crossed the street, she was walking out the door.

When she saw him approaching she stopped abruptly. Color washed over her face, then faded until her skin looked bleached. Her gaze darting frantically around him, she looked like a trapped animal searching for a way to escape.

"Good morning," he said softly, watching her.

She licked her lips. "Good morning, Chief." She stepped around him and started down the sidewalk, and he fell into step beside her.

"Why didn't you call me last night?" He spoke in a low voice, but she flinched as if he had yelled at the top of his lungs.

Walking a little faster, she answered without looking at him. "I did. Officer Williams was very helpful."

"I know you called Jack, and I'm glad you did. I meant, why didn't you call me at home after you talked to him?" He heard the anger swirling in his voice and tried to rein it in.

At that she looked at him, an incredulous expression on her face. "That would have been somewhat presumptuous of me, don't you think? After all, I hardly know you."

He wanted to reach for her hand, but knew he didn't dare. "You know I would have wanted you to, don't you?" he murmured.

"You weren't even home." She slanted him a look, her eyes wary. "Officer Williams told me he tried to call you."

"I was in the shower when Jack called." Glancing at the small police station, his lips thinned. "Next time, he'll call until he gets hold of me."

They walked in silence for a while, and he realized she was heading for her truck. "What are you doing in town today, anyway? Don't you have patients to see?"

"Even vets get a break for lunch." She glanced at him, her eyes still guarded. When he looked back, she immediately looked away. "I had to make sure the new postmaster knew I was living at the clinic. Most of my supplies will come by mail, and I can't afford to miss any shipments."

"Since this is your lunch hour, why don't we get something to eat while you're here? I'd like to ask you about what happened last night."

They'd almost reached her truck, and he could see her pause. After what seemed like a long time, she slowly nodded. "All right. I have some questions of my own."

They turned and headed toward the small café down the block from the police station. Neither of them spoke as they walked. He could almost feel the wall she'd thrown up between them, and wondered why.

As they reached the café her steps slowed, and she looked in the window. He reached for the door, but stopped as she stiffened beside him.

"What's wrong?"

She didn't answer, just continued to stare. Finally she turned to him. "I'm not really hungry, I guess. Would you mind if we went somewhere else to talk? Somewhere a little more private, maybe?"

He nodded. "That's probably a good idea." He struggled to keep his voice casual. "I don't particularly want our conversation overheard."

He saw the flash of relief in her face. "I'd rather no one else knows about what happened last night."

As she turned away, he looked into the small café. Three quarters of the booths were full, so there was no way of knowing who had spooked her. But someone had, he was sure.

His eyes scanned the crowd, cataloging it in his mind. As he started to walk away, his gaze connected with a pair of eyes that stared insolently at him. Bobby Duvall. He held the man's gaze for a moment, then looked past him to finish scanning the room. Was it Bobby who had made her retreat from the café?

"How about we go back to the station? There shouldn't be anyone there right now besides our dispatcher."

"That's fine," she said, shoving her hands into her pockets and looking at the sidewalk. He wondered what she was thinking.

Ten minutes later she sat next to his desk, her hands wrapped around a cup of coffee. All her attention was focused on the dark brown liquid.

"Tell me what happened last night, Tory."

Involuntarily she looked at him, then immediately she looked away. "I was walking back from the clinic," she began in an emotionless voice. "I don't think I heard anything, but just before I got to my front door I looked behind me. There was something standing at the edge of the woods. I watched it for a second, but I couldn't tell what it was. I don't even know if it was a person or an animal."

She took a long drink of the scalding coffee, and as she lowered her hand he could see it shaking. "Then it vanished. One moment it was there, and the next it was gone."

He picked up his coffee and sipped at it, never taking his eyes off her. "Jack Williams told me he didn't find any traces of anyone there. Are you sure you actually saw something?"

She set the ceramic mug on the edge of his desk with a small snap. Some of the coffee slopped onto the plastic surface. "I saw something. I just don't know what it was."

Her hands tightened in her lap, and she finally looked at him. Her dark green eyes were huge, and the shadows under them looked like purple bruises. Her long dark red hair, which yesterday had been meticulously braided, was pulled into a haphazard ponytail. Taking a deep breath, she said softly, "Was it you, Holt? Were you checking on me, to make sure I got to the house safely?"

"My God, Tory, I wouldn't do that to you," he exploded. He banged his coffee cup onto his desk and leaned forward in his chair. "Is that what you think?"

She stared at him for a long time. He saw the fear flicker in her eyes, shadowed by something else. Something that looked like the suspicion he'd seen in the eyes of a few other people in Eagle Ridge. "It was the only thing that made any sense," she whispered. "Who else could have any reason for watching me?"

"And why would I skulk in the woods to watch you, rather than just pull into your driveway?" He watched her as he spoke. "Did you think it was because I'm new to Eagle Ridge? Did the thought cross your mind that the two murders happened only since I arrived?"

She flushed, but she didn't look away. "You weren't home when the police officer called you," she said defensively. "What would you have thought under the circumstances?"

"Do you think I'm the murderer, Tory?"

She stared at him like a small animal trapped by a predator. "I don't know what to think," she whispered. "I don't know you at all."

"What do your instincts tell you?"

Her gaze dropped and she reached for her coffee. "My instincts have been wrong before."

Her hands still trembled as she held the mug cradled between them. He knew he shouldn't touch her, but he couldn't resist. He took her mug, then reached for her hands and curled his own around them. Her fingers felt ice cold. She tried to pull away from him, but he held on to her.

"Tory, listen to me. I was at home, taking a shower. If Jack had called me ten minutes before or after he did, he would have found me. I can't prove it, but that's where I was." He turned her hands over in his and stroked his thumb across her palm. When he felt her muscles quiver in response and jerk away from him, he tightened his grip on her.

"Although I have to admit I was tempted to go back and wait until you were finished in the clinic and safely in your house. I wish to hell I'd followed my instincts last night. If I had been there, this may not have happened at all."

She was staring at their joined hands almost as if she couldn't believe what she saw. "If it wasn't you out there, it wouldn't have mattered. Whoever was there would still have been there. I just wouldn't have seen him."

She sounded so certain that he turned her hands over and gripped them hard. "Why are you so sure, Tory?"

She shrugged, sliding her hands out of his. "I just am."

She gathered herself to stand up, then froze in her seat. "Who is that?"

"Who?" He leaned around her to look out the window.

"That man who just crossed the street. I can't see his face, but he looks familiar."

Holt looked at Tory, tensed in the chair, then out the

window again. "I don't know him, but then I haven't met everyone in town yet. Hey, Marge," he yelled. "Do you know that guy across the street?"

The middle-aged dispatcher stuck her head in the door. "No, but I've seen him around town a couple of times. I think he's a fisherman who's staying about ten miles out of town. I've seen him go into the bait store before."

"Thanks, Marge." Holt smiled at Tory. "You can see the benefits of having the head of the Eagle Ridge grapevine working for me. Do you know the guy?"

Tory shook her head slowly and took a deep breath. "No, I don't. For a second he reminded me of someone else."

Making a mental note to check on the man, Holt stood up. "I suppose you're going to have to be getting back to the clinic."

Tory's gaze flew to her watch, then she stood up, too. "Thank you for reminding me. I have an appointment in half an hour."

"How about I follow you back?" he suggested. "I can check out the spot where you saw the prowler. Daylight should make it a lot easier to see if anything's been disturbed there."

She nodded. "All right. I was going to check it myself this morning, but I was running late."

Her gaze dropped. From the way her face changed when she talked about the forest, he suspected it had been more than running late that had kept her from the woods this morning. He wanted to know what it was, but knew she wasn't ready to tell him.

"I'll meet you out there, then," he said, reaching for his keys and his hat.

She nodded, watched him for another moment, then turned and left. He watched her walk down the street before he followed her out the door.

Tory was too conscious of the black four-wheel-drive vehicle behind her as she drove down the tree-lined road toward her clinic. Every time she glanced in the rearview mirror, she saw Holt watching her. It was just the reflection of his mirrored sunglasses, she tried to tell herself, but the effect was unnerving. Almost as unnerving as having him take her hands in his office.

A powerful current had seemed to flow from his hands into her, both warming her and making her feel jittery and nervous. Sitting in his office, feeling the response he stirred in her, she had told herself her fears were ridiculous. The suspicions that had eaten away at her all night seemed foolish when she sat next to him.

But she didn't really know him, she warned herself. She'd sensed uncharted depths in Holt Adams the first time she'd met him, and she had no idea what hid beneath his reassuring facade. She wanted desperately to think he was only concerned about her safety, but she knew better than to trust a man just because he wore a policeman's uniform.

She slowed as she approached her driveway and breathed a sigh of relief to find the parking lot empty. Until her client showed up, she'd be free to help Holt look for clues. She ignored the small voice inside her that said she'd be able to make sure he didn't cover up any evidence of his own presence there last night.

Parking her truck in the tiny garage next to the house, she walked toward Holt's Blazer. He frowned as he watched her approach. "I thought you had a client to see."

"They're not here yet, so I thought I'd see what you found."

"Are you sure?" He watched her with a question in his eyes. "I got the impression that the woods bothered you."

Had she been that transparent? Or did he not want her to see what he found? "I'm just not used to being surrounded by them at night. They don't bother me in the daylight." That wasn't completely true, but she found that the prospect of entering the woods with Holt by her side was somehow much less frightening.

He looked at her, frowned again, then shrugged. "Okay, then, let's go."

The trees seemed to loom over her as they approached

the spot where she'd seen the intruder. Moving a step closer to Holt, she focused her attention where she'd seen the prowler disappear. Maybe if she didn't think about it, the woods wouldn't bother her.

They stepped into the woods and onto the blanket of pine needles that covered the ground, and she immediately felt cooler. She looked up involuntarily. The tall pines grew so close together that they seemed to block out every bit of the sky. For just a moment she felt trapped, her heart stumbling in panic.

Then she looked over and saw Holt next to her, and her heartbeat steadied. Swallowing hard, she forced herself to look around.

All she saw was an ocean of trees. There was no sense of menace, no force trying to pull her more deeply into the woods. She didn't feel the evil that seemed to emanate from these trees at night.

Which just goes to show that your imagination is working overtime, she told herself. Looking around as she walked, she didn't realize that Holt had stopped until she bumped into him. He didn't look at her. As he stared at the ground, she felt a shiver crawl up her back.

"What is it?" she asked, hearing the fear in her voice.

"Come and see."

Chapter 4

As he knelt in the pine needles, Tory moved closer and eased down next to him. "I don't see anything," she said after a moment, allowing herself to relax slightly.

"Look here," he said, pointing. "Don't you see these marks on the ground?"

She looked where he was pointing. All she could see was black earth showing through the covering of pine needles. "There's nothing there but dirt."

"Exactly." He turned to her, his face grim. "Look around, Tory. The ground has been covered by pine needles for years and years. Do you see dirt anywhere else?"

Slowly she scanned the area. "No, I guess not." She stared at the black patches again. "What does it mean?"

"It means someone was here last night. He was damned careful, but he was here." He pointed at the two scuffed-looking patches of dirt. "This is where he stood. He probably shuffled his feet a little to keep warm. He was damned careful not to leave any other signs, but the pine needles have definitely been disturbed."

Slowly Tory raised her head and looked around. She had

a clear view of both her house and her clinic. Feeling slightly sick, she looked at Holt. "How do you know it wasn't an animal? A deer could have made marks like that." She heard the desperation in her voice, but she didn't care.

"I haven't seen many two-legged deer, Tory." His eyes softened as he took her hand and pulled her to her feet. "Let's see if he left us any more clues."

She clung to the warmth of his hand for the moment it took her to rise, her fingers curling around his palm. Then she slowly let go. Was he really concerned, or was it all an act? Did he know exactly who had been standing here last night?

Holt moved deeper into the woods, and she couldn't contain her shudder. It was daylight. A dim green light filtered down to where she stood, but the terror she'd felt the night before came rushing back. She didn't want to take another step.

He looked at her. "Do you want to come with me or do you need to get back to the clinic?"

It would be so easy to tell him she had a client coming, to turn and run to the safety of her clinic. Swallowing hard, she shook her head. "I have a few more minutes. I'll come with you."

He waited for her to catch up with him, pretending not to notice how long it took her to walk through the trees. When he reached for her hand, she didn't resist. Her fear of the woods was stronger than her reservations about Holt, and the connection steadied her, reassuring her that she wasn't alone in the forest. His warm hand pulsed with life and strength, and she clung to him as the trees pressed closer.

She didn't let go as they walked along. He stopped occasionally to examine something on the ground, and every time he slowed down she tightened her grip on his hand. The wind moved restlessly through the pines, whispering her name, calling for her. If she let go of Holt she wouldn't be able to resist it.

If he thought she was acting strangely he didn't say anything. But every once in a while he smoothed his thumb across the palm of her hand, a slow, reassuring gesture. She would have thought it was unconscious on his part, except that when his wrist touched hers she felt his pulse leaping in his vein.

Finally he stopped and faced her. "Let's go back." He spoke abruptly, his eyes shuttered.

"What's the matter?" she breathed, her heart jumping in her chest. "Did you see something?"

He smoothed his thumb across her palm one more time and looked around, his lips tightening. "Nothing but these faint tracks heading deeper into the woods." He stood tensed and still for a moment, watching and listening. Almost, she thought, as if he could sense the same evil she felt.

He turned to her. "You've got a client coming. Why don't I take you back and continue by myself?"

Suspicion slithered into her mind like a snake, dark and ugly. "Why don't you want me to go with you?"

His eyes softened as he looked at her. "It's not a matter of wanting or not wanting. You told me you had a client coming soon, and I figured you needed to get back." He paused, his grip on her hand tightening. "And I know you're not comfortable in the woods."

His eyes were too knowing, and she tried to pull her hand away from his. "Since I've been holding on to you like a leech for the past fifteen minutes, I suppose that's a reasonable assumption. But like I told you earlier, I'm just not used to being surrounded by this many trees."

Moving his hands to her shoulders, he held her lightly in front of him. "It's more than that, Tory, and I know it. What's going on?"

She could feel the strength in his hands, knew he could tighten his hold and hurt her, but she knew he wouldn't. He watched her steadily with his silver eyes, and she read in them nothing but concern for her. The wind curled around her, but she barely felt it. His eyes held her mesmerized.

"I don't know what's going on, Holt," she heard herself saying. Fear shivered through her, but she realized it wasn't fear of Holt. Maybe that fear had simply been overwhelmed by her fear of the trees, but for now she didn't care. "The trees scare me."

His hands kneaded her shoulders, comforting and reassuring. "The woods make a lot of people uncomfortable, especially people who come from the city. I know you used to live here, but you've been gone a long time. Have you lived in Chicago the whole time?"

She nodded, lost in the sensation his hands were evoking on her skin. "Except for the time I was in vet school."

"Give it a while, Tory. You'll get used to them."

She shook her head but didn't back away from him. She couldn't bear to move away. "It's more than that. Something's trying to pull me into these woods, something that scares me. Something evil."

His hands tightened on her shoulders then dropped away. "What do you mean?" he asked in a low, urgent voice. His silver eyes turned to hard steel.

"I don't know what I mean." She bit her lip and looked at him, wishing she hadn't said anything. And wondering what she'd been thinking of. For all she knew, Holt was the evil she felt in these woods. "It's just my overactive imagination, I guess." She shrugged. "You're right, I should get back. My client will probably be waiting for me."

He stood watching her for a long moment as she avoided looking at him. Finally he said, "I won't let anything happen to you, Tory."

Her gaze flew to his. He wasn't laughing at her. There was no mockery in his eyes, no patronizing smile on his face. All she could see was concern, and something else hidden beneath that concern. Something hot and potent that both warmed her and frightened her. Something she didn't want to think about, much less acknowledge.

"What could happen to me out here?" Her words tripped over each other. "There's nothing here except trees, and they can't hurt me." To emphasize her words she reached out and spread her palm against the trunk of the closest pine. The rough bark felt cool and spiky under her fingers, and utterly lifeless. It wasn't a vessel of evil. It was only a tree.

He reached for her hand again. His fingers brushed hers, sending a tingle of warmth up her arm. She hesitated, and when he stepped closer she felt her arm bump against something cold and hard. When she looked down, she saw that it was his gun.

Instinctive fear washed over her, erasing any thought of the trees. Pulling her hand away from him, she began to walk in the direction of her clinic. She could feel him right behind her.

"Tory, wait."

Looking over her shoulder, she slowed down. But she didn't stop.

"What's wrong?"

She shook her head and kept walking. "Nothing. I just don't want to be late for my client."

He grabbed her hand and pulled her around to face him. "Something just happened, and I want to know what it is." His gaze bored into hers. "And don't give me that bull about being late."

Slowly she straightened and tugged her hand away from his. She fought to keep her eyes on his. "I remembered I have to get back to my clinic, that's all. I have a business to run, and I can't keep my patients waiting. Is that so hard to understand?"

He stared at her, then smiled. The look in his eyes made her uneasy, and she took a step away from him.

"I think I'm beginning to understand very well," he murmured, moving closer to her. "It's very convenient, isn't it, Tory? Having your business, being able to hide behind its shield." He was very close now, and the heat from his body warmed her in the cool woods. "I know all about that kind of hiding. Believe me, it doesn't work. I know.'' His eyes shuttered, but not before she saw the desolation. ''Tell me what you're hiding from.''

''I'm not hiding from anything.'' Her heart pounded, and the beat roared in her ears as he moved closer still. His belt buckle almost brushed her abdomen as he reached up and caught her shoulders.

''Prove it, Tory.''

Then his mouth was on hers. She stiffened and tried to pull away as blind panic surged through her veins. But his hands gentled on her shoulders and slowly smoothed down her arms, and unexpected arousal twined with the fear.

His mouth wasn't hard and demanding, as she'd expected. Instead, he nibbled lightly on her lower lip then touched her delicately with his tongue. The pressure of his teeth followed by the delicious wetness stirred something inside her.

She relaxed and softened as the fear seeped away, replaced by a heavy, languorous throbbing deep in her belly. When Holt pulled her closer she didn't resist. The muscles of his thigh were hard against hers, and she felt him trembling.

Slowly he moved his hands from her shoulders and slid them around her, drawing her against him. His fingers smoothed down her back, and she shivered. Her fear retreated to a far corner of her mind as she fisted her hands on his shirtsleeves.

His body tensed and his arms tightened around her. The light, almost teasing kiss deepened, until she found herself opening her mouth to him. His tongue swirled into her, tasting hot and male and dark. He thrust his hips against her, and she felt the unmistakable evidence of his desire for her.

A wave of heat crashed over her, engulfing her in fire. It raged deep in her abdomen, sending out rivers of flame along all her nerves. She forgot about the woods, forgot about her clients, forgot everything but the feel and taste of Holt. He groaned into her mouth and crushed her closer, and she went willingly.

Gradually she loosened her hands from their grip on his arms and lifted them to his neck. Making a low, guttural sound, he trailed his lips down her cheek and along her neck. Shivering, she wrapped her arms more tightly around him and tried to pull him closer.

Something sharp and cold pressed into her chest. It stabbed into her breast when she moved, right above her heart. When she tried to shift away from it, something caught in the pocket of her shirt.

"Hold on," Holt whispered. "Let me get you untangled."

Cautiously she opened her eyes and looked at her chest. It was his badge that had stabbed into her and caught in her clothes. As she looked at the dull glint of metal between them cold reason washed over her, replacing the passion that had fired her blood.

What was she thinking of? Her arms dropped away from his neck and she backed up, out of his reach. Holt was watching her, but she couldn't seem to look anywhere but at his badge. How could she have forgotten? The sight of his badge and gun made her feel slightly sick as she remembered her surrender to him.

"I have to go," she whispered. She ran blindly through the forest. If the trees whispered to her, she didn't hear them. All she heard was the pounding of her own heart, echoed in Holt's footsteps right behind her.

She burst into the empty parking lot in front of her clinic, panting. Her hair had fallen out of the careless ponytail she'd pulled it into that morning, and her face felt flushed. She didn't care. She had to get into her clinic.

Before she could open the door Holt was there. He stood in front of it, blocking her way.

"I want to know what happened back there."

"I should think it was fairly obvious. We kissed. No big deal."

She could feel his eyes studying her, but she wouldn't

meet his gaze. After what seemed like a long time, he murmured, "It was a big deal, Tory, and I think you know it." He paused, then said softly, "Why did you pull away from me?"

Shrugging, she forced herself to look at him. There was no anger in his eyes, no accusation. He watched her steadily. Her gaze slid away as she said, "I didn't realize how late it was. I had to get back."

He reached out for her and she took a step backward. He stared at his hands for a long time before balling them into fists and shoving them into his pockets. Then, leaning against the door frame, he lifted his gaze to her.

"I'll find out, you know," he said in a quiet voice. "Sooner or later, I'll find out what's wrong."

"Why does there have to be something wrong?" She lifted her chin and clasped her hands behind her back to hide their trembling. "Or does your ego find it impossible to believe I'm just not interested?"

One side of his mouth quirked up in a brief smile. "I might have bought that line ten minutes ago. But now you'll have to do better."

"I'm not interested in getting involved with anyone," she said, a desperate edge to her voice. "I have to concentrate on my practice."

He pushed himself away from the door to stand up straight. "You can't define yourself in only one way, Tory," he said. "If you do, you're setting yourself up for devastating disappointment." The raw pain that looked out at her from his eyes seared her soul, then he lowered his eyelids. When he opened them again his eyes were blank. "You're more than a vet, you're a woman, too. And I could taste the need in that woman, back there in the woods."

"I'm perfectly capable of deciding how to define myself, Holt. Just like I'm capable of deciding what I need in my life. And right now, what I need is to be left alone to practice veterinary medicine." She told herself her voice trembled because she was angry. It had nothing to do with Holt's almost frightening perception.

The noise of a car engine made both of them look toward the highway. A car was turning into Tory's driveway, and she closed her eyes with relief. As she tried to step around him to go into the clinic, he put one hand on her arm to stop her.

"I want to get to know you better, Tory. Tell me what I have to do."

A flame burned steadily deep in his eyes, and she swallowed hard. She couldn't seem to tear her gaze away from his. Then he moved forward. She wasn't sure what he intended, but the movement made the sunlight glint off his badge, and she quickly stepped away from him.

She stared for a long time at the dull gleam of metal on his chest. Then, looking at him, she said, "Take off the badge."

She stepped around him, opened the door of the clinic, went in and shut it quietly behind her.

Holt stood staring at the door until he heard someone behind him. An older woman with fluffy white hair clutching a small, fluffy white dog walked slowly toward the door of Tory's clinic. When she saw him, she smiled.

"Hello, Chief Adams. I didn't know you had a pet."

Holt scrambled to remember the woman's name. "I don't, Mrs...."

"Maude Kendall, Chief." The woman's smile widened. "I expect it's hard to remember everyone in town."

"Sorry, Mrs. Kendall. No, I don't have a pet." The remembered pain was small compared to the other, but still there. "It wouldn't be fair to an animal with the hours I keep."

Just like it hadn't been fair to his wife. The thought stabbed into him, bringing with it the familiar twist of guilt. Guilt that was just as sharp and painful as it had been two years ago.

Mrs. Kendall hadn't seemed to notice. "Things are different in Eagle Ridge than they are in Detroit, Chief Adams." She gave him a sweet smile. "Once you settle in, I'm sure you'll have time for all sorts of things."

He held the door open for her and watched her walk to the front desk. He knew Tory was there, even though he couldn't see her. Letting the door close he walked to his vehicle.

You'll have time for all sorts of things. As he drove slowly toward town, Holt thought about Mrs. Kendall's comment. He didn't want to have time. He'd thought that coming to Eagle Ridge would be his salvation, but he'd found instead that the slower pace of life was his torment. Even working twelve-hour shifts left him too much time to remember. And the two murders that had happened since he'd arrived only fed his guilt.

The only person he wanted more time with was Tory Falcon, and she'd made it plain she wasn't interested. Unless he took off his badge.

Frowning, he stared out the windshield and thought about her words. She'd told him to do the one thing she'd known he couldn't do. Was it only to let him know she was uninterested, or was there another reason?

He drove past the police station without stopping. Pulling into the parking lot of his small apartment building a few minutes later, he checked to make sure that the radio hanging from his belt was turned on. Then he swung out of the Blazer and hurried into his apartment.

There were only a couple of places his address book could be in the almost empty apartment. Looking around at the few pieces of furniture he'd brought with him, he decided to try the desk first.

A few minutes later he looked at the book in his hand with grim triumph. Paging through it slowly, he finally found the name he was looking for.

He dialed the phone number, ignoring the voice inside him that whispered what he was doing was an invasion of Tory's privacy. He was concerned about her, and if something had happened to her in Chicago he wanted to know about it.

"Sixth district, White speaking." The impersonal, hurried voice on the other end of the phone told him he'd reached a police station in Chicago.

"Is Detective Kelly there?" Holt asked.

"Hold on, I'll check."

Holt listened to the silence on the phone line for what seemed like forever until it clicked and another voice said, "Kelly here."

"John? This is Holt Adams, from Detroit homicide. We met at a conference a few years ago."

Holt could hear the other man thinking, trying to place him. Suddenly he said, his voice filling with warmth, "Adams! How're you doing?"

"I'm okay, Kelly. How about you?"

"Can't complain. What can I do for you?"

Holt took a deep breath. "I'm not in Detroit anymore. I'm the police chief in a small town in northern Michigan. I've got a woman who just moved here from Chicago and I need some information on her."

"What's her name?"

Holt gave him all the information he wanted, then talked with the other man for a few more minutes. Finally Kelly said, "I'll give you a call as soon as I have anything, but it could be a few days. We're up to our ears in alligators right now."

"Whenever you can get back to me is fine." After giving Kelly his phone number, he hung up the phone and stood staring out the window at the woods that ringed his apartment.

Tory was frightened of the trees. And unless his instincts were wrong, there were some other things Tory was frightened of, too. Telling himself again that his phone call to John Kelly was justified, he walked out of his apartment and drove to the police station.

Tory watched with relief as her last client walked out of the clinic late that afternoon. She waited for a few moments then went over and locked the door before checking to make sure that the back door was locked, also.

Alone in her clinic, she made notes on the animals she'd kept in the clinic, then went to check on them. As she stood in front of the cages, talking to the two cats and one dog, she knew she was just delaying the inevitable.

She would have to go into Eagle Ridge tonight. The food she had brought with her was gone, and she needed to get some groceries. She wished passionately that it didn't have to be tonight, but if she didn't shop she'd go hungry.

And she couldn't put it off forever. Sooner or later she'd have to go to the grocery store and the hardware store, where she'd be the center of attention. Everyone in town wanted to know why she'd decided to come back and what her plans were for the future. Each of her clients had asked her, some more diplomatically than others, and she knew that the first few times she went into Eagle Ridge she would be the jar of honey to all the town flies.

She'd managed to make it to the post office and back without being waylaid, but that was because she'd been caught by Holt. This time she'd be on her own.

After checking the animals one last time, she finally walked out into the crisp autumn air. It wouldn't be long before the sun went down, and before she got into her car she walked to her house and turned on all the outside lights. The last thing she wanted was to drive into her yard in total darkness.

She made it halfway through the grocery store without seeing anyone who recognized her. Congratulating herself on shopping while nearly everyone else was eating dinner, she turned into the next aisle and stopped dead in her tracks. Her stomach fluttered with fear.

Of all the people she'd imagined running into while she shopped, she hadn't thought of him. She didn't think Bobby Duvall knew what a grocery store was.

His back was to her as he studied a shelf. As she tried to turn her cart, she banged into a display of soup. When Bobby looked up and saw her, his small eyes narrowed, then he smiled.

"Well, well, well, look who's here. It's Eagle Ridge's

own celebrity. I thought you kicked over the traces of this town long ago, Tory."

Tory stared at the man who had tormented her all through school and slowly realized that he'd changed. Or she had. His massive frame no longer scared her. Instead of the bully she'd feared, she saw a man who hadn't taken care of himself and was running to fat. The mean glint in his eyes that had always made her run in terror now made her feel almost sorry for him. She had done something with her life. Bobby Duvall had stayed in Eagle Ridge and was still playing the part of town bully.

Tory smiled at him. "If I recall, the only thing I kicked in this town was you, Bobby." As she backed up her cart she saw his smirking smile disappear, replaced by the ugly, mean look that had always intimidated her. Now it only made her regret all the years she'd run from him.

There were some things to be said for living in Chicago, she thought as she paid for her groceries. Dealing with gang members and street toughs, as she had in her inner-city practice, made Bobby Duvall merely pathetic. She was smiling as she left the grocery store, her arms full of bags.

"It looks like you could use some help."

She stopped so suddenly that one of the bags started to slip. Holt lifted it from her in one smooth move and cradled it on his hip. He reached for another one, but she backed up a step.

"Thank you, but I can get them. You just startled me."

"Sorry." He nodded toward the grocery store. "You look like you enjoyed yourself in there."

She felt the smile creeping onto her face. "I ran into someone I knew when I was a kid."

An odd look flashed over his face, one she might have called jealousy if there had been any reason for it. Then he said carefully, "It's always nice to see old friends."

Her smile turned into a laugh. "I wouldn't exactly call him that."

"Him?" Holt's voice was quiet.

"I wouldn't describe him as a..." Her voice trailed off

as she saw someone dart around the corner behind Holt's back. There was something familiar about him, something that reminded her of the man she'd seen from the window of the police station. As she stared over his shoulder, Holt turned to see what she was looking at.

"What is it?"

She shook her head slowly. "I don't know. That person looked familiar." Staring at the spot for a moment, she finally shrugged her shoulders. "I guess there'll be a lot of people who trigger that reaction for a while. I won't remember everyone who was here when I left."

"But we remember you, Tory. We remember all about you."

The voice behind her was low and ugly, filled with the kind of threatening insinuations that used to make her cringe and run away. She turned to face Bobby Duvall.

"How sad for you, Bobby. Believe me, I haven't spent the last thirteen years thinking about you. I put that part of my past behind me." She paused, then said deliberately, "You might say I've kicked it behind me. I've had better things to do with my life."

The bewilderment on Bobby's face would have been amusing if it hadn't been followed by a look of pure rage. His eyes narrowed and glittered with fury as he looked at her.

"I'll see you around, Tory."

"I doubt it, Bobby. I'm very busy these days. I have a business to take care of."

His face turned purple as he stared at her, and she felt Holt tensing beside her. Then without another word Bobby turned and walked away.

"What was that all about?"

Tory watched Bobby disappear down the street. "That was Bobby Duvall."

"I know who it was. What the hell was going on?"

Tory felt her arms trembling. She tried to tell herself it was because she held the heavy bags of groceries, but she couldn't forget the rage and hatred in Bobby's face. He might not be able to make her turn tail and run anymore, but the look in his eyes would make anyone nervous. Everything that had happened in the last twenty-four hours came back with a rush.

"Bobby and I go way back," she said, her voice suddenly weary.

Holt pulled the bags of groceries from her arms, and she didn't object. "I could see that." His voice was gentle. "Do you want to tell me about it?"

Suddenly she did. "Bobby has always been a bully. He was in my grade in school, and I became his favorite victim. He tormented me almost until the day I left Eagle Ridge."

"Why did he pick on you?" Holt's voice was low and without expression.

She shrugged, hoping to look nonchalant. Her childhood in Eagle Ridge wasn't something she wanted to discuss with anyone. "Why does a bully pick any victim? But he kept it up because he could tell I was scared of him."

Holt exhaled slowly. "You didn't act too scared of him today."

She felt her muscles begin to relax. Holt was right, she realized. She allowed herself a small smile. "I wasn't. I met enough truly frightening people in Chicago to make me see that Bobby is just pathetic."

"Something else happened with Duvall, didn't it, Tory?" Holt asked as they neared her truck. "What was it?"

She opened the back of the truck without looking at him. "What makes you say that?"

"There was too much unspoken in your conversation. I could tell." Holt set her bags of groceries in the truck then turned to look at her. "He hates you, Tory. Deep down hatred. I saw it in his eyes. What happened?"

She took a deep breath and looked at the darkening sky, remembering the fear of her last encounter with Bobby before she left town as an eighteen-year-old. Remembered the fear and the terror, and the fierce surge of triumph when she'd thwarted him. There was no reason to keep quiet about it anymore. And as Eagle Ridge's new police chief, Holt had a right to know.

"He tried to rape me."

and your nephew.

way toward home. Could not, for reason he knew could
expect, experience what he Holt Stone's now power those
this and it will be home.
are unacceptable, the

Chapter 5

"He what?" Holt didn't raise his voice, but tension electrified the air as his knuckles whitened on the door of her truck.

Some part of her wanted to reach out to him and reassure, but instead she wrapped her arms around her waist to stop her instinctive trembling. As hard as she'd tried, she hadn't been able to forget about that particular spring evening.

"Don't worry, he didn't even come close to succeeding. In fact, the only reason I know that's what he intended was he told me so." Hating the sudden tremor in her voice, she paused for a moment before she continued. "I was stupid enough to take a shortcut home from school one day during my senior year in high school. He caught up with me behind the stadium. There wasn't anyone else around, and he tried to take his verbal harassment one step further."

"What happened?"

She straightened, remembering again the rush of anger and rage she'd turned on Bobby Duvall that spring night. And realized it had freed her forever from his domination.

"I kneed him in the groin. When I tried to get away he grabbed my ankle, so I kicked him again. He never touched me or looked at me after that."

"My God." Holt looked at her, his face tight and controlled. When she looked in his eyes, she saw dark, black anger. "Did you call the police?"

"His father was the chief of police." She turned away and rearranged the bags of groceries. "Do you think they would have listened to me?" Even then she'd known the answer. The Falcon family had been notorious in Eagle Ridge.

"You mean you let him get away with it?" His incredulous voice rose in the still, twilight air.

"He didn't get away with it. He limped for two weeks afterward."

"That's not what I mean, and you know it. You should have called the police."

"I didn't, and now it's ancient history. I'd rather not discuss it anymore, Holt. You know now, and I'm sure Bobby will figure out that you know. Let's drop it."

She could feel his eyes on her as she opened her door. Before she could slide onto the seat, he touched her arm.

"Stay in town and have dinner with me. It's getting late to go home and fix a meal."

A few bright stars were visible in the navy blue sky. The thought of driving home alone and parking her truck in the dark made a ripple of fear climb her back. Wanting to postpone that moment was almost enough to make her agree to have dinner with him.

Almost, but not quite. Given a choice between Holt and the dark, she realized she was less afraid of the dark. At least the dark didn't threaten to take away all the control she'd tried to rebuild so carefully over the past few months.

"Thank you, but no. I need to get back."

To her surprise he didn't try to argue with her. Instead, he nodded and waited for her to get into the truck. "I'll follow you to your house, then, to make sure everything's all right."

She hated the relief that overwhelmed her, hated knowing how much she'd dreaded going to her house alone in the darkness. Hated the involuntary burst of joy she felt hearing that Holt would be there, too.

Her hand tightened on the key and she shoved it into the ignition. "Thank you." She didn't look up as he closed the door of her truck and walked away.

She drove along the tree-lined road through the gathering darkness, watching his headlights in her rearview mirror. It was absurd how comforting two points of light could be.

She would never admit it to Holt, but she was damn glad he was there. Seeing Bobby Duvall again, telling Holt what had happened thirteen years ago, had opened the dam on a rush of memories. Most of them she would have preferred to forget.

But in facing Bobby that evening, she had realized, finally, that he was merely pathetic. The remembered fear would never go away, but there would be no new terror to replace it. Her hands tightened on the steering wheel in exultation, then relaxed. She was free. Bobby Duvall was one ghost she had managed to exorcise.

Seeing the reflector that marked the entrance to her driveway, she slowed and turned onto her property. When she stopped the car and turned off the engine, the sudden silence seemed to throb with night sounds. An owl hooted somewhere in the distance, two branches rubbed together in the surrounding forest, and the ever-present wind sighed through the trees. The pungent scent of pine surrounded her, and she hurried to the back of her truck without looking at the trees.

"Let me get a couple of those bags."

Holt walked toward her in the darkness. She began trembling again, but this time it wasn't from fear. Wanting to tell him no, to ask him to leave, she swallowed hard and shoved a bag into his arms. He had followed her home, after all, to make sure that nothing had happened at her house or clinic. She knew he wouldn't leave until he was satisfied everything was all right. "Thank you," she muttered.

He followed her silently with his arms full of groceries. When she fumbled with the lock on her door, he eased one of the bags out of her hands. Even though she turned her back on him while she opened the door, she was acutely aware of him right behind her. His scent filled her senses, obliterating the smell of pine. Heat and energy seemed to roll off him and surround her. She felt as if he'd planted himself between her and the woods, using his body as a buffer between her and whatever evil lingered out there.

The door opened with a jerk, and she half-stumbled into the living room. One of Holt's hands snaked out and caught her wrist, steadying her. "Take it easy," he murmured. She looked at his fingers encircling her and waited for the fear to come.

Instead all she felt was his hard, callused palm on her arm. That, and a warmth that seemed to penetrate her skin and sink all the way into her bones. She stared at his hand for a long time, wondering why a policeman affected her this way

He let her go and shifted the bags in his arms. "You want these in the kitchen?" he asked, nodding toward the other room.

Heat suffused her face. "Just set the bags on the counter. I'll put everything away later."

He slid the brown paper bags onto the counter, then stepped back and shoved his hands into his pockets. If she didn't know better, she'd think he was as unsure of himself as she felt.

"Would you like me to check the house for you?"

Her pulse leaped, and she told herself it was fear. Merely thinking about Holt looking in all the rooms of her house couldn't make her heart pound.

"I'm sure you'll find everything is all right, but check if you like." He disappeared from the kitchen, and she busied herself with putting away the groceries. When she found herself straining to hear his footsteps she snapped a paper bag and folded it noisily, then squatted to shove it into a cabinet.

A few moments later he appeared in the doorway. "Everything looks fine here." He paused for a moment until she reluctantly stood up and faced him. "Do you have to go back to the clinic tonight?"

"Yes," she answered. "But I thought I'd do it later." She needed time to get up enough nerve to step into the darkness, where she would be unprotected and surrounded by the trees.

He watched her steadily. "Any reason you can't do it now?"

"I suppose not," she said.

"Good. I'll walk over there with you and wait until you've finished."

"You don't have to do that, Holt." She knew her voice sounded weak and unconvincing. Her nerves crawled as she thought about walking to the clinic and back, wondering who or what was hiding in the trees, watching her.

"I know I don't have to do it. I'm going with you because I want to."

She shrugged into her coat, trying to disguise a rush of relief so profound her arms trembled. Even before he touched her, she knew he'd moved behind her.

"Let me help you." His voice sounded more gentle than she'd ever heard it as he settled the coat over her shoulders, and she ducked her head as she pushed the buttons through the buttonholes. What a fool she must be making of herself.

"There's nothing to be ashamed of, Tory." He spoke from behind her, resting his hands on her shoulders, and she imagined she felt his warm breath caressing the nape of her neck. "You have a reason to be frightened out there. Someone was in the woods last night, watching you. Any normal person would be scared."

She looked at the keys in her hand and her knuckles whitened. "I have to get over it sometime."

"Some things are easier to get over if you don't have to face them alone." His hands tightened painfully on her shoulders, then dropped away. The pain in his voice made her face him.

He'd shuttered his face. The man who looked at her was cold and remote, not the man with the gentle voice who had tried to soothe her just moments ago. His hard, set expression and the badge gleaming on his chest were the marks of a policeman, but she suddenly realized she wasn't afraid of him. She was looking at Holt, a man who tried too hard to disguise the pain in his eyes.

"Holt?" She heard the question in her voice but wasn't sure what she was asking. Apparently he didn't want to answer, because he headed for her door.

"Let's go. The longer you think about it, the harder it'll be to walk out there."

He was halfway out the front door when she caught up with him. The porch light cast a golden glow that spilled onto the steps and the first few feet of driveway. After that there was nothing but darkness and the faint, glittery light from the stars.

Taking a deep breath, Tory pulled the door closed behind her and clutched the ring of keys in her pocket like a talisman. Holt waited for her at the bottom of the stairs. She hurried down the steps and headed for the clinic.

"I didn't see anything over there," he murmured, nodding toward the woods.

She knew he was referring to the place where the watcher had stood yesterday. "Thank you for checking." She heard the wobble in her voice and cleared her throat. "I'm sure whoever it was won't be back, now that he knows we've seen him."

"I hope you're right." His grim voice told her he wasn't so sure. "How're you doing?"

"I'm okay." She was surprised to realize it was the truth. The sense of menace that seemed to reach out from the trees was missing tonight. They still made her nervous, but she wasn't terrified of the forest. "Whatever was spooking me seems to have gone away."

She could feel him looking at her, sense his sudden stillness. "What do you mean?"

"I'm not sure," she said, shrugging her shoulders. "It just doesn't feel the same tonight as it did last night." She reached for the door of the clinic with relief. Even though the terror was gone, the woods still made her uncomfortable. "Maybe I was so scared because I was picking up on whatever or whoever was watching me. And maybe I'm not so scared tonight because they're not in the woods."

"Maybe." He slanted her a glance as she turned on the light in the reception area. "And maybe he's not in the woods because he's here in the clinic with you."

Her heart contracted with terror, then she realized he was referring to himself. Slowly she turned to him. "You already told me it wasn't you," she whispered. "Were you telling the truth?"

"What do you think?" His voice echoed off the walls of the deserted building.

As she stared at him, she realized she desperately wanted to believe it wasn't Holt. But she didn't really know him, didn't understand the pain that sometimes looked out of his eyes. "I don't know," she whispered, her words loud in the silent building. "Tell me, Holt. Tell me it wasn't you."

"Would it matter? Would you believe me, Tory?"

The silence stretched between them, slowly hardening into suspicion and doubt. Finally Holt moved away, his eyes flat and unreadable. "I'll check the clinic. Wait here until I'm finished."

He disappeared into her office. In a few moments he came back to the reception area. "Nothing's been disturbed, as far as I can tell."

She nodded, watching him. She wanted to tell him she didn't think it was him in the woods, but the words wouldn't come. A small, ugly kernel of doubt lingered in her mind, making the words stick in her throat. What did she know about this man, after all? He was a stranger to her.

"I'll check on the animals, then." She walked around

him, passing close enough to feel the energy coiled in his muscles.

"I'll wait here for you." She shot him a surprised look, and something flashed in his eyes. "I told you I'd stay until you were finished, and I meant it. Unless you'd rather I didn't stay?"

Flushing, she shook her head. "No. I'd like you to wait. It shouldn't take me long."

A few minutes later, satisfied that her patients would be all right overnight, she turned off the light in the kennel and walked into the waiting room. Holt stood at the window, staring at the woods that surrounded them. When the swinging door whooshed he turned around.

"All set?"

She nodded. "They're all fine."

She locked the door behind them and headed for the house. The chilly night air stirred, brushing across her face with icy fingers, and she shivered. Burrowing more deeply into her jacket, she forced herself to concentrate on the tea she would make when she got indoors rather than on the menace that emanated from the trees around her.

"I still think you should move into town." He spoke abruptly and without looking at her.

Startled, Tory glanced at him. He stared at the woods surrounding them, his back ramrod straight and his hands clenched at his sides. Without looking at her, he added, "There are a couple of women who rent out rooms. I'll bring you their names."

They'd reached her front porch. She wrapped one arm around the post that framed the stairs, the cool, solid lumber steadying her. "Thank you, Holt, but I'm staying here. I told you yesterday that even if I wanted to move into town—which I don't—I couldn't afford it."

When he turned to look at her, his eyes were dark and troubled. "That was before you saw someone watching you. Isn't that enough to change your mind?"

She shook her head. "I can't leave. This is my home now, and I won't turn tail and run just because I'm scared."

She wouldn't run away like she had thirteen years ago. She'd come back to regain control of her life, not surrender it to another bully.

Holt turned from her and scanned the surrounding forest. "Call me if you hear or see anything…anything at all."

"I called last night, didn't I?"

"You didn't call me." He looked at her, his eyes unfathomable.

"I called the police. Officer Williams was very prompt."

He stared at her, then said softly, "Call Jack first if it makes you feel better. But then call me."

Heat flared in her face. "I didn't mean…"

"It doesn't matter. Just call me."

"All right."

Her whispered words seemed to ease some of the tension in the air. Nodding toward the house, he said, "Do you want me to check the house again before I leave?"

"I'm sure it's fine. Thank you, though."

He nodded once more. "I'll see you tomorrow, Tory."

Without another word he got into his Blazer and drove away. She watched the beam from his headlights bouncing through the pines until it disappeared, then went slowly up the stairs and into the house.

Locking the door behind her, she went into the kitchen and put on the kettle for some tea. As she waited for the water to boil, she looked out the window at the forest that stared back at her. She hadn't felt this alone in a long time.

True to his word, Holt came out to her house the next night and the one after that. He showed up just as she was closing the clinic, walked her to her house and checked all the rooms before he left. He reappeared a couple of hours later to walk to the clinic with her in the darkness.

The suspicion she couldn't quite banish from her mind hung over them like dark, ugly clouds. Holt was careful not to touch her or even come too close. He checked her house, walked her to the clinic, then left, leaving her alone with the trees and her own thoughts.

On the third night she was running late, sitting in the office writing up the records for the last patient she'd seen, when the front door opened. Without looking she knew it was Holt. She dropped her pen and walked to the waiting room. He stood looking out the window.

She hadn't made a sound, but he turned. Something flickered in his eyes as his gaze drifted over her disheveled lab coat, then his expression was carefully blank again. "Take your time. I'm off duty."

He looked more remote and unreachable than ever. *Tell me,* a voice inside her wanted to whisper. *Tell me it wasn't you in the woods that night.* But she knew he wouldn't say anything.

"I'll be finished in a minute. A couple of emergencies came in, but I'm almost done."

"I'll check the back while I'm waiting."

Holt pushed through the swinging doors and disappeared. She looked at the doors for a moment, trying to banish the ball of regret that swelled in her throat. She'd learned the hard way not to trust people. And Holt especially represented everything she feared. Maybe it was better to have this wall between them.

By the time she finished her paperwork, he was back in the reception room. As she shrugged into her coat and turned off the lights, she realized that the sky outside, which had been blue and cloudless at noon, was an ominous steel gray.

When she stepped outside, a cold wind slashed at her coat, whipping it around her legs. The tops of the pine trees were bent over by the force of the wind, and a low moan seemed to rise from the surrounding woods.

"It looks like it's going to rain," she said, glancing at Holt. "Don't worry about coming back tonight. No one would bother us in a storm."

He looked at her for a moment, then at the trees. "I'll be back." His flat voice sounded final.

When they reached her front porch she paused before climbing the stairs, wondering what to say. "Thank you,

Holt," she finally murmured. "I appreciate your coming out here every day."

He watched her for a moment, his eyes still unreadable. "I'll see you in a couple of hours," he said, turning and walking away.

Even though it wasn't dark yet, he turned on his headlights as he drove out of her driveway. All they did was illuminate the gray gloom that had enveloped the forest, making shadows dart among the trees. Tory retreated into her house and pulled the curtains firmly closed. Holt was gone, and the trees were already calling her name. Maybe if she didn't look at them, she could ignore their voices.

When the phone rang twenty minutes later she grabbed it with relief. Even dealing with an emergency would be better than sitting here, trying not to think about the forest.

"Hello?"

"Is this the vet?" The voice sounded disembodied, neither male nor female. One part of her brain registered that fact, and the rest went into her professional mode.

"Yes, this is Dr. Falcon. Can I help you?"

"There's a dog lying by the side of the road about a mile north of your clinic. I think it was hit by a car. I couldn't catch it."

"Who is this?"

"It's not my dog. I thought you would want to help." The phone clicked in her ear as the receiver was replaced at the other end of the line.

Tory stared at the phone as she replaced it slowly in its cradle. No one lived on the road a mile north of the clinic, but it was possible that a dog from town had strayed out that far. As she wondered what to do, the wind whistled through an ill-fitting window in the kitchen with a lonely, mournful sound.

The sky outside had turned a glowering, gunmetal gray, and dark, heavy clouds scuttled across the sky. Tory knew she didn't have a choice. It was going to storm, and soon. The thought of a dog lying injured and scared by the side of the road made her grab her coat and car keys. It would only take a few minutes to go out and pick him up.

She ran to the clinic, grabbed her emergency bag then jumped into her car. The sun wasn't supposed to set for another hour yet, but the sky was already as dark as twilight. Turning on her headlights, she drove slowly down the road, peering into the gloom as she looked for the injured animal.

She drove two miles north, then stopped and turned around. There was no sign of a dog. Driving even more cautiously, she finally spotted what looked like a skid mark on the road and pulled onto the shoulder.

Nothing moved in the semidarkness except the trees, swaying in the wind. She rolled down her window and listened intently. Except for the sighing of the trees, she didn't hear a thing. The smell of the approaching storm surrounded her, sharp and fresh, and she knew it wouldn't be long before it began to rain.

After another look revealed nothing but forest, she eased out of the cab of her truck, clutching her keys in one hand. An injured animal would probably have tried to drag itself into the woods. She had to check the bushes that lined the road, then the clearing just beyond them.

The trees that encircled the small clearing seemed to know her as well as the ones around her house and clinic. For a moment she stood still, pressed against the side of the truck, and listened to them moan her name. Then, telling herself firmly not to be a fool, she pushed away from the reassuring bulk of her truck and stepped toward the bushes.

She had only forced herself to take a few steps when the glare of headlights stabbed through the deepening gloom. Without thinking, Tory scrambled into her truck and rolled up her window, then reached with a shaking hand to make sure both doors were locked. The approaching car slowed, then stopped in front of her.

Her hand trembled so badly that it took a moment to shove the key into the ignition. By then, the door of the vehicle in front of her had opened and Holt was striding toward her.

"What are you doing out here?"

Even though she hadn't opened her window, she heard his voice. Rolling down the window just enough to answer him, she said, "I got a phone call that there was an injured dog out here. I'm trying to find him."

"It's going to storm any minute."

"I know. That's why I hurried out here. I wanted to find him before the storm hit."

Holt rested his fingers in the open crack of the window and leaned toward her. "Don't you know better than to stop on a deserted road in the dark? Or have you forgotten what's been going on around here?"

"I haven't forgotten. I didn't go more than five feet away from my car."

His hands tightened on her window. She smelled the faint tang of the soap he used as his fingers blanched white only inches from her eyes. "You shouldn't have gotten out of the car at all. God only knows who could be waiting for you in those woods."

His words sent a chill swirling through her and made her stomach tighten. "Don't be ridiculous," she muttered. "I'm only looking for a dog."

"Who called you? Did they give you a name, or did you recognize the voice?"

"No," she admitted. "I couldn't tell if it was a man or a woman, and when I asked who it was they hung up."

"Damn it, Tory," he exploded. "I thought you had more sense than this."

"A lot of people don't want to give their name when they report an injured animal," she protested. "They think that if they do, we'll assume it's theirs and make them pay the bills."

"I doubt whoever was on the phone was worried about being dunned for money." His voice was grim. "Why didn't you call me? I would have come out here with you."

"How do I know it wasn't you on the phone?" The

words were out of her mouth before she could stop them, and he let go of her window and straightened.

"You don't. And if I were you I'd leave now, while you still can. I'll look around and see if I can find any signs of a dog." His hand hovered lightly on the butt of his gun. "But I don't expect that I will."

Her heart pounded in her chest. He towered over her, his uniform dark and menacing in the dim light, and for a moment she was back on a Chicago expressway with another policeman standing over her, his hand resting on his gun.

Swallowing hard, she forced herself to look at him. This was Holt, and she was in Eagle Ridge, Michigan. "I'm sorry," she whispered. "I didn't mean—"

"It doesn't matter what you meant," he cut her off. "Go home. Get away from here. Lock yourself into your house and call Jack Williams to come and sit in front of it until I get there."

She wanted to tell him she didn't need Jack Williams, that she didn't think Holt was the one who'd called her, but the words wouldn't come out. Every time she tried to say them, the sight of his uniform silenced her.

"Roll up your window, Tory, and drive like hell." His harsh voice stabbed into her, pricking her with pain. "Go on—"

Suddenly he snapped his head up. When she opened her mouth to speak, he held up his hand for silence. Staring into the darkness that had seeped into the forest, he stood motionless and tense, listening.

"Roll up your windows, lock your doors and start your engine," he finally whispered. "If you see anything or anyone but me come out of the woods, hit the gas and don't stop until you're at the police station in Eagle Ridge. Tell Jack Williams where I am, then wait there. *Do not* go back to your house."

Without another word he moved into the woods. After a few steps he disappeared, swallowed by the trees and the darkness.

Chapter 6

Tory clutched the steering wheel of her truck and stared into the woods. The approaching storm had sucked all the light out of the forest, leaving nothing but an impenetrable wall of blackness.

Her hands tightened on the hard vinyl. Holt was in there somewhere, and the gun that hung by his side was a pitiful weapon against the menace that rolled off the trees like a thick fog.

The truck rocked gently in the wind, as if swayed by a giant, invisible hand. The tips of the pines bent closer to the ground, their boughs waving like arms beckoning for her. The familiar edginess that she associated with the trees sliced through her. The forest was a giant magnet, pulling her relentlessly into its heart. Her hand shifted to the door handle before she pulled it back in horror.

What was the matter with her? What was out there, in the darkness of the forest, that seemed to be able to creep into her mind? She closed her eyes, as if by shutting out the sight of the trees she could take away their power. The truck shifted subtly again, as if someone had bumped it, and her eyes flew open.

There was no one out there in the gloom. No sign of Holt or a dog, no stranger standing next to her truck. She might have been the only living soul for hundreds of miles, alone except for the trees that called her name.

Her hand shaking, she reached for the radio. She needed company, and music would have to do. A rollicking honky-tonk song by Joe Diffie blared out of the speakers, and she abruptly switched the radio off. More than company, she needed to be able to listen, to hear if anyone approached her truck.

Another blast of wind made the truck tremble, then two fat raindrops hit the windshield. The next moment the heavens opened and a wall of water crashed down on her. The rain poured out of the sky, so heavy she couldn't see the front of her truck. She peered out the window, worried about Holt, wondering if anyone was approaching her truck in the driving rain.

A figure appeared suddenly at her door and she jumped, reaching for the gearshift. Before she could jam the truck into gear and drive away, she realized it was Holt. His arms were full of something gray and wet.

When she rolled down the window the rained streamed in, soaking her jacket and face. "What's that?" she shouted over the wind.

"Your dog." She could hear the grimness in his voice even over the noise of the storm.

"Is it alive?"

"Barely. I'll put him in my truck and follow you to the clinic. Don't get out of your truck until I get there."

Without another word he disappeared into the darkness. When Tory heard his Blazer start, she eased her truck into gear and pulled onto the road. She strained to see through the gloom and the rain. Why had Holt told her not to get out of her truck until he got to the clinic? Surely the fact that he'd found the dog meant the phone call was legitimate and not a trap to lure her into the woods.

It took hours to reach the clinic. At least Tory felt like she'd been driving that long when she finally pulled in. Night had fallen, and she realized that in her hurry to get to the injured dog she'd forgotten to turn on the porch lights. Her house and the clinic looked blank and unwelcoming, dark and deserted and surrounded by the forest.

It only took a minute for Holt's truck to pull into the driveway behind hers. Her hand tightened around the door handle as she watched his headlights pierce the blackness of the storm as he approached. She felt absurdly reassured by his presence. By the time he'd stopped the engine and gotten out of the Blazer, she had scrambled out of her truck and was standing inside the clinic, holding the door open.

Holt ran in, clutching the gray bundle to his chest. "Where do you want him?" he asked, shaking a strand of wet hair out of his face.

"Bring him into the operating room." Tory hurried ahead of Holt and turned on the lights, reaching for the long metal pole that held two bags of intravenous fluids. She turned in time to see Holt ease the dog out of his arms and onto the stainless steel table. Holt's hand smoothed the dog's head once, then he stepped back and looked at her, his face grim.

"It's a damn good thing that I came along when I did. Look." Tory took a step closer. Her stomach jumped with pain as she looked at the animal.

His front and rear legs were tied together with thin pieces of twine pulled cruelly tight. All four of the animal's feet were swollen and red. A similar piece of twine was wrapped around the dog's neck. It, too, was too tight, and the string had dug deeply into the skin of his neck. Dried blood had crusted over the string, burying it deep in his flesh.

Tory laid a reassuring hand on the dog's head as she turned horrified eyes to Holt. "Where did you find him?"

Holt's mouth tightened as he looked at the dog. "About twenty yards into the woods. Far enough that he couldn't be seen from the road, but close enough that you probably would have found him. And found whoever put him there.''

Tory stared at Holt, fear stirring in her belly. ''What do you mean?'' she whispered.

''Do you think it was a coincidence that this dog was in the woods tonight, after you got that phone call?'' he said roughly. ''Think about it for a minute. What do you think would have happened if I hadn't shown up and you had gone into those woods alone?''

''I don't know. What do *you* think would have happened?'' She stared at the man next to her, seeing the black anger in his eyes.

''I think someone would have found you with your throat cut.'' His voice was brutal. ''This dog was left in the woods to lure you to someone. There's no other explanation.''

''Maybe someone saw him and didn't want to get involved,'' she protested. Her mind refused to accept the other possibility. ''Maybe the person who called knows who did it and just wanted the animal taken care of.''

''And maybe there haven't been two murders in Eagle Ridge in the last month and a half.'' His voice rose and he took a step closer to her. ''Come on, Tory, the person who called you wasn't concerned about this dog. He was just using it to get to you. What more has to happen before you realize that you're in danger? Someone tried to break into your clinic, you saw someone watching you, and now someone called you to come out to the woods. Face the facts. You're in danger here.''

Tory didn't look at him. Instead she watched the dog as her hand stroked his side, feeling his bony ribs and painfully thin body. One part of her acknowledged that Holt was probably right. This dog didn't belong to anyone. He had the gaunt, ragged appearance of a stray. She'd seen too many of them in her practice in Chicago not to know.

Then the dog turned his head to look at her, his brown eyes glassy with shock, and she forgot about what or who waited for her in the woods. Her stomach twisted with pain as she looked at the suffering animal. Her own fears receded. "I need to take care of this dog," she murmured, reaching for a pair of scissors.

The dog laid quietly as she cut through the twine that bound his feet together. His legs twitched a couple of times, and he tried to raise his head from the table. Then he settled onto the cold steel.

"What can I do?" Holt's quiet voice cut through her concentration, and she looked at him, startled.

"You don't have to stay, you know. I'm used to working alone."

"I know I don't have to stay. I want to."

She nodded. "Go into the kennel. Get some towels, and in the cabinet over the sink you'll find a bunch of big plastic bottles. Fill them with hot water and bring them here. We need to get him warmed up."

Without another word he disappeared, and Tory turned her attention to the dog. By the time Holt returned, his arms full of bottles and towels, she'd started intravenous fluids in the dog's leg and given him a couple of shots for the shock. She barely looked up when Holt walked into the surgery room.

"I'm going to lift him up," she said, speaking in a low voice. "Slide one of those towels underneath him, then wrap the others around the hot water bottles." Silently he did as she told him, then handed her the wrapped bottles one by one. They warmed her chilled hands, and she placed them gently around the dog's body, finally covering him with the last towel.

"What do we do now?" Holt asked.

She looked at him. "First we take that string off his neck and treat the wound, then we wait."

"For what?"

"To see if he's going to recover from the shock."

She saw his mouth tighten as he looked at the helpless animal. "How long before you can tell?"

"If he's going to make it he should show some signs of improvement in an hour or so. If he survives the night he'll probably be all right."

"Tell me what you need me to do."

She watched him as he looked at the dog, and something shifted inside her. He didn't have to stay here and help her. He could have left her alone with the dog and gone to the comfort of his own house. Nine out of ten people who found an injured dog would have done just that.

A cynical, disbelieving voice pointed out that he was only trying to score points with her. But another part of her didn't think so. His jaw clenched tight, he stared at the animal with dark anger in his eyes. Anger, and a deep, deep pain that for once he didn't try to disguise.

She looked away, uncomfortable with his raw emotion. "Getting this string off his neck is probably going to hurt him. Why don't you steady his head and try to keep him still?"

He nodded once and bent over, resting his elbows on the table. Taking the dog's head in his big hands, he stroked the dirty, wet hair and murmured something low and soothing. The dog's tail lifted feebly and thumped twice against the table.

Her chest tightened and a hot ball of tears swelled in her throat. The trusting brown eyes of the dog were fixed on Holt's suddenly soft gray ones. The fear and mistrust of Holt that had lodged inside her like a jagged lump of ice for the past few days blurred and began to melt. She turned away, fumbling with the instruments she'd need to remove the string.

When the suture scissors clattered to the floor she left the room, gathering her composure as she found a clean pair. When she returned, Holt looked at her, his eyes dark with worry.

"He's shaking."

Laying her hand on the dog, she felt his tremors and nodded, relief flooding through her. "That's good," she said, giving Holt a tiny smile. "It means he's warming up. He'll keep shivering until his body temperature is close to normal."

Holt relaxed and placed one hand gently on the dog's rib cage. "I was afraid it meant he was getting worse."

She shook her head and reached for the pan of warm antiseptic solution she'd made up. "Worse would be if he didn't start shivering. It would mean the shock was deepening."

She pulled on a pair of latex gloves, rested her hand lightly on the dog's neck and looked at him. "I'm afraid this is going to hurt, fella," she murmured. Lifting her gaze to Holt, she added, "If you'd rather wait in the other room until I'm done, I'll understand."

Holt looked at her, his eyes dark and his gaze unfathomable. "I'll stay."

Nodding, she reached for the stack of gauze pads she'd placed on the tray with her instruments and the antiseptic solution. "Talk to him, then, while I work."

As she cleaned the wound on the animal's neck, Holt stroked the dog's head and murmured to him. When she finally cut the string and eased it off, both the dog and Holt flinched, but Holt held the animal's head steady and his voice never faltered.

It only took a few more minutes for Tory to tend the wound and cover it with an antibiotic ointment, then bandage it. Straightening, she looked at Holt. One hand was clenched tight around the edge of the table, his knuckles showing white against the tan of his skin. The other smoothed gently over the dog's head and ears, his touch light as thistledown.

"I'm finished," she said softly.

His hand stilled on the dog. "Now what?"

The dog's shivering had slowed down until only an occasional shudder wracked his body. His eyes were beginning to look more alert. Hope blossomed in her chest. "Now we wait and see how he is in the morning."

"How do you think he'll be in the morning?"

"The standard line is that he isn't out of danger yet." Her gaze slid from the dog to Holt, and her mouth relaxed in a slight smile. "But if I was a betting woman I'd say he's probably going to be fine."

Holt stood. "Thank you, Tory," he said quietly.

"For what? His treatment was routine. I didn't do anything special."

"Yes, you did. You cared about what happened to him. I saw how gentle your hands were as you worked on him, how you tried not to hurt him."

Shrugging, she turned away to clean up the mess she'd made. "Of course I tried not to hurt him. I wanted to help him."

His hand closed around her arm, preventing her from moving away from him. Heat pulsed into her from his fingers, starting a throbbing deep inside her. Slowly, reluctant to let him see her reaction to his touch, she looked at him.

"Not everyone would have." Holt's voice was a low murmur, intimate even in the brightly lit, stark room. "Not even every vet would have done what you did tonight. A lot of people wouldn't have given a damn about a dirty stray dog."

"You did." The words seemed to come out of her on their own.

He looked away from her and let her go, shoving his hands into his pockets. Clearing his throat, he glanced at the dog on the table. "Yeah, well, he's evidence." When he looked at her, the shutters were in his eyes, blocking her view of his soul. But she'd seen it earlier, and it was a sight she knew she would never forget.

In silence he helped her clean up. The residue from the brief moment when he'd touched her lingered in the air, making it thick and heavy with expectation. It was almost impossible to move in the small surgery room without accidentally brushing against him, and each time she did she jumped away from the spark that seemed to arc between them.

When all the instruments had been washed and she had no other excuses for ignoring him, she forced herself to face him. It unnerved her to find him watching her. Trying to ignore the sensation fluttering in her chest, she said, "I'm not going to leave him here in the clinic tonight. Would you help me carry him over to the house?"

"Of course," he said as he pushed himself away from the table. Watching her steadily, he added, "Do you take all of your patients to your house at night?"

Ignoring the question, she said, "It'll be easier than running back over here every couple of hours." She looked at the dog rather than at Holt. "If he's in a cage in my kitchen I won't have to go as far."

"Uh-huh." He paused, then murmured quietly, "Just routine, I know," and she realized she hadn't fooled him at all.

She didn't want Holt to be able to read her so easily. It implied a dangerous level of intimacy, and that was the last thing she wanted. There was no room for intimacy in her life right now, especially with a cop.

But what had happened tonight had shattered forever the myth that all cops were alike. Shifting uneasily, she looked away from Holt's hand, still resting on the dog's head. Holt had allowed her to see a tender side of him that she suspected few other people knew about.

"If you'll carry the IV stand, I'll carry the dog. Don't worry about the lights. I'll have to make another trip over here."

As she slid her hands underneath the dog, Holt obligingly picked up the long metal rod that held the intravenous solution. The dog yelped once, then relaxed as she shifted him in her arms. He was a pitifully light burden.

As soon as she walked out the door of the clinic, the sense of menace slammed into her. The rain had stopped, but the wind had gotten stronger and now it howled through the trees, screeching her name as it demanded her presence among them.

Holt stopped. "What is it? And don't tell me nothing. You flinched as if someone had just hit you."

"I don't know," she whispered. "The trees. There's something there. I can feel it."

Shifting the intravenous pole to his left hand, he let his right hand hover over the butt of his gun. Staring into the woods for a long time, he finally turned to her. "I don't see anything."

"I don't, either. But it's there."

"Let's get to your house. I'll call Jack Williams and have him come out and look while I stay with you."

Feeling the trees pressing closer to her, she began to walk toward the house, wishing passionately that she'd turned on the lights before she'd left to find the dog. She wasn't sure which was worse, entering a completely dark house or staying out here with the trees. For the first time, she began to wonder if maybe she shouldn't listen to Holt and move into town, at least until she'd regained some of her equilibrium.

"Where are your keys?" Holt's voice murmured into her ear, his breath soft and warm against her cheek.

"In my pocket." As she tried to shift the dog and grab them, he reached out and slid his hand into her pocket. The feel of his fingers pressed against her hip sent a flash of heat through her. When he closed his hand around the keys and pulled them out of her pocket, she moved away from him with an awkward step.

Holt opened her front door and flipped on both the outside and inside lights before he stepped aside to let her enter. As she headed for the kitchen, he touched her arm. "Wait."

A few seconds later he reappeared. "The kitchen's fine." Taking the IV stand in his hand again, he led her toward the kitchen. After she'd laid the dog on the floor he said, "I'm going to check the rest of the house."

Her fear began to ease as she sat on the floor next to the dog and watched Holt disappear up the stairs. In a few minutes he reappeared. "Nothing's been disturbed, as far as I can tell."

"Thank you for checking. You've been…it makes me feel better when you check," she finished with a rush, embarrassed to admit that she was scared in her own house.

He squatted next to her. "I'm worried about you, out

here alone. Especially after this.'' He looked at the dog, then at her. ''Are you sure you can't find someplace else to live?''

''I'll think about it.'' It was all she could promise. Even though she was scared out here, if she left she would somehow be admitting that she couldn't handle it. She would be admitting that the policeman in Chicago had taken much more from her than a little blood and flesh.

''Do you want me to call Jack and have him come check the woods?''

She shook her head. ''He didn't find anything the other night, and I suspect he wouldn't find anything tonight. I'm sure with the storm he has other things to worry about.''

''Do you want me to go look?''

''No!'' Clearing her throat, she lowered her voice. ''No, you don't have to go outside again. You're just getting dry now.'' His shirt stuck to his chest in a few spots, and she told herself to look away. She didn't want to notice how the damp material clung to his broad shoulders, or how the wet denim of his jeans only molded them more perfectly to his long thighs. Forcing herself to look at the gun strapped to his right hip, she tried to focus on that.

Holt eased himself to the floor and leaned against a cabinet as he watched her. ''Tell me about the trees.''

She turned to the dog, checking his IV and rearranging his blanket. ''There's not much to tell. I'm just not used to living in the woods. The only trees in Chicago are either in the parks or carefully spaced on the parkways.''

''I think there is something to tell,'' he said quietly. ''I don't think you're a woman who spooks easily, but you're spooked by those trees. You told me there was something evil in them, and I want to know what it is.''

''So do I,'' she cried. ''I don't want it in my mind. If I knew what it was I could stop it.'' She clamped her mouth shut, appalled at what she'd revealed. It was only because of the strain of the evening, she told herself. She was tired, and she wasn't guarding her tongue.

Leaning forward, Holt said, "What exactly do you feel out there, Tory?"

She stared at him for a long moment before shrugging. He wouldn't stop until she'd told him. It was humiliating to have to admit her fears, but humiliation wouldn't kill her. And maybe, a tiny voice deep inside her murmured, telling someone else would take away the fear and the mystery.

"I feel scared. I feel like there's something in those trees that's calling me, something that wants me. Sometimes I even start walking toward them. When the wind blows, I can hear the trees calling my name." She slanted him a look, then turned away. "Tell me I'm just a neurotic city woman."

He was silent for a long time. Finally he said, "I don't think you're neurotic. I have no idea what's going on, but I'm not going to tell you to ignore your feelings. Sometimes all you have is your instincts."

"I'm sure it's just getting used to living here," she said, illogically reassured by his refusal to dismiss her feelings as silly. "It's about as far removed from Chicago as you can get."

"Maybe, maybe not. Do me a favor, Tory. Stay out of the woods."

She gave a shaky laugh. "You don't have to worry about that. I'm not going anywhere near those trees."

"Now that we have that settled, what are we going to do with him?" Holt nodded toward the dog.

"I have a crate in the basement. I'll put him in there for the night so he doesn't wander around and pull out his IV line. Then we'll see how he is in the morning."

"Do you want me to get the crate for you?"

She nodded gratefully. She hadn't been looking forward to wrestling it up the basement stairs. "Thanks. It's sitting in the corner."

A few minutes later the dog was installed in the crate on a bed of old towels. As they stood staring at him, Holt murmured, "What's going to happen to him?"

She knew what he was asking, but she didn't want to tell him what had already crossed her mind. "First he has to survive. Then I'll worry about what to do with him." She shifted her gaze to Holt. "Do you want him?"

His eyes softened for a moment, then he tightened his lips and shook his head once. "I have no right to get a dog. I'm gone for twelve hours at a time, and that's on a good day. It wouldn't be fair to any animal."

"A dog would think that was paradise compared to running the streets of Eagle Ridge, scrounging for scraps."

"No. I can't take him."

Looking at his set face, Tory saw the pain again. Pain that his brusque answer couldn't quite cover up. "Have you ever had a dog?"

This time the pain that seared his face was raw, as if she'd torn the scab off a healing wound. "Once, a few years ago. It died."

"It can take a while to get over the loss of a pet," she said softly. "But eventually most people want to get another one."

"I'm not taking this dog, Tory. I don't have time in my life to deal with a pet."

His anguish seemed out of proportion to the loss of a pet a few years ago. "What happened, Holt?" she asked softly. She didn't question her need to know. Suddenly it seemed very important to be able to offer him some comfort, the way he'd comforted her when she'd confided her fears about the trees.

He turned away. "I had a dog and he died. That's all there is to it. It's not important anymore."

"I think it is. It might help to talk about it."

"It won't." His voice was flat and final. "Drop it, Tory."

"All right." She searched for something to say that would cut the tension swirling through the air. "Will I see you tomorrow?" She felt her face redden, and added quickly, "To check on the dog, I mean."

"What do you think, Tory?"

He watched her steadily, and her heartbeat increased to a heavy, primitive rhythm against her ribs. She wanted to look away, but his gaze captured hers and held her captive. She watched, helpless, as his gray eyes turned dark and smoldered with heat.

"I guess you will. After all, he's evidence in your case," she said lightly, hoping her flippant answer would ease the tension in the room.

It didn't. "Is that why you think I've been coming out here every night? Because of what's been going on in Eagle Ridge?" His low voice sounded like black velvet. "I thought you were smarter than that, Tory."

When he reached for her she didn't even think of resisting. His strong hands gripped her shoulders, and he pulled her toward him. "Let me show you why I've been coming out here."

He stared at her, then his mouth closed over hers. This time his lips didn't tempt and tease. His kiss was dark and hot, possessing her and firing her blood. When his tongue traced her lips, she opened to him immediately and he plunged into her mouth.

There was no room for fear as heat and desire crashed over her, leaving her trembling and aching for more of him. "Holt," she whispered into his mouth.

In answer he pulled her closer, easing her along the length of him. His hands skimmed her back, touching her as if he was savoring every inch of her. She felt his muscles quiver, felt the control he imposed upon himself as he slowly wrapped his arms around her.

She realized he was holding himself back so he wouldn't frighten her, and a wave of tenderness washed over her. It mixed with the desire and made her ache inside, made her want him with an intensity she'd never felt before.

Winding her arms around his neck, she pulled him closer and touched his lips with her tongue. He groaned, deep in his throat, and shifted so she stood in the cradle of his legs. He throbbed against her belly, hard and hot, and another burst of liquid heat turned her legs to jelly.

Pushing her against the counter, he slid one hand to her waist and slowly pulled her shirt free of her slacks. His hand slipped inside and touched her bare skin, and she couldn't disguise the tremor that shook her. Feeling her response, he thrust against her as his hand crept up her back, leaving a trail of fire wherever he touched.

As his hand slid over her ribs and around to her belly, she clung to him, lost in the sensations. His tongue thrust deeply into her mouth, mimicking the motion of his hips. When he cupped her breast in his palm she moaned, tightening her hold on him. Pleasure so intense it was almost pain speared through her as he gently squeezed her nipple.

He released her breast and, drugged with desire, she opened her eyes to look at him. He stared at her, his face tight with passion, as he slowly unbuttoned her blouse.

She watched him as he spread her blouse open. He touched the hollow above her collarbone and let his fingers trail down the valley between her breasts and over her belly. Then, raising his eyes to hers, he murmured, "I've wanted you since the first day I met you."

Her tongue was thick and heavy in her mouth. She couldn't speak. Every part of her brain was short-circuited except for the part that poured overwhelming pleasure through her veins. He looked at her chest again, and slowly reached out and released the hook on her bra.

Brushing the flimsy material aside, he let her breasts spill out into his palms. She stood there holding on to him, trapped between his legs and the counter, watching him hold her breasts in his hands, and knew that not even in her dreams had she ever felt or seen anything so erotic. It didn't matter that they stood under the harsh fluorescent lights of the kitchen, or that both of them were still fully clothed. She was more aroused than she'd ever been in her life.

Until he bent and took her nipple into his mouth. Arching back against the counter, she heard soft cries in the quiet of the room and realized they were coming from her.

"Oh, yes, Tory," he murmured against her breast, his

tongue flicking out to circle her nipple again. "Tell me what you like. Tell me what you want."

Slowly she slid her hands down his back until she cupped his buttocks in her palms. His muscles felt rock hard beneath her fingers. When she pressed him closer to her, it was his turn to groan her name.

His hands slid down her stomach and fumbled with the button of her slacks. Her breath caught in her throat as she instinctively pushed against him, throbbing as she anticipated his touch.

As his hand slid beneath the waistband of her slacks she heard a growl behind them. Holt's hand stilled, then he slowly withdrew it and moved away from her.

She opened her eyes to see the dog swaying on his feet, staring at the front door, all the hair on his back raised and his lip curled in a snarl.

Chapter 7

Holt eased his gun out of its holster and glanced at her. "Stay in this room and don't go near the window." Without another word he headed for the front door.

She stood rooted to the floor, her body still quivering with the passion he'd unleashed, and watched him disappear into the night. As the throbbing receded she felt strangely unconnected, as if her body was an alien thing, a shell totally unfamiliar to her. Finally, hearing the dog growl again, she looked at his crate then moved awkwardly to kneel on the floor next to it.

His dirty, matted gray hair was still raised in a line that extended the length of his back. Although he shifted from one foot to another, as if it hurt to stand too long on his swollen paws, he was oddly still and intent as he stared at the front door. Primitive bloodlust vibrated through him, and as she watched him the hair rose on the back of her neck.

"Hey, fella, it's all right," she murmured, leaning closer to the crate.

Slowly, reluctantly, the dog turned to look at her. The

aggression that burned in his eyes slowly faded as she continued to talk to him. When she was sure he wouldn't bite her, she reached in and stroked the top of his head.

At her touch his tail wagged once then he dropped in a heap on the towels in the crate. The hair on his back smoothed, and he lowered his head to his paws. Tory continued to pet him and murmur to him until she heard Holt come in the front door.

"I didn't see a thing." He stepped into the kitchen, bringing a whiff of the fresh, storm-washed air. "If anyone was there, he was gone by the time I got outside."

Tory looked up from where she sat by the dog's cage. "The dog certainly acted like he heard something outside, but maybe he was just dreaming." She hesitated, her face reddening as she added, "I wasn't paying much attention to him before he started to growl."

Holt let his eyes travel down Tory's body, and his voice got huskier. "I wasn't paying much attention to him, either."

Tory looked down to see where his gaze lingered, and realized that her shirt and bra were still hanging open. Flushing again, she pushed herself away from the dog crate and stumbled to her feet, turning away from Holt.

He grasped her shoulders and turned her to face him. She didn't meet his gaze as she struggled to button her blouse. Gently pushing her hands away, he reached out to fasten her bra. Her skin burned when he touched her, and the desire he'd ignited earlier flamed to life.

"You have nothing to be ashamed of, Tory." His hands lingered in the valley between her breasts, then reached for the edges of her blouse. "In fact, I owe you an apology. I was so out of control that if the dog hadn't growled I would have taken you on the kitchen counter."

She closed her eyes as he pushed the last button through its hole, her body throbbing with the memory of his strong thighs pressing against hers. His taste lingered in her mouth, and her breasts still burned from his caresses. But most of all her heart ached for the tenderness she'd felt beneath his rigid control.

As his hands slid down her arms she opened her eyes. "I don't recall that I was doing a lot of objecting."

His lips brushed her cheek. "Casual sex on a kitchen counter isn't your style, Tory. I know that. The fact that I want you, that I have from the beginning, doesn't change that." His fingers trailed down her cheek and across her mouth in a tender, almost unconscious gesture, then he shoved his hands into the pockets of his jeans. "I'm sorry I lost control."

She wanted to tell him she wasn't, that she meant every minute of it, but she didn't. He was right. Casual sex never had been and never would be her style. And if that was all it would have been to him, she was thankful the dog had stopped them before she'd made an even bigger fool out of herself.

Her gaze lingered on him, taking in every detail. The gun made her pause, but she didn't feel the revulsion she expected. Something had changed tonight. Seeing Holt with the dog had forever altered her image of him. The dog had trusted him, and so, on some level, had she. There was no way she could ever think of him merely as a policeman again.

The thought scared her senseless. When he was one of them he was easy to dismiss. Now that barrier was shaky, and he was becoming a formidable threat to her need for control. If the dog hadn't growled, she probably would have made love with him.

Except that it wouldn't have been making love, she told herself. It would have been sex. Hot, passionate, burning-her-alive sex, but sex just the same.

She shoved her shirttail into her slacks as she kept her back carefully turned. "Thank you for checking outside. I'll sleep easier now." Who was she trying to fool? If she managed to fall asleep at all tonight it would be a miracle.

"Tory..." She could hear him taking a step toward her,

and she stiffened. He stopped behind her, but he didn't touch her.

"I have nothing to give you," he said, so softly she had to strain to hear him. "And even if I did, I'm a cop. Don't forget that."

Slowly she turned to face him. "I haven't. Thank you for helping with the dog, Holt. I'll see you tomorrow."

She stood stiff and straight in front of him, daring him to say anything else. After a moment he nodded and walked away. When he reached the front door he turned and looked at her, but whatever words he intended to say didn't come out. Instead, he raised one hand and slipped out the door.

Standing by the counter, her heart and body aching, she listened to the sound of his Blazer fade into the distance. When she couldn't hear it any longer, she pushed away and moved to the kitchen window.

The lights were still on in her clinic. For a second panic slid over her at the thought of walking alone in the darkness to turn them off. Then she stood up straighter. There was no reason the lights couldn't stay on all night tonight. After what had happened earlier this evening, she would be a fool to go outside alone.

And she hadn't been a fool for a long time. Not until she met Holt Adams.

Holt drove along the rain-slick road, his headlights slicing thin wedges of illumination through the darkness. He didn't pass another car in either direction as he drove toward Eagle Ridge. Most people were smart enough to stay home on a night like this.

As he approached the spot where he'd found Tory earlier that evening he slowed down and stopped. Any evidence of a third vehicle on the shoulder of the road was long since washed away by the rain. He doubted there had been any in the first place. The murderer, he was beginning to realize, was far more than lucky. He was damned clever.

Holt burned to get out and plunge into the woods, to search the area where he'd found the dog for any evidence.

He stayed in his truck. Between the rain and the darkness, he didn't have a snowball's chance in hell of finding anything. Shoving the Blazer in gear, he headed to town. Tomorrow would be soon enough to look. He'd have a better chance of finding what was there in the daylight. But he held out slim hopes of finding anything. Whoever had left the dog in the woods for Tory to find was a master at leaving nothing behind.

He had no doubt the person who'd called her and told her about the dog was the person responsible for the two murders. His hands clutched the steering wheel and he pushed the accelerator a little harder. She'd been in Eagle Ridge less than a week, and the murderer had already noticed her. Panic clawed at his chest, and his stomach tightened with fear.

It was happening all over again, and he felt helpless to stop it. Two women had died. How many more would be killed before he caught the person responsible?

Tory would not be one of them. He sped down the quiet streets of Eagle Ridge, exceeding the legal speed limit by a considerable amount. When he reached the small apartment building where Bobby Duvall lived, he slowed down, searching for his car in the parking lot.

It was there, sitting in a corner, covered with drops of moisture from the rain. There were no signs of mud on the fenders or the tires, but the rainstorm could account for that. The windows in Bobby's apartment were all dark. He sat in the truck for a while, then slowly drove off.

There wasn't a soul on the street tonight. All the citizens of Eagle Ridge appeared to be at home, staying dry and minding their own business. All but one. Which of them was it? Who had been in the woods earlier, binding the dog's legs together, waiting for Tory to come looking for it?

Easing to a halt in front of the police station, he looked around the quiet, seemingly peaceful town for a few minutes before getting out of his truck. He walked inside to find Jack Williams sitting in his chair, his boots propped up on his desk.

Jack's feet dropped to the floor and he stood up, a faint streak of red on his cheeks. "I wasn't expecting you, Chief."

"I noticed." Ignoring the young policeman's discomfort, he asked, "Any reports of prowlers tonight?"

Jack relaxed slightly. "Not a thing. Nobody goes too far from home on a night like this. It's been quiet as a tomb."

"I suppose that's an appropriate analogy, considering what's been happening here."

Jack flushed again and shifted his feet. "There haven't been any problems tonight," he insisted. "I've only gotten a couple of calls, and they were both about the storm knocking out the power." He looked at Holt again and slowly tensed. "Is there something wrong? Is that why you're here?"

Even though he was young, Jack Williams was no fool. Holt shook his head. "I just stopped by to let you know I'm going to do a little patrolling tonight. If you need to get hold of me, use the radio because I won't be home."

Williams said quietly, "It wasn't your fault, you know."

Holt jerked his head toward the younger man. "What the hell is that supposed to mean?"

"It means I know why you never go home and that you hardly ever sleep. You're not responsible for the two women who were killed. No one expects the police to prevent all crimes." His face crinkled in a trace of a smile. "Not even the city council."

Holt looked away, unable to watch the knowing compassion in the other man's eyes. "I may not be responsible for their deaths, but I sure as hell am responsible for making sure it doesn't happen again. If you get any calls that sound even the least bit suspicious, call me on the radio."

He walked out of the office before Williams could answer or give him any more of his theories about responsibility. The kid didn't know a damn thing. He may not have been responsible for the first death, but the second had opened a wound that was still raw. And if there was a third...

If there was a third it would be Tory Falcon. He jammed the key into the ignition of the Blazer and let the engine roar to life. Tory was the target of this madman. He knew it, felt it in his bones. And he intended to do everything in his power to stop him.

By the time he reached the clinic he'd squashed the panic, turning the fear into cold, calculating anger. Letting his truck idle on the road, he looked down the driveway and saw that the lights were still on inside the clinic. "Thank God," he muttered, realizing she'd at least had enough sense not to go to the clinic to turn them off.

Turning his attention to her house, he saw lights blazing out of every first-floor window. Either she hadn't gone to bed yet or she was trying hard to make it look that way. Easing his truck into gear, he headed down her driveway and cut the engine as he glided silently to her front door.

As he shoved the seat as far back as it would go and struggled to get comfortable, he stared at the lights, wondering what she was doing. And told himself with his next breath it didn't matter, as long as she was safe.

Why was someone stalking Tory Falcon? Was it simply because she was new to the community, with few friends and no family, living in an isolated location? Was it because she was an easy target? Or was there another, darker reason?

Holt's hands curled around the steering wheel as he stared at the woods surrounding Tory's house, dread curdling in his stomach. He had been spending a lot of time at the veterinary clinic. To a casual observer, it would appear he was interested in the new vet.

Had the murderer's attention focused on Tory because of Holt's interest in her? Had he somehow drawn Tory into the battle between himself and the murderer? Or was the grudge more personal, the hatred focused more directly?

Holt thought again of the look on Bobby Duvall's face as they'd stood outside the grocery store three days ago.

Bobby had a lot of reasons for hating both Tory and Holt. And what better way to settle two scores at once?

Slowly Holt looked at Tory's house. Was his continual presence out here putting her in more danger? If he never came out here again, would she be safe? And was he willing to take that chance?

He wasn't. He knew it instantly. Regardless of his feelings about her, she was a citizen of Eagle Ridge, and he was sworn to protect her. If this madman had focused on her—and Holt knew, deep down, that he had—then he had no choice but to watch her.

And what were his feelings for her? It was no more than physical wanting, he told himself. Never again would he get emotionally bound up with a woman. It would cause nothing but pain for either of them. No, his feelings for Tory Falcon went no deeper than lust.

Lust was merely an urge, and like all urges it was subject to his will. Wanting her physically he could control and keep separate from the rest of his life. Never again would he hand over his heart to a woman. He'd rather pluck it out of his chest himself. That would hurt far less.

He looked at her house, once more trying to ignore the faint ache beneath his breast.

The baton flashed at her and the pain burst inside her head, making her cry out in agony. But no sound came out of her throat except a choking gurgle. The metallic taste of blood flooded her mouth, and she pushed herself to her knees.

The face of the police officer towering over her was vague and blurry. As she stared, the shadows suddenly shifted and his face came into focus. Holt Adams stood looking at her. There was no baton in his hand, and the expression on his face wasn't one of rage, but Tory felt the fear expanding deep inside her.

He extended one of his hands to her. She stared at it for a long time, hope struggling against the fear that pulsed all around her. Gravel dug into her hands until she lifted them off the road. As she tentatively reached toward Holt, he disappeared into a swirling fog.

Tory opened her eyes to the darkness in her room, her heart drumming in her chest. The fear from the dream seeped away, leaving a dull longing in its place.

The dream had never varied before. As she stared at the white walls of her room, willing her heart to calm down, Holt's face lingered in her mind. Why had he appeared in her nightmare? And what would she have found if she'd managed to take his hand before he vanished? Comfort or more pain? Hope or despair?

She didn't know. Throwing her comforter to the side, she slipped out of bed and told herself that she didn't want to know. Holt Adams was dangerous to her. After the way he'd handled the dog earlier that evening her physical fear of him had eased, but he could inflict a mortal blow to her heart and her soul. And he would be fatal to her attempt to regain control of her life.

Shaking with cold even wrapped in the warmth of the thick robe, she started down the stairs. Thank goodness she'd left the lights on, she thought, shivering. When the third step from the bottom creaked, she only hesitated for a moment. Then she heard the dog stirring and hurried to the kitchen.

He lifted his head when she walked into the room, and thumped his tail once. The sound was muffled against the towels, but she felt her throat swell and tighten. Her eyes burned as she knelt next to him and opened the crate.

"How're you doing, guy? Are you feeling better?"

The dog thumped his tail again in answer and swiped at her hand with his tongue, and Tory smiled mistily as one tear rolled down her face. He was going to be all right. She turned off the flow of fluids from the bag suspended over his head, capped the catheter in his leg then sat back and watched as he stood up.

He moved stiffly and tentatively, obviously reluctant to put any weight on his feet. She let him take a few steps, then gently lowered him to the floor.

"I bet you need to go outside, don't you?" she said softly, and was rewarded with another thump of his tail. She thought about opening the front door and taking him out, and her gaze shifted involuntarily to the kitchen window. Only the tips of the trees were visible, but she swallowed hard. "You'll have to make do with papers tonight, buddy."

It only took a minute to pile newspapers in one corner of the kitchen. The dog seemed to know what they were for, and in another minute had finished relieving himself. Tory bundled the soiled papers into a plastic garbage bag, set it by the back door and turned to the dog, petting him again.

Wide awake, she walked into the living room and settled on the couch. She wasn't surprised when the dog followed her and plopped down on the floor at her feet. As she watched him, a picture of Holt insinuated itself into her head, stroking the dog and murmuring to him in a low voice.

So what if the dog liked him and Holt liked dogs? she asked herself defiantly. It didn't prove anything.

Except that it probably hadn't been Holt who'd put the dog in the woods in the first place. An animal would remember the person who'd tied him up so cruelly. He certainly wouldn't wag his tail the next time he saw him.

Tory sighed and rested her head against the back of the couch. Questions about Holt could chase through her head forever like squirrels in a cage, and it wouldn't make any difference. He'd made his position very clear earlier that evening. He was only interested in one thing, and she'd never been interested in sex for its own sake. And if by chance he decided he wanted more, she wasn't able to give it to him anyway.

A low growl came from the dog at her feet, and she shot up on the couch. He was staring at the front of the house, but his hair wasn't standing on end the way it had earlier.

"You hear something out there, don't you, buddy?" She heard the pleading in her voice and swallowed hard. When he didn't look away from the door she reluctantly slid off the couch, looking from the telephone to the door.

She compromised by getting the phone before she looked out the window. If she saw anything suspicious she could punch in the number for the police station immediately. Clutching the receiver in one clammy hand, she edged over to the window and pressed her back to the wall. Taking several deep breaths, she finally lifted the edge of the curtain and peeked out the window.

A black truck stood in front of her house, blocking the stairs. The phone fell from her hand and clattered to the floor as she stared out, unable to move. Finally she dropped the curtain and fell to her knees, scrabbling for the receiver. Her shaking hands couldn't hold on to it as she frantically tried to press the numbers on the dial.

"Tory, it's me. Open the door."

Holt's voice penetrated the front door, and for a moment she was afraid her imagination was playing a cruel trick on her. As she stared at the door, his voice came through the wood again, louder this time.

"Open the door, Tory. I saw you at the window."

The dog wobbled to the door, tail wagging, and looked at Tory impatiently. Clutching the receiver to her chest, she stood up slowly and walked to the door. Her hand hovered over the doorknob as she called out, "Holt?"

"It's all right, Tory. Unlock the door."

Her damp palm slipped on the cool metal of the doorknob as she fumbled with the lock. She finally got the door open, and Holt stepped into her living room and closed the door behind him.

His gaze traveled down her robe, and she felt heat creep across her cheeks as she pulled the lapels together with one hand. "What are you doing here?" she managed to say. "You scared me to death."

"I'm sorry, I didn't mean to frighten you. I didn't even mean to let you know I was here." He nodded to the couch. "Mind if I sit down? The truck isn't built for comfort."

"Of course," she said instantly, waiting for him to sit

down then choosing the place on the couch farthest from him. He looked like he'd been sitting in the truck most of the night, she thought, watching him. His jacket and shirt were rumpled and twisted, as if he'd shifted in the small seat innumerable times, trying to get comfortable. His skin was gray with fatigue, and his eyes were black coals burning out of deep pits. He rested his head against the back of the couch and closed his eyes.

"Why are you here, Holt?" she asked softly.

Without moving his head he opened his eyes and looked at her. "Because I was worried. Because whoever called you about the dog tonight came too damn close to getting you, and I wasn't about to give him a second chance."

She stared at him, an unexpected mix of feelings stirring in her. He had given up sleeping in his bed so he could sit and guard her door. Tenderness stirred in her chest, along with something else she hurried to label gratitude.

Along with it came another burst of fear. "Things like this aren't supposed to happen in places like Eagle Ridge," she whispered.

"Tell that to Sally Phillips and Carrie Stevens," he retorted, his voice blunt and hard. "They didn't think so, either."

"What should I do, Holt?" Her voice sounded small and frightened, and she cringed. It was hard to be strong and heroic at three o'clock in the morning. Especially when the police chief sat on your couch telling you that you were the target of a killer.

"Leave. Get out of here as fast as you can."

"I can't do that." She looked at her hands, locked together in her lap to prevent him from seeing their trembling. "All my money is tied up in this clinic. I have to stay here and keep it going." Closing her eyes, she willed herself to control the panic. She was trying to rebuild her life on the fragile foundation of this clinic. If she left now, she would be admitting that she couldn't do it.

"Then you're going to have to be more careful," he said, his voice a low growl. "For starters, you keep that clinic door locked and only let in people who have appointments. You don't go outside at night by yourself, even if it's just to walk to the clinic. If someone calls you after hours with an emergency, you put them off until the morning. And you never, ever open the door to your house to anyone. I don't care who they are."

She felt the blood draining from her face as she stared at him. "You're making me a prisoner here," she whispered. "I can't live like that."

"Then you'll die like those other two women," he said, his voice harsh. "That's your choice, Tory. Either cooperate with me or take your chances with the killer."

"But I have to go to the clinic at night if I have a patient in the hospital. And some emergencies won't wait until the morning. What am I supposed to do then?"

"I'll be here every night to walk you to the clinic. And if you get a legitimate emergency, call me and I'll come out." His voice softened. "I know you wouldn't turn an animal away if it needed help, and I don't expect you to do that. But I'm sure the killer knows that, too. It would be far too easy to lure you out of your house some night with a phony emergency call. And you wouldn't think twice about responding to it, would you?"

"Probably not," she admitted. Clenching her hands together in her lap, she stared at her twined fingers. "But you can't spend all your time out here, Holt." Her voice was quiet. "You have other responsibilities and other people to protect. What if the murderer decides to go after someone else?"

He was quiet for a long time. Finally, his voice sounding strained, he said, "I don't think he will. The only prowlers that have been reported since you've been back have been out here. You were the one he tried to lure into the woods with the dog. No, like it or not, this guy seems to be after you. So I'm going to be your shadow."

"You're frightening me." The words seemed to linger in the air of the quiet house, echoing around her ears.

"I'm trying to be realistic. You won't leave, so I have to do what I can to protect you."

She could feel him watching her, but she refused to look at him.

"I don't want you to die, Tory."

At that she did look at him. His gray eyes were distant and forbidding, and he was looking right through her. He was a man lost in grim memories.

She looked away, unable to bear the pain on his face. "I guess I don't have a choice. I would be a fool to refuse to do what you're asking."

"And you're not a fool, are you, Tory?" he murmured.

"I hope not," she whispered. But she was. Only a fool would want things she couldn't have, things she knew would be bad for her. Only a fool would wish the dog hadn't growled and interrupted them earlier.

He pushed himself off the couch. "You should get some sleep," he muttered. "I'll go out to the car and leave you alone."

As if there was the slightest chance she'd get back to sleep tonight, she thought, closing her eyes. When she opened them she was looking into Holt's tired gray eyes.

"You don't have to sleep in the truck." The words were out of her mouth before she had a chance to bite them back. "Why don't you just stay on the couch?"

He paused at the door. "What?"

"If you're going to stay out here, you'd be more comfortable on the couch than in your truck. You're welcome to use it." An odd expression flitted across his face, and she hurried to add, "If you want to, of course."

"I'd want to. You're couch is a damn sight more comfortable than that truck."

He moved toward her, and she told herself to back up, to go upstairs, but she couldn't seem to move. He stopped inches from her. "Thank you, Tory." His gravelly voice was low and intimate in the quiet house. It sounded as if everything in the room was holding its breath. "Good night."

His breath whispered against her cheek, and she found herself swaying toward him. Jerking away, she turned and stumbled on the hem of her robe. His hand clamped around her arm to steady her, but she couldn't bring herself to look at him. She waited until he released her, then hurried to the stairs.

"Good night, Holt." She hated the breathless sound of her voice. "Make yourself at home."

Stupid thing to say, she told herself as she practically ran up the stairs. The last thing she wanted him to feel was at home on her couch. In her room, she began to ease the door shut, then hesitated as she caught a glimpse of the night and the trees outside her window.

Maybe she didn't want to close herself completely inside this room. Leaving the door open a crack, she listened to Holt moving around downstairs for a while, feeling strangely comforted. Finally she slipped off her robe and got into bed.

It wasn't thoughts of the dream and the killer outside that kept her awake, though. All she could think about was Holt lying on the couch in her living room. As she turned over one more time during the endless hours until dawn, she thought that memories of her dream would have been more comfortable than the thoughts burning in her mind tonight.

Chapter 8

The alarm clock shrilled in her ear, and Tory opened her eyes with a silent groan. Her head throbbed from lack of sleep and she wanted nothing more than to roll over and close her eyes again. But the weak light of dawn streamed through her window, mercilessly illuminating the face of her clock. Her first patient would arrive at the clinic all too soon.

Stepping out of the bedroom, she froze as the lights from the living room blazed at her. Then she remembered. Holt was there, standing guard in her living room. Waiting for the murderer to come for her.

The heat clicked on in the house, the warm air rising out of the register at her feet and blowing at the hem of the skimpy nightshirt she wore. It reminded her that she wasn't dressed for company. She hurried into the bathroom and closed the door firmly behind her.

Twenty minutes later she walked downstairs to find the living room empty. A cushion from the couch lay jammed into one end, bunched and rumpled. The rest of the couch was rumpled, too. In fact, as she stared at it, she imagined she could see the faint outline of Holt's body on the cushions. If she sat on the couch, she was sure she would feel the heat from his body wrapping around her.

"Good morning." His slightly husky voice came from the kitchen door, and she jerked her head up to find him watching her. The tails of his flannel shirt were loose, as were the top two buttons. His hair was tousled and his face was shadowed with a day's growth of beard. He looked incredibly sexy as he leaned against the door frame with a cup of coffee in his hand.

She swallowed. "Good morning. Did you sleep well on the couch?"

"Like a rock." He watched her for a moment, then murmured, "It was a lot more comfortable than the seat of the truck." *But not as comfortable as your bed would have been.*

It was as if she could read his mind. His eyes said everything he left unspoken, and she felt her face flame as she stared at him, unable to look away. Something shifted and softened in the gray depths of Holt's gaze, then he blinked and his face hardened. A whimper drew her gaze from Holt, and she looked down to see the dog standing next to him. She seized on the distraction, crouching and trying to concentrate on the dog.

"He looks a lot better this morning," she finally said, surprised to find her voice steady.

"He's looking for food, so I suspect he'll survive."

She looked up sharply at Holt's casual tone. He was staring at the dog, though, and the look in his eyes was anything but casual. As she watched, he bent and ruffled the hair on the dog's back. His hand lingered on the dog's head before he straightened and looked at her.

"He was dancing by the back door, whining, so I let him outside. I hope that's all right."

"It was fine, thanks." Rising, she looked around the kitchen, searching for an excuse to escape. The early-morning intimacy was incredibly awkward. Standing in the kitchen with him only reminded her of what had happened between them the night before. She wasn't sure she'd ever be able to look at the kitchen counter without blushing, and now he was casually leaning against it.

The rumpled couch in the room behind her and his early-morning appearance made her think of things she'd vowed to forget. They stirred longings in her that she'd thought she'd talked herself out of during the long night. Jamming her hands into her pockets, she turned abruptly and walked into the living room, reaching for her coat. "I'm going to run over to the clinic and get some food for him."

"Hold on, I'll go with you."

She heard the faint scrape of denim as he pushed himself away from the counter, then the padding of his stockinged feet as he headed for the living room. The coffee he'd started gurgled in the coffee maker, and the enticing aroma drifted out to her, reminding her again of just how intimate the whole business really was. "That's all right," she said hurriedly, reaching for the door. "I'll be fine."

Before she could turn the knob, he slid his body in front of her. "I'll go with you." His tone of voice told her it would be useless to argue.

She let her hand drop to her side and backed up a step as she looked at his hard, chiseled features. "Aren't you getting carried away? After all, it's daylight and other people will be coming to the clinic soon."

"Soon is the operative word. No one else is there right now, and I'm not going to let you go in there alone."

Her hand tightened around the keys she held until their sharp edges bit into her palm. "You're going to have to leave me alone at some point. You can't keep me safe twenty-four hours a day, you know." Her feeble protest sounded incredibly weak even to her own ears.

He looked up at her as he tied his boots. "I can try."

She didn't say anything as he pulled on his jacket. Her mouth dried as she watched him pull the material away from the holster at his side, leaving his gun exposed. What had seemed melodramatic and unreal at night was becoming grim reality in the hard light of day. Holt was convinced that some maniac was after her and that her life was in danger.

He glanced at her before he opened the door. "I'm going to look around before we go outside, so don't get your shorts in a knot."

"The dog is the only one who's getting his shorts in a knot," she retorted. "He'd like to eat sometime before he has grandchildren."

"He'll survive." The words were clipped and short as Holt opened the door. A blast of cool air greeted her, a hint of the frigid weather that would soon be moving into the Upper Peninsula. Autumn was short in the north woods, and winter long and hard.

She studied his back, watching the way he moved his head slowly from side to side. He wouldn't miss much, of that she was sure. He might be a hard man, and harder to understand, but he was good at his job. He took his responsibilities seriously and did his best to fulfill them. If there really was someone out there stalking her, she could do a lot worse than having Holt on her side.

The tension in his shoulders eased by a fraction. Apparently he hadn't noticed anything out of the ordinary in the woods surrounding the house. Letting his hand move away from his gun, he took a step forward onto her porch.

Then he froze.

He stared down for what seemed like forever, then turned and pushed her into the house. When she tried to look around him, to see what was out there, he took her by the shoulders and moved her away from the door, kicking it shut behind them.

"Go into the kitchen and call the station. Tell whoever's there to get out here with the evidence kit. And you stay in here. Don't look out the windows, don't try to sneak out the back door. Stay in the kitchen."

"What's on my porch?" she whispered.

"Something you don't want to see," he answered, his voice grim.

"Is it...has there been another murder?"

"No, thank God. It's not that."

"Then what's out there? I want to know," she insisted as he hesitated. "It's my front porch."

"A dead cat," he finally said. There was no inflection in his voice. "It's throat's been cut."

Bile welled up in her throat, threatening to overwhelm her. Pressing one hand against her stomach, she stared at Holt, nausea and fear roiling together inside her, swelling until they threatened to suffocate her. "Maybe someone accidentally hit it with a car and brought it here."

"This was no accident." His arm slid around her shoulders, and his fingers brushed over her arm in a brief caress as he led her into the kitchen and eased her into a chair. The red light from the coffee maker glowed at her with an unblinking stare as Holt poured a mug of coffee and set it in front of her. The rich smell made her stomach turn over again, and she jumped up abruptly.

"Maybe the cat's not dead. Maybe it's just hurt. Why don't I take a look and see?"

He put his hand on her arm and gently pushed her into the chair. "No, Tory. There's nothing you can do." His hand tightened on her. "Don't go out there. Please."

He stared at her until she nodded, then let go and picked up the phone. She stared at him as he spoke in a low voice to one of his officers. It seemed like he talked for a long time before he hung up and turned to her.

"I'm going outside. Will you be all right here by yourself?"

She nodded. "I have to get over to the clinic pretty soon, though." She swallowed. "Clients will be coming."

"I'll walk you over later. Stay here for now."

She stared at the front door for a long time after he disappeared, listening to the silence. Not even the wind disturbed the quiet. Wondering what he was doing, trying not to think about the animal on her front porch, she looked down to find her hand wrapped around the mug of coffee.

She always had coffee in the morning. She had to get on track, get ready to see the clients who would be arriving soon. Taking a deep breath, she lifted the mug and took a sip. The acidic taste burned all the way down her throat.

As she set the mug of coffee on the table she saw droplets of oil floating on the black surface, shimmery and iridescent under the lights. They reminded her of the way blood glistened when it spilled out onto an aluminum exam table, and she shuddered, pushing the mug away.

The walls of the kitchen closed in around her. She had to get out of here. She needed to go to the clinic and get ready for her day, take care of the patients who'd been hospitalized. Bolting for the door, unable to stay in the house for another moment, she had her hand on the doorknob when she heard a car pulling into the driveway.

Another police officer had arrived. The thought was like a splash of cold water on her overheated face. Holt and the other policeman would be crouched on the porch, staring at the poor cat. She didn't want to think about that cat. Trying to banish the image from her mind, she slowly backed into the kitchen.

The dog whined, and she turned to him gratefully. "I know you must be hungry, buddy. The dog food supply is temporarily cut off, but let's see what I can find for you." She opened cabinets randomly, forcing herself to think about the dog and not about what was happening on her porch. "How about a can of chicken?"

The dog whined again as if he'd understood her, and she turned to face him. "I don't want to hear any complaints if you get diarrhea, do you understand?"

He wagged his tail, and Tory swallowed the lump in her throat. At least she and Holt had managed to save this animal from whoever had killed the cat, she thought with fierce triumph. She opened the can and emptied the contents into a bowl, then watched with satisfaction as the dog gulped it down.

"We're going to have to think of a name for you," she said to the dog, who wagged his tail again but didn't stop eating. She looked at his gentle face and skinny body with the dirty, matted hair and remembered the night before.

Staring at the door and growling, his hair raised, he'd been a different animal, primitive and fierce and frightening. No Chicago watchdog had anything on him. "How about Spike?"

Spike wagged his tail again and kept on eating. Tory leaned against the counter and watched him for a while, then pushed away and began to gather what she needed to take to the clinic with her. If Holt wasn't finished soon, she would have to tell him she had to go.

The front door opened and he walked through it and into the kitchen. He poured himself a cup of coffee, and Tory shuddered as she watched him drink it. After two gulps he set the cup on the counter and turned to her. "I need a bucket and a scrub brush."

Her insides twisted as she realized what he needed them for. "In the laundry room by the back door," she answered tightly.

As he moved past her, she reached out and touched his arm. "Tell me."

For a moment she thought he would refuse, but finally he turned to her. "I won't be able to tell until we get the report back from the pathologist, but my guess would be it was the same knife used on the two women. The cat's body was laid out the same way." He looked at her and his mouth tightened. "It was a message, Tory. It was supposed to have been you, and if you had gone into the woods last night, it would have been."

"I don't understand," she whispered. "I haven't even been here a week, and the only people I've talked to besides you are my clients. Why has he picked me?"

His mouth flattened to a grim line. "These madmen don't have to have a reason. It could be nothing more than your looks, or your age, or even just the fact that you're alone and an easy target." Watching her carefully, he added, "Are you sure you don't want to leave?"

Yes, she wanted to shout. She wanted to run away from these trees that knew her name and the nightmares that haunted her sleep. Her hand tightened on the keys she still held, the keys to her clinic. "If someone is trying to kill me, who's to say he won't follow me if I leave?"

Holt's eyes darkened and he stared out the window. "That's possible," he said after a while. "Who knows what someone like this would do? He might follow you, or maybe he would just pick another victim here in Eagle Ridge. Maybe you're better off here, where at least I can keep an eye on you."

Her suspicions concerning Holt, the ones she thought had died the day before, came creeping back. "Are you saying now that I should stay? Are you trying to tell me I'll be safer here?"

"I have no idea, Tory." He turned to her, and she noticed the lines of exhaustion that radiated from his eyes, the deep purple shadows underneath them. "It's a crapshoot, as far as I'm concerned. I'm not sure where you'll be safe. You have to make that decision yourself."

"It's already made. I can't leave."

She thought the look in his eyes was relief, but it was gone so quickly she wasn't sure. "Then I'll do my damnedest to make sure you're safe."

And he would. Suddenly she was convinced of that. The suspicions that had wormed their way into her mind dissipated like mist in the sunlight. She had been right the night before. Holt wasn't the one who put the dog in the woods, and therefore he hadn't put the cat on her porch, either. She was convinced of that.

He continued to stare at her, and the atmosphere in the kitchen thickened until it was almost impossible to breathe. Her heart pounded and her body tensed, throbbing with the beat it had discovered the night before. Holt's eyes changed as he watched her, the signs of exhaustion fading to be replaced by another kind of tension.

Slowly he reached for her. She swayed toward him, unable to look away. His fingers skimmed her face, lingering on her lips, then curved around her neck. He pulled her closer and pressed his mouth against hers.

Desire shot through her and she whispered his name

against his lips. His hand tightened on her neck and she felt his body harden. Heat flared off him. Then he uncurled his fingers from the back of her neck and stepped away.

"I'll walk you to the clinic. Let's go."

She opened her eyes to find him heading for her back door. Dazed, she touched her fingers to her lips, where his taste still lingered, and watched as he opened the door. Bright sunlight spilled into the room, and the dog scurried past her and dashed out the door.

Gathering herself, she looked around for the clinic keys before she realized she still had them in her hand. She grabbed her jacket and slipped it on, then shut the door behind her.

"Don't lock it."

She looked up, startled at Holt's words. "Why not?"

"I'm coming back after you're settled in the clinic, remember? To clean up."

"I'd forgotten." Incredibly, she had. The brief kiss they'd shared in the kitchen had pushed the other memories of the morning out of her mind. She forced herself not to look in the direction of her front porch. "Here." She shoved the keys into his hand. "You'll need these."

She stood to one side while he unlocked the door to the clinic. Standing in the reception area and waiting while he checked the rest of the building was almost old hat by now. In a few minutes he came back.

"Everything looks fine. I'll bring your keys back when I've finished."

"Thank you, Holt," she said quietly.

He was almost at the door. "Thank me when I've caught this guy." Without another word he disappeared out the door, letting it close quietly behind him.

Holt scrubbed furiously at the wood on Tory's front porch, trying to erase more than the ugly stain. He wanted to wipe the taste of her from his memory, to scrub until he couldn't feel her soft moan against his mouth. If he could, he'd wash away everything that had happened this morning.

The need that gnawed at him when he touched her frightened the hell out of him. It wasn't supposed to be like that. It was supposed to be nothing more than physical gratification, a mutual giving of pleasure that ceased to have meaning as soon as it was finished. He hadn't bargained for the tenderness he felt when he touched her, or the ache that welled up inside him when he let her go. She wasn't supposed to mean anything to him.

She couldn't mean anything to him. He dipped the scrub brush into the bucket of hot water and detergent, then attacked the wood again. He scrubbed until the oval patch was spotless, until his arm ached. He didn't want to leave any reminders of this morning.

Gravel crunched on the driveway behind him, and he turned and watched as a dented and rusted old automobile drove slowly to the clinic. The kid who drove glanced at him, then looked away.

But not before Holt had seen the look of fear flash across his face. He stared at the car as it disappeared around the side of the clinic, then dropped his brush into the bucket and started after the car.

By the time he rounded the clinic the kid was almost in the back door. "Who are you?" Holt asked sharply, stopping the kid in his tracks.

"Teddy Larson, sir." The boy slowly turned and faced Holt. "I work for Dr. Falcon."

The kid's freckled face was pale beneath his red hair, and Holt studied him. "Yeah, I guess I remember you. Is this the time you normally arrive at work?"

Teddy's face got even paler, and he licked his lips once before his gaze drifted away from Holt. "No, I'm, ah, a little late today." His gaze shot to Holt's face and he turned completely white. "Did Dr. Falcon call you because I was late?"

"Should she have?"

Teddy shook his head quickly. "No, of course not. I just overslept."

Holt studied the young man, making a mental note to check out just what Teddy Larson had been doing the night before. "You should be telling that to Dr. Falcon, shouldn't you?" he asked softly.

"Yes, sir. I will." He hesitated, as if expecting Holt to say something more, then he disappeared inside the clinic. Holt stared at the back door for a moment before he turned and walked toward Tory's house.

An hour later he slid into his Blazer and headed to town. The blood was gone from Tory's porch, and he had searched the woods thoroughly and found absolutely nothing. Not that he'd expected to, he reminded himself. Between the storm the night before and the general lack of evidence he'd found in this case, he hadn't expected much. But the absence of even one sign of anyone in the woods puzzled and worried him.

No ghost had murdered Sally Phillips and Carrie Stevens. And no ghost had tied up the dog and slit the cat's throat. But the lack of clues was becoming almost spooky. It was almost as if the murderer knew exactly what the police would look for, then made sure it wasn't there.

Holt stared out the windshield, seeing Bobby Duvall's face instead of the road in front of him. Someone intimately familiar with police work would know just what not to do. Someone like an ex-policeman.

He'd gradually increased his speed as he drove, and he tapped on the brakes as he approached the houses on the edge of Eagle Ridge. Any man who could try to rape a high school kid was capable of a lot of ugly things. From now on, Bobby Duvall was going to feel like he was living underneath a microscope, Holt thought savagely. He wouldn't be able to go to the bathroom without Holt knowing about it.

Holt pulled into the parking lot of his apartment building, eased out of the truck and headed for his door. He needed a hot shower and cool sheets, in that order, but first he'd call the station and tell them to keep an eye on Bobby. He was tired enough that he just might be able to sleep for a few hours.

His message light was blinking as he reached to pick up the phone. No one ever left messages for him, and he paused as he watched it. Dialing the number of the station, he stared at the red light as he gave the officer on duty a brief message about Bobby.

After a pause, he punched the play button and waited while it rewound. "Adams, this is John Kelly in Chicago. I've got some information for you that's interesting, to say the least. Give me a call." The machine whirred in the silence of his apartment as Holt felt himself tensing. What kind of information could Kelly have that he would find interesting?

He couldn't quite keep his hand from shaking as he punched in Kelly's number, and the clerk who answered the phone seemed to take forever to locate Kelly. Finally his friend's weary voice came over the line.

"Kelly here."

"John, this is Holt Adams in Michigan. You've got some information for me?"

The silence from the other end of the phone was deafening. "Yeah," Kelly finally said, "I do. Are you asking for personal or professional reasons?"

"Both." Holt's voice was clipped.

Kelly sighed. "I was afraid of that. It's not a pretty story, but here it is."

Fifteen minutes later Holt let the phone drop into its cradle and stared into the distance as he tried to tame the murderous rage building inside him. No wonder Tory had looked at him like he was the devil incarnate. Kelly's story sure as hell explained a lot of things.

His first instinct was to drive to Tory's clinic and confront her about what he'd learned. He was halfway out of his chair before he forced himself to sit back down. She would be busy with her clients and her clinic right now. It wasn't the time to discuss what had happened to her in Chicago.

He sat in the chair until the rage had passed, leaving him feeling drained and helpless. He was the one person Tory would be unlikely to accept comfort from. Hell, when it came right down to it, he was surprised she'd even given him the time of day.

Finally, stiff and sick at heart, he rose and stumbled into the shower. Afterward he lay on his bed, knowing he should sleep but unable to do anything but stare at the ceiling.

Ten hours later, he gripped the steering wheel of his police Blazer tightly as the headlights of an oncoming car blinded him momentarily. His eyelids felt like sandpaper when he blinked, and his nerves were strung out from lack of sleep. But his exhaustion didn't matter. Nothing mattered except making sure that Tory was all right.

When he turned into her driveway he saw no cars in her small parking lot. The lights in her clinic still blazed, though, and her house was dark and still. At least she hadn't tried to go home by herself.

The front door to her clinic was locked. His stomach tightened as he knocked on the door, then relaxed as he heard her call out, "Who is it?"

"It's me, Tory."

A moment later the door opened, and she stood there with a tentative smile on her face. It faded just a little as she noticed his grim face. Stepping back, she said, "Hi, Holt. Come on in. I'm glad you were a little later than usual tonight. I had a lot of paperwork to do."

"I'll go check the rest of the clinic while you finish it up."

"I already locked both the doors."

"I know." He turned and tried to smile at her. "I just want to double-check."

Nodding, she headed toward her office. He watched her go, battling the urge to pull her into his arms and promise her she would be safe with him, that never again would she have to endure pain and terror. But he didn't move. He couldn't.

Even if he had the right to comfort her like that, he had no assurance that what he said was the truth. Whoever had committed these murders and was now stalking her was both smart and clever. As he shoved through the door into the kennel, he vowed that no one would get to her unless they went through him first.

The back door was securely locked, as were all the windows. He stood in the semidarkness of the kennel, listening to the rustle of the animals in their cages, and looked at the woods that surrounded the building. They just looked like trees to him, but Tory was terrified of them.

He watched them sway in the wind for a while, listening to their sighs. The trees had comforted him when he'd first arrived in Eagle Ridge, his spirit battered and nearly broken. They'd been a symbol of endurance and hope. They had survived countless storms, weathered fires and the constant punishment of the seasons, and still stood straight and proud. He should be able to do the same.

He'd thought he'd been recovering, because his pain and guilt weren't constant companions anymore. They snuck up on him at night, when his guard was down, but during the day he could keep the memories away. He'd taken it as a good sign.

Until he met Tory. Met her and wanted her with a passion he couldn't remember ever feeling before, not even for his wife. It scared the hell out of him and brought all the pain crashing in on him. And the guilt had returned, too, along with the pain.

Now another kind of guilt ate at him. Was Tory a target for the murderer because of him? Had he somehow drawn the murderer's attention to her?

He had to keep his distance from her, emotionally if not physically. It was his only hope of keeping her safe. But first he had to make sure she realized that he wasn't a threat to her, at least not the way the cop in Chicago had been.

The swinging door behind him creaked, and he turned to find her standing in the doorway. "I was beginning to worry," she said, and he could hear the effort she made to keep her voice light. "You came back here and never came out."

"I was communing with nature," he said, walking toward her. "Trying to figure out what bothers you about the trees."

Her face tensed and her hand tightened on the door. "I thought we'd agreed I was just imagining things."

"I never said that, Tory." He watched her as she turned off the lights and shrugged into her jacket. "I told you to trust your instincts."

"My instincts tell me that I'm out of my mind to be afraid of a bunch of trees," she said lightly. Bending her head, not looking at him, she snapped her fingers and called, "Come here, Spike," and the dog came running out of her office.

"Spike?" He looked from the small dog to Tory in disbelief.

"It suits him." Giving him a look that dared him to contradict her, she reached for a leash and snapped it on a red harness around his chest. "We're ready," she said.

Holt looked at the dog, who stared at Tory with adoration in his eyes, and felt his heart crumble just a little. Bending down, he scratched the dog's head and realized that Tory had changed his bandage and given him a bath. "He looks like a different animal."

She skimmed her fingers over the strips of white adhesive tape around the dog's neck. "He is. The wound on his neck is healing very nicely. In a few days he probably won't even need the bandage anymore, and his feet look like they're almost back to normal."

"What are you going to do with him?" He held his breath, waiting for her answer.

"Keep him, of course." She looked at him as if challenging him to tell her otherwise. "I always wanted a dog when I worked in the city, but didn't have the room for one. Now I do.''

"I'm glad," he said simply. A strange surge of emotion washed over him. He'd become attached to the dog from the moment he saw him lying in the woods, and it seemed right that Tory was going to keep him.

He opened the door and they stepped into the early evening air. Tory clutched the leash in her hand and avoided looking at the woods. It didn't take a genius to feel the fear that rolled off her in waves as she hurried to the refuge of her house. When they walked up to the front door, he noticed that she avoided looking at the porch.

It only took a few minutes to check the house. By the time he'd finished, she had hung up her jacket and poured out a pan of food for the dog in the kitchen. When he came down the stairs, she stood waiting in the living room, her hands clasped in front of her.

"Thank you for checking the house for me," she said softly. "I know you can't stay tonight, because you must have gotten very little sleep last night. I appreciate you coming all the way out here when you must be wishing you were sleeping in your own bed."

"I'm not going anywhere, at least for a while," he said bluntly. "We need to talk."

"About what?"

"About what happened in Chicago."

Chapter 9

Tory felt herself pale as she stared at Holt. "What do you mean, talk about what happened in Chicago? You don't want to hear about the practice I worked in while I was there," she said desperately.

He held her gaze as he took a step closer to her. "You're right, I don't. I want to hear about what happened with Ed Barber." He took another step and reached for her hand. "I want you to tell me about that evening on the expressway."

"You know." She could barely get the words out of her mouth.

"Yes." His hands were gentle on hers, cradling her suddenly cold fingers between his two large, warm palms. "I know the official story. I want you to tell me what happened."

"Why?" she whispered. "Why did you pry into my life? I didn't intend for anyone here to know about Chicago."

"Because I needed to know, Tory. I knew something was frightening you, and I wanted to know what it was." His hands shifted, and he laced his fingers with hers. "The last thing I wanted was to scare you."

"So you went behind my back and got all the sordid details? You had no right to do that, Holt."

"I knew something was wrong. If I had asked you, would you have told me yourself?"

Tory knew she wouldn't have. Holt read her answer in her face and he gripped her hands harder. "I knew you wouldn't. No one else will find out, Tory, believe me. I won't tell a soul."

God help her, she believed him. Deep down, she knew Holt could be trusted with her secrets, because he was a man with secrets of his own. But that didn't change anything.

"I know you won't tell anyone else. That's not why I didn't want to tell you."

"Why, then?" She'd never heard his voice so gentle.

Pulling her hands away from his, she turned her back to him and stared blindly at the wall. "Because it's so humiliating. And because I don't like to be reminded how little control I have over my own life."

"There's nothing to be humiliated about, Tory."

She whirled to face him. "Isn't there? How would you know, Holt? You've always been the one on the other side of the baton."

"Don't put me in the same category as Barber. Most cops are decent people who would be appalled by what he did."

"Most cops would defend one of their own," she answered bitterly. "I know."

"Tell me what happened, Tory."

She stared through him, seeing dusk on a Chicago expressway once again. "Have you ever been beaten on the side of the road, knowing that people in their cars were slowing down to watch?" she whispered. "Knowing that none of them would stop to help you because they all thought you'd done something to deserve it, that you were a criminal of some sort?"

He took a step forward, but she moved away from him. "You want to know what happened? I'll tell you. Ed Barber pulled me over because he thought I was speeding. I was going the same exact speed as everyone else, and I didn't notice him behind me because I was thinking about work. When I finally noticed him and stopped, he told me to get out of my car. I tried to talk to him, but he started yelling that I was fleeing from him and resisting arrest. The next thing I knew, he yanked out his baton and hit me in the face." She swallowed as she brought her hand up to instinctively cup her left cheek. "When I fell down he hit me again. I tried to grab his baton, and he bit me."

She would never forget the sight of the policeman standing over her, licking her blood from his lips. It was the scene that had haunted her dreams and made her shake every time she saw a policeman.

"How did you get away from him?" Holt's hands were clenched into fists, his knuckles showing white.

"A state police officer drove up and saw what was happening. He was able to subdue Barber." She fingered the small scar on her cheekbone. "I was lucky. He could have killed me before anyone stopped to help."

"Do you know what happened to the bastard?"

"Didn't you find that out, too?" Suddenly sick and shaking inside from remembering, she wrapped her arms around herself and wanted to tell him to stop. She didn't want to talk about this anymore.

"He was fired, Tory. You know that, don't you?"

"They wanted to put him on disability and let him draw his pension," she said bitterly. "Because he was obviously a sick man, they said."

"That didn't happen. He's gone. No pension, no benefits, nothing."

She closed her eyes. "I didn't want to know," she whispered. "I was afraid I wouldn't be able to handle it if I found out he was still getting paid by the police force."

"He was a bad cop. There are a few of them, Tory, just

like there are a few bad veterinarians. It doesn't mean that every cop is going to abuse his power.''

Drawing a deep, shuddering breath, she opened her eyes and looked at Holt. "I know," she whispered. "In my head, I know that. But in my heart, it's hard not to be scared."

Slowly he lifted his hand and traced the scar on her face. "I know. And I'll try not to do anything to scare you."

His touch lingered for a moment, then he dropped his hand. Turning, he shoved his hands into his pockets and stared out her window.

Watching the back of his head for a painfully long moment, she asked in a low voice, "Why did you bother, Holt? Why did you want to know?" Suddenly it was important that she find out.

He was silent for a long time. Then, without turning, he said, "I won't lie to you, Tory. It's been a long time since I've wanted anyone like I wanted you. But I knew you were frightened of me, and it didn't make sense. That's why I called my friend in Chicago. I wanted a weapon to break through your fear."

"And now do you think you have it?"

He turned to face her. "Now I expect you to say you never want to see me again. Hearing about what happened from another cop isn't the same as hearing it from you."

This was it. She could tell him to disappear from her life, and he would do it. Oh, he would protect her from the murderer in Eagle Ridge, but there would be no more kisses, no more brief touches of his hand. He wouldn't look at her with that heat in his eyes, burning her inside.

She couldn't do it. Her heart swelled with fear, then began pounding in her chest. She could send him away and he would go, but she couldn't bring herself to say the words.

"I'm not sure I want to tell you to leave."

Her voice was barely audible in the quiet of the house, but he jerked around to look at her, his eyes blazing. "Tell me to leave, Tory."

"I can't."

"I'm not what you need," he said, his voice harsh and raspy. "There's nothing left inside me to share with anyone, and you need more from a man than mere physical pleasure."

"You're right, I do." She didn't even blink at his brutally frank words. "And I'm scared to death of you. Not because you want me, but because you make me want more than just sex."

"For me it would be sex and nothing more. Don't try to fool yourself."

"I guess I'm willing to take a chance and find out for myself."

"Why, Tory? Why are you saying this?"

"Why did you go to the trouble of finding out what happened to me in Chicago?"

"To get you into bed."

She shook her head. "I don't think so. I think there was more to it than that." Biting her lip, she forced herself to meet his eyes. "I was angry at first that you'd invaded my privacy. I'm not anymore. Now I'm touched that you went to the trouble."

He stared at her with a mixture of wariness and sadness. Then he sighed and looked away. "I'm not the person you think I am, Tory. Don't make me into a paragon of virtue, because nothing could be further from the truth."

It was time to lighten up, or she would say things neither of them wanted to hear. "All right, you're the scum of the earth. Incredibly sexy, but still scum. Are you satisfied now?"

One of his rare smiles flitted across his face, then faded. "It's closer to the truth, at least."

She watched him for what seemed like a long time, then turned away. The order she'd been gradually rebuilding in her life was looking very shaky right now, and she needed to take a deep breath and regroup. Trying to keep her voice light, she changed the subject. "I was going to make spaghetti for dinner. Would you like some?"

She could feel the struggle in him behind her, could almost hear him shrug. "Thanks. Since I'm going to be here anyway, I guess it would make sense."

Whirling to face him, she said, "What do you mean, you're going to be here anyway? You're dead on your feet. You need to go home and sleep."

"How much sleep do you think I'd get, wondering if that madman had managed to find a way into your house? No, I'm staying here. If you don't want me on the couch, I'll sit in the truck again."

"Of course you can stay on the couch." She wouldn't tell him how reassuring his presence was. Hidden fears could be denied. "I'll even dig up a blanket and a pillow for you." She whirled and headed up the stairs, relieved to have an excuse to leave the room. She'd said things to Holt she wouldn't have dreamed of saying to anyone, and she needed time to collect herself.

"Wait a minute, Tory."

He spoke from the bottom of the stairs, and she reluctantly stopped. "What?"

"That can wait. I want to talk to you."

"About what?"

"About Barber."

Talking about Barber was light conversation compared to the minefield they'd been skirting. She let him lead her to the couch. "What about him?" she asked after they were both seated.

"Do you think he might have followed you up here?"

She stared at him, astounded at the idea. "I don't know how he could have," she finally answered. "He knew nothing about me, not even my name. I was a random victim. He pulled me over simply because he could single me out of the pack, and he probably wouldn't have lost it with me if I had stopped immediately."

"I'm sure he knows your name now," Holt retorted, his voice grim. "Did you ever see him again after he beat you?"

She shook her head. "No. I talked to a lot of people in

the police department, but I never confronted him. I would have refused if they had asked me to. I couldn't bear the thought of it.''

"I know from John Kelly that he was suspended for a few weeks while they investigated, then he was fired. No one in Chicago seems to know what happened to the guy.'' He leaned forward, his elbows on his knees. "Maybe he came up here after you.''

She shook her head again. "I don't know how he could have. I didn't tell anyone but my closest friends where I was going, and they knew what had happened. They wouldn't have told anyone where I had gone. I didn't even tell my bosses at the clinic where I worked.''

"Why were you so secretive about coming back here?''

Biting her lip, she looked away. Finally she answered in a soft voice, "After it happened, I felt like my whole life was falling apart. It's always been important to me to feel like I was in control of my life, and after the beating I felt like I had lost that completely. I thought that the only way to recover my control was to start over, fresh, in a place where no one knew what had happened. That's why I came here.''

"I've been wondering why you came to Eagle Ridge. It's not like you have any close friends or family here. You hadn't been back once since you left when you were eighteen. In fact, after what you told me about Bobby Duvall, I can't believe you have many good memories of this town. Why here? Why not some other small, anonymous town in Michigan or Wisconsin?''

She wasn't ready to tell him her reasons, so she shrugged and stared at the dog at her feet. "Because I knew the town, I guess. And which one of us doesn't want to go back to our hometown as a success?''

He didn't say anything, but she could feel his gaze on her. If she looked up, she knew, it would cut through her half-truths like a razor. To her surprise, he didn't challenge her. Instead, he said, "So you don't think Barber could have found out where you went?''

"I doubt it. I quit my job in Chicago early in the summer and pretty much dropped out of sight. I came here for a few weeks when I bought the practice, but other than that I didn't do much." She touched the scar on her cheek. "I didn't want to go out around people until my face had healed. And that took a while."

Holt moved closer and gently pulled her hand away from the scar, then pressed his fingers against it. "Does it hurt?"

"No." *Only in my dreams,* she wanted to tell him, but pressed her lips together. She wasn't ready to share that with him yet.

Holt searched her eyes with his soft gray gaze, then trailed his fingers down her cheek before letting his hand drop away. "It's not very noticeable, Tory."

She tried to smile and failed miserably. "I know it's hard to see, but to me it's a symbol of how little control I have over my life. To me it's enormous."

"Why is it so important to feel in control all the time?" he asked softly. "No one is always in control."

"I know." She shifted restlessly on the couch and looked toward the kitchen. "It just is, that's all. I guess I was more shaken up by the whole thing than I realized at the time." She stood up, and headed for the kitchen. "I think it's time to start dinner. Want to help?"

He stood, too, and the look in his eyes told her he wasn't fooled by her change of subject. But he didn't pursue his question. Following her into the kitchen, he said, "What do you want me to do?"

"How about making a salad?"

"I think I can handle that."

They worked together in silence, and gradually she relaxed. They'd skated dangerously close to subjects she didn't want to share with anyone. The truth about her childhood in Eagle Ridge was something she didn't want to talk about, not now and maybe not ever. Even with Holt. Maybe especially with Holt.

A thin shard of moonlight sliced through the pines, silvering the brown needles on the ground. Something moved slowly between the trees, weighted down by the thing dragging behind it. The wind sighed restlessly, murmuring its approval as it wrapped its tentacles around her. It held her in place, unable to move, as the dark shadow and its burden came closer.

She tried to close her eyes, but the wind and the trees wouldn't allow it. Her mind filled with terror as the darkness approached, but she stood rooted to the ground.

It stepped into a clearing, and the moon shone clearly on the thing dragged behind it. Pale moonlight had become blood. Everything was red. The dark color soaked the pine needles and reflected off the trunks of the trees, changing what had once been human to a ghastly caricature.

She wanted to look at the person standing over the lifeless body on the ground, but she couldn't do it. She couldn't tear her eyes away from the horror. Revulsion rose inside her, thick and hot, battling with the power she felt radiating from the other figure in the clearing. Power and an intoxicating ecstasy swirled over her, reaching out for her. *He wanted her.*

''No!'' The scream was torn out of her mouth as she bolted upright in her bed. She opened her eyes and looked around wildly. The trees were gone, and so was the horrible thing on the ground. Only the white walls of her bedroom surrounded her.

The third stair creaked as footsteps pounded toward her room. Shrinking back on her bed, she reached for the telephone on her nightstand without taking her eyes off the door. She had dialed the first four numbers of the police station when Holt burst through her door, his gun drawn.

''What's wrong?'' He took one close look at her then spun around, and peered into all the corners of her room and pulled open her closet door. When he dropped to his knees to look under her bed, she reached out for him with a trembling hand.

''Nothing's wrong, Holt. There's no one here but us.''

Sitting back on his heels, he examined her face then slid

his gun into the holster. "What happened, Tory? And don't tell me nothing. They probably heard you scream in the next county."

She looked at her hands, clutching the edge of her comforter. Deliberately she loosened her grip and smoothed the wrinkles. "I had a nightmare, that's all. I'm sorry I disturbed you."

He watched her, then sat on the bed next to her. Awkwardly pulling her onto his lap, he wrapped his arms around her and held on tight. She resisted for a moment, then she melted into him.

Burying her face in the crook of his neck, she took a deep, trembling breath. He smelled warm and musky, like he'd been sleeping when she screamed and hadn't completely awakened yet. His pulse beat beneath her cheek, steady and reassuring. He was warm and alive, and the nightmare was only a dream.

The stiffness and uncertainty in his hands gradually softened. Slowly he rubbed her back, his fingers hot and hard but surprisingly gentle through the thin material of her nightshirt. The movement was hypnotizing as he moved up and down and up again. Warmth from his body gradually replaced the cold that encased her, and she felt her trembling decrease.

"Do you want to talk about it?"

"No!" She shivered as the memory of the blood filled her mind again. "I just want to forget it."

Easing her away from him, he looked into her eyes. "Did you dream about Barber because we talked about him tonight?"

She closed her eyes, afraid he could see straight into her soul and watch the dream unfold. "No."

His breath ruffled the hair next to her ear, and she knew he was watching her. "Don't hold it inside, Tory. Let it out. Once they're exposed to the light, most dreams fade away into the darkness where they belong."

A shudder racked her, and she shook her head. "Not this one. There was so much blood, Holt," she whispered, reaching out blindly for him. He took her hand in his strong grip, then pulled her close.

"Tell me."

And suddenly she needed to tell him. The words fell over each other as they tumbled out of her. "I was in the trees. Surrounded by them. They were talking to me, keeping me there. Then it came through the trees, dragging something behind it. There was so much blood, but I'm sure it was a person. Dead. And I knew that whoever had spilled that blood wanted me, too."

His arms tightened around her. "Are you saying you saw someone in the woods with a dead body?"

"That's what they want, Holt," she whispered. "That's why the trees have been calling me. Whoever did that is waiting out there for me."

"Where was this, Tory?" Urgency filled his voice. "Did you recognize the place?"

She shook her head, pressing her face against his neck again. "The trees all look the same."

He held her for a while longer, then gently disentangled himself. She made a sound of protest deep in her throat, and he took her hand. "I'm not going anywhere. I just need to use your phone."

Clinging to his hand, she watched as he dialed the familiar number for the police station. "Jack?" His voice was crisp and no-nonsense. "Call Lenny and Tom in. We may have another murder on our hands. Start combing the woods." Hesitating, he looked at her. "Start near the vet's place and work your way toward town. I'll catch up to you as soon as I can."

He didn't take his eyes off her as he set the phone in its cradle, and she felt the fear blossom in the pit of her stomach. "You don't think there's really been another murder, do you?" she whispered.

"I don't know what to think." He hesitated, then reached out and cupped her cheek. "Your dream sounded awfully vivid. I don't believe in any of that mind-transference hooey or any baloney about psychic visions, but it won't hurt to check. I'd do the same if I got an anonymous tip over the phone or in the mail.''

After a moment, she nodded and slid away from him. Her bed suddenly seemed enormous, wrapped in a chill that would never go away. She hadn't realized how comforted she felt with him here and how alone she would feel when he left.

He didn't move from the edge of her bed, and finally she said, ''You'd better get going. Your men are probably waiting for you.''

At that he turned to face her directly. ''I'm not going anywhere until daylight. I told them I'd catch up to them as soon as I could, and that's after you leave for the clinic. I'm not going to leave you alone, Tory.''

She tried to ignore the tremendous wave of relief she felt. ''I'm sure I'll be fine. If there has been another murder...'' She swallowed and tried to force the image of the dream out of her mind. ''If someone has been killed, don't you need to be there?''

''Don't worry. If my men find anything, they won't do a thing until they get in touch with me. Until then, I'm staying here.''

Her breath trembled out in a sigh. ''Thank you, Holt,'' she murmured in a ragged voice. ''I don't want to be alone after that...that dream.''

His eyes softened and the scowl disappeared from his face. ''I'm not going anywhere. Why don't you try to get more sleep?''

Her heart contracted with fear at the thought of sleep. While she was sleeping she was helpless to prevent the dreams. ''Maybe I'll get a cup of tea instead and do some reading. Would you like some coffee?''

He reached out and touched her arm as she threw the comforter to the side and tried to scramble out of bed. ''I'll stay here and sit with you, Tory. I won't leave you alone.''

She stared at him, stricken to realize that he knew. He had seen beyond her words and recognized the cowardice hidden beneath them. ''It's all right,'' he said gently. ''It would be strange if you were eager to go back to sleep after a dream like that.'' As she sat motionless, staring at him, he added, ''And I don't want any coffee.''

He drew the comforter over her and waited for her to lie down. She slowly slid beneath the covers and watched him as he eased against the headboard, crossing his arms behind his head.

Tory rolled onto her back and stared at the ceiling. She knew that if she turned her head just a little to the left, the trees would be in her line of sight. Careful not to move in that direction, she listened to the sound of Holt breathing and waited for her body to relax.

Agonizingly long minutes ticked past until finally she turned to look at Holt. He didn't seem to be any more relaxed than she was. ''Are you going to sit there and stay awake for the rest of the night?'' she asked, her low voice echoing off the walls.

He turned to look at her. ''I'm not going to leave, if that's what you're asking.''

She swallowed and said, ''Why don't you lie down, then? It'll be more comfortable for you.''

She couldn't meet his eyes, although she knew he was looking at her. Finally he slid down onto the comforter next to her. Even though she was beneath the covers and he was on top of them, he filled the bed with his presence. ''I've dreamed about you saying those words more times than I can count. Somehow, though, it was never under these circumstances.''

His low, husky voice shivered through her, very close to her ear. Longing stirred, banishing the chill from her bed as it fueled the ache inside her. He was lying on his back next to her and said, ''Will you hold me, Holt?''

Slowly he turned to look at her. ''What are you asking, Tory?''

Flushing, she refused to look away. ''Just that. I don't want to be alone tonight. I need to feel connected to someone besides the person in my dreams.''

His face tightened as he watched her, and she was sure

he would refuse. Suddenly, without a word, he threw back the comforter and slid between the sheets next to her. Reaching out, he pulled her to him and held her cupped against him. They were like two spoons nesting together. All his muscles were rock-hard with tension, and his erection throbbed against her buttocks.

She felt tension rising. "Holt," she began, but he interrupted her.

"Go to sleep, Tory," he said, his voice harsh and strained. "You know I want you, and you can't expect me to lie here with you and not get aroused. But that's my problem, not yours. Go to sleep."

As if she could, she thought. But as he tucked his arm around her and held her snugly against him, the weariness that had seeped into her bones overwhelmed her. Her last conscious thought as she snuggled closer to him was how good he felt lying next to her, how right it somehow seemed.

The alarm clock didn't go off at its regular time. She awoke alone in the bed to the clear light of morning streaming into her room. Rolling over, she saw the rumpled sheets next to her and the indentation in the pillow that was scrunched into a ball. Holt's scent clung to the pillow, a heady mixture of soap and man. She lay there for a moment, allowing herself to soak it up, then reluctantly stumbled out of bed.

They might have slept in the same bed, but she wasn't about to go downstairs dressed only in her nightshirt and robe. Throwing on some clothes, she hurried into the bathroom and washed her face.

How would he act this morning? Her face flamed as she remembered how she'd pressed against him, glorying in the feel of his body next to hers. The memory of his arousal burned into her, as it had burned into her flesh the night before. He'd made no bones about the fact that he wanted her.

The smell of coffee drifted to her from the kitchen as she descended the stairs. Spike greeted her enthusiastically, then trotted back to lie down next to Holt. He was seated on the couch, a grim look on his face.

"What happened?" She held her breath, waiting for his answer.

"I have to go." He avoided her eyes as he laced his boots. "I called Teddy, and he'll be here in a few minutes."

"What happened, Holt?"

She didn't think he was going to answer. Finally he looked up at her, his eyes full of pain. "Jack Williams radioed me a half hour ago. They found a body in the woods."

Chapter 10

Holt watched Tory walk into her office. Her slender frame
was like a tightly strung bow, humming with tension. It
would be a long time before he forgot the shock that had
filled her eyes when he'd told her the news. Her face had
blanched white and she had recoiled like she'd received a
physical blow.

He walked into the kennel to see that Teddy Larson had
begun to walk the dogs and clean their cages. Right now
he was standing outside with a dog on a leash. Holt stepped
through the back door.

"'Morning, Teddy.''

Teddy looked up from the dog he was watching. "Oh,
good morning, Chief Adams.''

As Holt studied him, the young man's eyes drifted to the
dog. "I appreciate you coming in early," Holt murmured.

Teddy's gaze flew to him. "I'd do anything for Dr. Falcon,'' he said fervently. Too fervently, Holt thought, ob-
serving him with narrowed eyes.

Watching the boy, thoughtfully, he asked, "How far do
you go when you walk the dogs?''

Teddy gaped at him for a moment, as if he didn't understand what Holt was asking, then his gaze darted around the small area behind the clinic. "Not much farther than this, I guess," he muttered.

"You ever out of sight of the back door?"

Teddy considered the question, then shook his head. "Some of the dogs go as far as the trees, but I don't go into the woods. So I guess not."

Holt nodded. "If you can't see the door, you lock it behind you, understand?"

Teddy nodded slowly, although it was clear he didn't understand. "If that's what Doc Falcon wants me to do."

Holt felt a flash of admiration for the boy who was trying to stand up to him by stating his loyalties so clearly. "That's what she wants," he said in a gentler voice. "You stay here with her today until I get back. Can you do that?"

"Yeah." Trying to disguise the look of relief that flashed across his face, Teddy shoved his hands into his pockets. "That'd be fine."

Something was bothering Teddy, but Holt didn't think it was murder. His adoration for Tory was too obvious. When he had time, he'd question the boy and try to find out what it was. Right now he had other priorities.

"Thanks, Teddy."

"I'll watch out for her, Chief," the boy called out as he turned to leave.

Inside the clinic he found Tory seated at her desk, staring out the window at the forest surrounding her. When he walked in, she turned to look at him. "Where did they find the body, Holt?"

"In the woods." He wouldn't—couldn't—lie to her.

"Where in the woods?"

But he could hedge. "I'm not sure yet. I'll be able to tell you better after I've been there."

"It's close by, isn't it?" she whispered.

"Eagle Ridge is a small town. Everything is close."

"It's close to me. I know it is, Holt. He wanted to kill me, and some other woman lost her life instead."

"You don't know that, Tory. And you never will know for sure. You can't blame yourself." All the blame was his, anyway. He'd been so sure Tory was the person in danger that he'd neglected to protect the rest of the town. And now another woman was dead.

"I have to go. I told Teddy to stay here with you until I get back tonight. And for God's sake, lock your door today. Don't let anyone in who doesn't have an appointment, and make sure Teddy's with you whenever you see a client."

Her green eyes were huge and dark and full of pain. "All right. Be careful, Holt."

He paused at the door to look at her as she sat at the cluttered desk, her dark red hair turned to flame by the aureole of light from the window. One part of his mind was so relieved she was safe that he was ashamed. Ashamed and guilty. Because he'd been so obsessed with her safety, someone else had died. "It's too late for that now."

He pulled out of the parking lot and pointed his Blazer toward the spot Jack had described. Too little time had elapsed before he was standing in a small clearing in the woods, staring grimly at a sheet-covered mound on the ground.

"Let me see."

Without a word Jack pulled off the sheet and Holt stared at the body. God, there was so much blood. Turning away, he looked at Jack. "Do you know who it is?"

Jack swallowed and nodded, covering the body again. "Her name is Eve Blackston. She was visiting her aunt in Eagle Ridge." Biting his lip, he stared at the sheet again, then looked at Holt. "According to the local gossip, she was pretty wild. Went to a different bar every night, left with a different man each time." He shifted his feet, uncomfortable. "You know how it is in a small town. That kind of behavior doesn't go unnoticed."

"By either the townspeople or the murderer, you mean."

Jack shrugged. "If he was looking for an easy victim, she sure fit the bill."

"Whatever she did, she didn't deserve this." Holt's voice was harsh. "Is the evidence crew from the state on its way?"

"They should be here any minute."

"I'll be back before they leave. Someone's got to tell her aunt before she hears about it through the grapevine."

Holt walked out of the clearing, pain tearing at his heart. He had failed again, and another innocent woman had paid the price. Memories swarmed over him, tormenting him with images he would never forget. Watching the ground, trying to make sure he didn't obliterate any evidence, he let the grief and the guilt pound at him as he walked.

He finally looked up, expecting to see his truck. Instead, he saw Tory's house and clinic.

The grief disappeared, replaced by fear. He had obviously walked the wrong way, but he hadn't realized how close the murder scene was to her house. Retracing his steps, his gut contracted as he stepped into the small clearing. The body was lying almost exactly where he had kissed Tory that afternoon that seemed so long ago.

"I thought you were leaving," Jack Williams said.

"I am. How many men have been in here?"

"Just me. As soon as I found her, I radioed you and the other guys. They went to the station."

"Keep everyone away. When the evidence technicians get here, make them search the perimeter until they find something. This body wasn't just dropped here out of the blue."

"I know that, Chief." Williams looked at him, insulted, and Holt sighed.

"I know you do, Jack." He looked around the clearing, and his jaw tightened. "We have to find something this time."

"The ground is still soft from the rain the other night. There'll be something, Chief."

Williams sounded more confident than Holt felt. Nodding, he turned and headed in the direction of his car. This time he found it with no trouble. Sliding behind the steering wheel, he looked out at the woods before starting the engine. What the hell had Tory seen in her dream last night? And why was the body in that particular spot?

A curl of dread tightened his gut. This was all tied up with Tory somehow. Tory, who feared the trees, who felt that they spoke to her, calling her to a dreadful fate that awaited her if she listened to them. The fear threatened to overwhelm him for a moment, and he battled it down. There was nothing supernatural about these murders. A human hand had wielded the weapon and committed these crimes.

Swearing under his breath, he revved his engine and headed toward town, preparing himself for the grief he knew he would encounter. And as he drove he cursed himself for the relief he hadn't been able to suppress.

Tory sat at her desk, listlessly sorting through the pile of mail and listening to Teddy whistle as he mopped the floor in the reception area. The kennel boy had been her shadow all morning. She'd barely been able to get into an exam room without him. Normally Teddy disappeared into the kennel or the surgery areas, cleaning and tending to the animals, and she wondered why his behavior had changed today.

Holt. Her hand paused over a brochure advertising a special on suture material as a curl of warmth penetrated the chill that encased her. He must have told Teddy to stick close to her. She had been terrified that morning, and Holt must have known it. His bleak eyes had mirrored his reluctance to leave her coupled with the knowledge that he had no choice. Having Teddy watch her must have been Holt's only alternative.

"You okay, Doc?" Teddy stuck his head in the door of her office and watched her anxiously.

She managed a wan smile. "I'm fine, Teddy. Are you ready to leave for lunch?"

He shook his head. "How about we order a pizza today? I still have some things to do in the back."

Her heart warmed. "That sounds like a good idea. Why don't you go ahead and order it? I'm sure the clinic can cover the cost of having a pizza delivered."

A wide grin split the boy's face. "Sure thing, Doc." He disappeared, and a minute later she heard him on the phone. Leaning back in her chair, she felt some of her tension dissipate as she thought about Holt and Teddy conspiring to keep her in the clinic today.

Teddy had the right idea. She had things to do today, too. She shuffled through the pile of letters and threw all the junk mail into a recycling box on the floor. She laid the remaining three envelopes on the desk and stared at them.

Two of them had return addresses of clients she'd seen in the past week. They were probably payments for her services. The third envelope had no return address, although it had been mailed in Eagle Ridge.

A chill shivered down her spine as she looked at her name and address, printed in pencil in large block letters. Setting that envelope aside, she opened the other two then walked to the desk with the checks they held.

When she walked into her office, the envelope on her desk seemed to jump out at her. For a moment she wanted to throw it away without even opening it. Calling herself an idiot, she made herself pick it up and slice it open. It was probably from a client, either holding another check or asking a question.

The envelope held a single sheet of paper folded in half. Tory held it for a long time, staring at the blank whiteness and the crisp crease. Another chill rippled over her skin as she slowly unfolded it.

There were only a few words, printed in the same block letters as the envelope. Closing her eyes, she swallowed hard and took a deep breath before reluctantly looking at it.

"He killed his wife in Detroit. Are you going to be next?"

The sheet of paper fluttered out of her hand and landed

on the desk. She stared at it, frozen in place, as her heart contracted with horror.

"He killed his wife. He killed his wife."

The words battered at her heart like hail on a tin roof, relentless and unstoppable. She wanted to wad up the paper with its ugly message and throw it in the garbage, carry it to the incinerator and turn it into ash. Instead she stared at it, looking at the words that were already indelibly burned onto her brain, knowing that nothing would ever be the same again.

It was an anonymous note and should be treated with scorn, she told herself. The writer didn't even have the courage to sign his or her name. But something prevented her from ignoring it. The pain she'd seen in Holt's eyes was all too real, as was the guilt.

Small towns were known for their petty gossip. God knew she could testify to that. But they were also known for their almost uncanny ability to uncover the truth. If Holt had fled to Eagle Ridge hoping to leave his past behind, he'd made a major mistake. Had that miscalculation just come home to roost?

She couldn't move, couldn't breathe. The words grew wavy and indistinct as she stared at them. Who had sent her this letter? Which of the residents of Eagle Ridge hated Holt or her enough to send an anonymous note?

Unable to bear the sight of the letter for another moment, she picked it up and replaced it in its envelope. Then she locked it in her file drawer. Until she decided what to do with it, she didn't want anyone else to see it.

Gravel crunched on the driveway, and she heard Teddy scrambling to open the front door. The next minute he poked his head around the corner of her office and grinned at her.

"Pizza's here, Doc."

Her stomach turned over at the thought of food. Biting her lip, she managed to give Teddy a weak smile. "You go ahead and start eating. I'll be right there. I just have a few things to finish up in here."

* * *

It was six-fifteen, and Teddy sat in one of the chairs in the reception area, idly thumbing through a magazine. Tory looked at him from behind the front desk. "You can go on home, Teddy. Chief Adams will be here soon."

Teddy shook his head, a stubborn look in his eyes. "I'm fine. I wanted to read this article anyway."

"I didn't realize you were interested in Olympic diving, Teddy." A tender, reluctant smile curved her lips. She was very glad she'd hired Teddy.

A flush suffused his face and he looked at the glossy sports magazine he held. "I saw it on television last time the Olympics were on," he muttered.

A car pulled up to the front door, and they both raised their heads at the same time. Tory's eyes flitted to the doorknob, assuring herself the front door was locked. The tension in the room rose as they waited for the knock, and she resisted the urge to run into her office and look out the window to see who was there. She didn't want to scare Teddy.

"It's me, Tory." Holt's voice was muffled by the door.

Teddy threw down the magazine and stood as Tory hurried to open the door. Holt stepped into the clinic in his uniform, and Tory sucked in her breath as she saw him.

His normally clean, pressed uniform was wrinkled and dirty. When he took off his hat his hair was rumpled, as if he'd run his hands through it more than once during the course of the day. His eyes were two cold, hard lumps of ice, and harsh lines scored his cheeks, making his face look as if it had been carved out of granite.

She imagined his eyes softened fractionally as they looked at her, then Holt turned to Teddy. "I'll see you tomorrow morning."

Teddy seemed to stand up straighter as an unspoken message passed between the two males. "I'll be here, Chief."

Holt nodded as he watched Teddy leave. Neither he nor Tory spoke until they heard Teddy's old automobile sputtering as he left the parking area. Finally Holt turned to her.

"Was everything all right today?"

Everything was all wrong, she wanted to cry. The anonymous note sat in the briefcase clutched in her hand. The weight of it pulled on her heart and made the leather bag feel like it was filled with lead bricks.

"No problems. Just a routine day." She managed to say it without flinching. "Are you ready to leave?"

"Are you?"

Nodding, she called for Spike and headed for the door. "I'm finished here."

The dog scampered between them as they walked to her house. Tory kept her eyes on the gravel beneath her feet, unable to bear the sight of the trees around her. Their voices whispered to her on the wind, gloating about their triumph of the night before. Suddenly she saw Spike veering toward the woods and she called out sharply, "Spike! Come here!"

"He probably needs to relieve himself," Holt said, laying his hand on her arm. "Why don't you wait on the porch and I'll go get him."

She shifted the briefcase to her other hand as she watched Holt lope after the dog. The animal turned and wagged his entire body as Holt caught up with him. Watching them with suddenly blurry eyes, she felt the weight of the briefcase increase a hundredfold.

When they went into the house, Holt checked every room while she fed Spike. By the time he returned to the kitchen, she stood staring at the briefcase, wondering what she should do.

Raising her eyes to him, she said, "What happened today?"

His eyes went flat again. Turning away from her, he opened a cabinet, took down a glass and filled it with water. After he'd drained the glass, he looked at her again.

"Another woman was murdered. Same way as the other

two." His lips thinned. "We found a couple of clues this time, though. Maybe we can get the bastard."

Terror wrapped its tentacles around her chest as she stared at him. "Where was she found?" she asked in a low voice.

"In the woods. Just like in your dream."

"Where in the woods?"

His hand tightened around the water glass. For a long time she didn't think he was going to answer. Finally he looked at her, and the expression in his eyes was as bleak and desolate as a desert wasteland.

"In a small clearing not too far from here. The place where I kissed you."

The tentacles tightened another notch. "Why, Holt? Why was the body found there?"

"You tell me, Tory. You're the one wired into this guy."

She blanched and took a step backward as if he'd struck out at her. "What's that supposed to mean?"

Holt closed his eyes, and when he opened them again she saw weary contrition in their gray depths. "I'm sorry, Tory. I didn't mean that. I'm just so damned frustrated that I can't think straight."

Tory realized she was shaking, and she lowered herself into a chair. "You're right, though." Her voice was almost a whisper. "It does look like I saw what happened last night. Why, Holt? Why did I have that dream?"

"Hell if I know." His voice was rough with fatigue. "Don't you think I've been worrying at that all day, like a dog with a bone? I want to know what the hell is going on in Eagle Ridge."

"A lot of things, apparently." Fumbling in her briefcase, she took out the envelope and looked at it again. She had to show him. After this last murder, she had no choice. Someone in Eagle Ridge thought he was a murderer. And she needed him to tell her that the contents of that note were nothing but a lie.

"I got this in the mail today." She extended the envelope in his direction, noting with detachment her shaking hand.

Holt unfolded it slowly. His face hardened as he read it, and he didn't look up for a long time. Finally he raised his face to look at her, and she was shocked by the truth she saw there.

"It can't be true," she whispered. "Tell me it's nothing more than a lie."

"I can't do that, Tory. It's the truth."

"I don't believe it. You couldn't kill anyone," she cried.

"I killed her. Oh, I didn't fire a gun at her or stab her with a knife. But I killed her, as surely as if I had."

For the first time since she'd received the note, she felt the knot in her chest loosening. "What happened?"

He slowly crumbled the sheet of paper in his fist. He looked at the ball of white in his hand, then at her. His eyes were full of self-loathing. "My wife committed suicide."

She sucked in her breath as she stared at him, aching for the pain in his eyes. "Oh, Holt, I'm so sorry."

"Don't feel sorry for me. Feel sorry for Barb. I wasn't there when she needed me."

"It's not your fault she committed suicide, Holt."

"Then whose fault is it?" he demanded. "I wasn't there for her. It's that simple. She needed me, and I wasn't there."

She couldn't answer. There were no words that would erase the agony from his face. She longed to comfort him, to ease his pain, but she forced herself to stay in the chair. It was clear he wouldn't accept comfort.

"Do you want to talk about it?"

"Not particularly. But I will."

"You don't have to tell me, you know."

She thought the hard look in his eyes softened a little. "Yeah, I do, if only so you'll understand just how big a bastard I really am. Your sympathy is wasted on me, Tory. I got what I deserved."

"No one deserves to carry around a load of guilt for the rest of his life because of what someone did in a moment of despair." She spoke firmly, but her heart ached for him.

"You haven't heard the story yet. You'd better reserve your judgment."

"Tell me," she said softly.

He stared out the kitchen window, but Tory knew he didn't see the trees. He was looking into himself, at something that had happened long ago.

"Barb wanted kids," he began, finally looking at her. His eyes were full of sorrow. "Hell, so did I. After a year or so with no luck, she began to get desperate. Went to all kinds of specialists, made us both take all kinds of tests." His jaw tightened painfully. "The final diagnosis was infertility of unknown cause. In other words, she couldn't have kids, but they really didn't know why."

"I'm sorry," she murmured. She knew the pain of wanting something that wasn't possible.

"At first Barb was numb with shock." He shrugged, but he couldn't hide the pain in his eyes. "She'd always been fragile and easily upset, and she couldn't cope with the news. When it finally sunk in, she just lost it. When she wasn't crying she was begging me to find a way to fix it."

"The fact that she couldn't get pregnant was nobody's fault, not hers or yours," Tory said softly.

"I knew that, and maybe deep down she did, too. But it didn't matter anymore. The more she clung, the more I withdrew." His voice was savage. "I could have been more understanding, could have given her more support. Hell, I could have held her while she cried."

"What happened?"

"There was a case." He looked out the window again. "A serial killer who preyed on prostitutes. It was my case, and I was obsessed with catching the guy. And the case intensified as Barb disintegrated."

He looked at her with self-loathing in his eyes. "I wanted kids, too, Tory. I desperately wanted to have children. And when I found out that we couldn't have any, something died inside me. But my way of handling it was to submerge myself in my cases. And it wasn't tough to do. This killer was picking out the most vulnerable of the city's prostitutes, the young girls. I went a little more crazy each day that went by without catching the guy."

"And you withdrew a little more from your wife."

He nodded. "A real nice guy, wasn't I? She wanted to repeat the tests, find another doctor who would tell her what she wanted to hear. But we'd been to the best, and I knew it wasn't any use. We had to put it behind us and get on with our lives. And for me, that was my work." The muscles of his jaw worked. "To the exclusion of everything else."

"But Barb couldn't put it behind her."

"No. And part of the reason was me. I could have helped her cope with it. She couldn't bear it that she had failed at the thing she'd made the most important part of her life. For two years, she'd been completely focused on getting pregnant. When she finally stopped talking about it, I was relieved she'd accepted the fact that it wasn't going to happen. I thought she'd handled it. I was dead wrong."

Not wanting to hear, but knowing that she had to, Tory whispered, "What happened?"

"I came home one day and found her in the garage with the car motor running. She was holding on to our dog, hugging it. They were both dead by the time I got there. All she left was a note that said, 'Forgive me.'"

"I'm so sorry, Holt." She moved toward him, but he stood up and walked away from her.

"I caught the killer of those prostitutes a few days later. The day after I buried my wife. And do you know what bothered me most at the time? The fact that he'd killed two more girls before I was able to catch him. How's that for a cold-blooded bastard?"

"It sounds like you were trying to cope with your pain in the only way you could."

"Don't try to make excuses for me, Tory. A chapter of my life was closed the day I caught that bastard. I looked at him behind the bars of the county jail and realized I'd sacrificed my wife to catch him. I stayed on the police force until he was convicted, then I quit. I came up here, hoping I could forget.''

"Instead you're in the same situation as in Detroit.'' She ached for him, heart and soul.

"This is a small town, Tory. It's nothing like the situation in Detroit. There aren't that many places for a killer to hide in Eagle Ridge.''

"But you still blame yourself for what's happening, don't you? Just like you blame yourself for your wife's death.''

"My wife has nothing to do with Eagle Ridge. And yes, I am to blame. Not for the first woman, maybe, but for Sally Phillips and now this one. I should have caught this guy before now.''

"But you said yourself that there aren't many clues.''

"That in itself is a clue. There aren't many people in Eagle Ridge who have the knowledge to do this and get away with it. I should be able to connect it with one of them.''

"You want it to be Bobby Duvall, don't you?''

He stared at her. "Why do you say that?''

"It's pretty obvious. He has a grudge against you. The whole town knows that. Heck, I hadn't been here for more than a couple of days when my clients filled me in on that bit of gossip. And he used to be a policeman, so he knows what kinds of clues you look for.''

"Yeah,'' he said slowly, "I want it to be Bobby. It would be so simple and so clean. But there's no proof that it's him. My wanting to get this case solved isn't evidence. In the end, it boils down to one thing. Three women have been murdered, and I'm no closer to figuring out who did it.''

"So when were you appointed God?''

Eyes narrowing, he stared at her. "What's that supposed to mean?'' His voice was ominously low.

"It means you're not responsible for everything that happens in the world. Your wife killed herself because she couldn't live with her pain. That was a fault inside her, not you. As much as we might love someone, we can't be responsible for what they do. The blame has to rest on their own shoulders.''

"It's not that easy, Tory. Don't you think I want it to be? Don't you think I'd like to tell myself that it was Barb's fault, not mine? She may have decided to turn on the car in that garage, but I'm at least partially responsible for not being there when she needed me.''

"Maybe that wouldn't have made any difference.''

"Maybe not, but I'll never know. And I didn't give her a chance to find out.''

"So you're going to flog yourself over this for the rest of your life?''

"I'm sure as hell not going to get involved with anyone else, if that's what you're asking.''

"It wasn't, but since you brought the subject up, why not?''

"Because it hurts too damn much, that's why. Because I don't ever want to hurt someone that way again.''

"That's not the real reason, Holt, and you know it.''

"It's not?'' The pain had been replaced by anger in his eyes. "Since you know so much, Doc, why don't you tell me?''

"You're a coward, Holt Adams. That's the real reason.''

Chapter 11

"A coward?"

A smarter person would have backed off from the fury in his eyes, but anger flared inside her, a searing streak of heat that burned her heart and made her furious for the wasteland he chose to make of his life. "You're a coward, afraid of getting hurt if you get involved with anyone. I bet you don't even have any friends in Eagle Ridge. Do you?" she challenged.

He didn't answer, just stared at her, tight-lipped. She heard a whimper at her feet and looked at the dog, waiting impatiently for the rest of his dinner. Another spurt of anger pushed to the surface. "You wouldn't even let Spike into your life because you were afraid to get attached to him."

"That had nothing to do with it," he said furiously. "I didn't want to put him in a situation where he'd be confined to a small apartment for twelve or more hours every day. That's just common sense and kindness to him."

"That's bull, and you know it. You told me you didn't want another dog because the last one you had died."

Some of the fury faded from his face, and he turned

away. "You're right. But at least I admit it. I'm hell on relationships, and it's safer for everyone else if I don't get involved."

"Safer for you, you mean."

He turned to her, his eyes full of anger and pain. "I'm trying to protect you, Tory. Can't you see that?"

"Maybe I don't want to be protected."

"Then you're a fool."

"Maybe so." Her anger dissipated, replaced by futility. "But I don't think you're responsible for either your wife's death or what's been happening in Eagle Ridge. In fact, if anyone's responsible for this, maybe it's me. I'm the one having the dreams. Maybe I'm the focus of what's been going on."

"Tory, you're not responsible for another person's actions. You can't think you're to blame for this killer."

"Isn't that what you're doing to yourself about your wife's death?" she said softly.

He froze. Slowly he reached out to touch her cheek, letting his hand fall to his side at the last moment. "You don't understand," he whispered. "I would rather die than hurt you, and that's what would happen." He stared at her for a moment longer, then shoved his hands into his pockets and whirled around to look out the window at the fading sunset. "And on top of that, what if this killer has targeted you because of your connection to me? Have you thought about that?"

She hadn't. But watching his profile, silhouetted in the fiery setting sun, her heart swelled in her chest and she realized it didn't matter. "In that case, I might as well be hung for a wolf as a lamb," she said, taking a step toward him. "If I'm going to do the time, I can at least enjoy the crime."

He swung around to face her. "I don't want you out of pity, Tory."

"Who says it would be pity?"

"You hate cops."

"I don't hate you."

"I can't give you anything more than one night at a time. I can't make any promises."

"I don't recall asking for any."

He took a step closer to her. "I'm trying to do the right thing here, Tory, and you're not making it any easier for me."

"Do you think this is easy for me?" she demanded. "I'm not exactly used to throwing myself at a man."

"Is that what you're doing?" His eyes softened as he watched her.

"What would you call it?" Taking a step backward, she began to walk out of the room. Lost in the passion of the moment, she had spoken before thinking. Now the words quivered in the air between them, making the atmosphere vibrate with tension, and she longed to snatch them back.

He caught her arm and held her, preventing her from moving away. He murmured, "I'd call it the sexiest thing I've ever heard."

"Your social life must be sadly lacking, then," she retorted.

"It has been. Because I wanted it that way." Some of the harshness in his face disappeared as his lips curved slightly upward. "Until I met you, that is." His eyes devoured her as he gently pushed a strand of hair from her face. "I want you, Tory, but I'm scared. Scared of what might happen to you."

He wasn't talking about the murderer who haunted Eagle Ridge. And he wasn't only scared for her. Tenderness swelled inside her at his words, words she was sure he rarely spoke. "I'm scared too, Holt." But the need in his eyes gave her the strength to reach out to him. Cupping his cheek with her palm, she stood on her toes and brushed her mouth over his.

He hesitated for an agonizingly long moment, then he curled his arms around her and pulled her against him. Instead of kissing her, he looked at her, his face taut with control.

"Are you sure this is what you want?" he whispered, his breath feathering over her cheek.

"Yes." She answered without hesitating, her heart thundering as she read the desire in his eyes. "I'm very sure."

He watched her as he lowered his mouth to her lips. The pewter of his eyes shone as though a fire burned in their silver depths, and she felt an answering heat unfurl deep inside her. When his mouth met hers she closed her eyes, savoring his taste.

She could feel the effort it took for him to keep his mouth gentle on hers. His rock-hard muscles trembled with the strain wherever she touched him, and his hands on her back were tense and stiff. Her heart expanded as she realized that he was holding himself in check so he wouldn't frighten her.

Opening her mouth, she scraped her teeth over his lower lip then soothed the spot with her tongue. Holt groaned, his shaking arms pulling her closer to him. When she slowly traced his lips with the tip of her tongue, he shuddered violently then suddenly crushed her against him.

His control shattered. He took possession of her mouth, rocking his lips against hers as his tongue demanded entrance. She opened to him willingly, helpless to resist, his male taste filling her senses and stirring a response deep inside her. He'd had this power over her from the beginning, from the first time he'd walked into the clinic. She'd been imagining this moment ever since.

Now she wanted to glory in it, to grab hold of it with both hands and not let go. She wanted to give herself up to the sensations singing through her veins, to let herself drown in the passion that swirled around them.

His hands roamed over her back, tracing the hollows of her spine and pressing against the curves of her ribs as though he could drink in her essence through the cotton of her blouse. Tentatively she flexed her hands on his back, needing to touch him, too. She ached to test the strength of his muscles and slide her fingertips over his sweat-slicked back, to feel his heat blending with hers as skin touched skin.

Groaning, he tore his mouth away from hers and pressed his head against her shoulder, his hands tightening around her ribs. "Tell me to stop, Tory." The words were wrenched out of him, his breathing harsh and rapid and hot against the skin of her neck. "Tell me to stop now, because in another second I'm not going to be able to stop."

The heavy evidence of his arousal throbbed against her abdomen, burning her through the material of her slacks, and tongues of fire licked at her everywhere they touched. "I can't," she whispered. "Don't stop, Holt."

He lifted his head and looked at her, and she drew in a breath when his eyes fixed on hers. They were molten silver, the flames of desire and passion burning fiercely. Slowly he eased himself away from her.

"Tell me you want me, Tory."

He wasn't going to make it easy for her, for either of them. She wouldn't be able to look at him tomorrow morning and tell herself they had been swept away. Making love had to be a conscious choice—her choice.

Her heart pounded harder, filling her chest, anxiety mixing with desire. Keeping her eyes fixed on his, watching the flame that burned there, she allowed it to steady her. To reassure her. Laying her palms on his chest, she whispered, "I want you, Holt."

Closing his eyes, he leaned his forehead against hers. "I've dreamed of hearing those words. Even when I knew I had no right and no business wanting them."

"I've wanted to say them to you," she murmured, touching his face. "Even when I told myself I couldn't mean it, I wanted you."

A sigh shuddered through him. "I can't promise I'll never hurt you, Tory. But I'll try my damnedest."

"I know." Leaning forward, she pressed her mouth against his, not wanting to hear any more promises he might not be able to keep. He captured her lips, taking the kiss deeper and deeper, until she felt the tide of passion crashing over her head, pulling her under to the unknown depths that waited to claim her.

When she thought she would never be able to draw another breath and didn't care, he pulled away from her. Dragging her eyes open, she watched his face as he slid his hands down her arms. Squeezing her fingers once, he let her arms drop and reached for his own chest.

Puzzled, she opened her mouth to ask what he was doing, then caught her breath. Watching her all the time, he unfastened the badge that was pinned to the left side of his chest. The kitchen was so quiet that she heard the faint rasp of metal against material as he slid the pin out of the cloth. Then, still holding her gaze with his own, he laid the badge on the counter next to them.

Barriers in her heart crumbled as she watched him. He was telling her he would never use his superior strength against her or try to use his power to control her. Nothing could have moved her more or touched her more deeply. Biting her lip to hold back the tears that welled in her eyes, she raised her hand to cup his cheek.

The trace of stubble on his cheek bristled against her palm, and his scent surrounded her, filling her with need. "You didn't have to do that," she whispered. "I see only you now, not the badge."

"That's good, Tory," he murmured as he reached for her again. "Because that's what I want. No one but you. Only you, with nothing standing between us."

He kissed her again, but there was no struggle for self-control this time, no holding himself back. Tory tasted his passion in the pressure of his lips, felt his desire in the strength of his arms. Crushed against his chest, she felt nothing but his heart beating fast and strong against hers. There was no cold metal badge pressing into her, pushing her away from him, and no bitter memories throwing up fences around her heart.

With a murmur deep in her throat, she wrapped her arms around his neck and burrowed closer. His arms tightened almost painfully, then he let her go and took her hand.

"As much as I've fantasized about this counter since the other night, I've fantasized about your bed even more." Leading her out of the kitchen, he headed up the stairs to the darkened second floor. Stopping outside her door, he looked at her one more time.

He didn't say a word, but she understood what he was asking. Once they crossed this threshold, nothing would be the same. He was giving her one last chance to change her mind. Taking his hand, she led him into her bedroom.

Moonlight dappled the white comforter and filled the corners of the room. The moon was close to full and it spread its light unselfishly. Tory led him to the side of her bed, then paused, suddenly unsure of herself.

Leaning over her, Holt kissed her gently as he began to unbutton her blouse. In a moment, the soft material flowed apart and his hands stilled as he stared at her. The lacy bra she wore gleamed in the dim light, bright white against her shadowed skin.

She felt his hands shaking as he slid the blouse down her arms then unsnapped her bra. When she stood in front of him, naked from the waist up, he looked at her for what seemed like a long time then raised his eyes to hers.

"I've never seen anything more beautiful in my life." His voice was husky with feeling. Looking down again, he reached out and cupped her breasts with his hands.

Sensation speared through her, and her breath caught in her throat. Moving blindly, she pressed closer to him, needing to feel his flesh against her own. Her hands fumbled with the buttons on his uniform. She suddenly desperately needed to get rid of the barrier.

Letting her go, he helped her push the buttons through their holes. When he finally dropped his shirt next to hers she drank in the sight of him.

He was lean and hard, his muscles sleek rather than bulky. They corded on his shoulders and his arms, rippling with fluid grace every time he moved. Tory reached out tentatively to touch the mat of dark hair on his chest. It was soft and silky, and she followed it as it thinned and arrowed down his flat belly, stopping where it disappeared beneath the waistband of his slacks.

Her fingers lingered at his waist as she looked at him. His eyes were closed and his face was rigid. As if he could feel her gaze on him, he opened his eyes and stared at her, his face taut with desire.

"It's all right," he said, his voice thick. "I want you to touch me."

When she didn't move, he took her hand in his and slowly slid it down until it covered the hard ridge of flesh that strained at the front of his slacks. Groaning deep in his throat, he shuddered as she curled her fingers around him. Then, suddenly, he pulled her hand away and reached out for her, fumbling with the fastening of her slacks.

It took only seconds for him to sweep the last of the barriers down her legs. Slacks and panties pooled on the floor in the moonlight, joined moments later by the rest of his uniform. Finally they stood facing each other, naked, and as she felt his eyes on her she allowed herself to drink in the sight of him.

His hips were narrow and his legs long and lean. His hard, corded muscles were dusted with the same dark hairs that covered his chest. She imagined those powerful legs twined around her, pulling her closer to him, and a heavy wave of desire flowed through her belly and legs like thick honey. Letting her gaze rise higher, heat flooded her as she stared for a moment at his rigid male flesh, straining upward. Finally she looked again at his face.

"I want you, Tory," he whispered. "I want every bit of you." Reaching out a shaking hand, he undid the braid in her hair and let its waves flow over his hands. Then suddenly he scooped her up in his arms and laid her on the bed.

His mouth was everywhere, teasing her lips and feathering over her face, then sliding down her neck so his tongue could dip into the hollow above her collarbone. His hands closed over her breasts again, his thumbs finding her nipples and pulling on them gently. He swallowed her cry of pleasure with his mouth, his tongue plunging into her with the rhythm of his hands caressing her breasts.

Her hands tightened on his back, and she kneaded his hard, tense muscles with her fingers. His skin was sleek as satin as her hands slid over it. She let her fingers caress his ribs and the ridges of his spine. When she reached lower, cupping her hand over his buttocks, she felt the trembling he didn't even try to hide.

Raising his head from her mouth, he looked at her with glittering eyes for a moment before he slowly moved down her body. His thumbs flicked across her nipples one more time before his mouth took their place. Suckling gently on her, he curled his tongue first around one nipple, then the other as she writhed helplessly against him.

Every bit of sensation was centered in her core with a throbbing that demanded to be satisfied. Nothing had ever felt like this before. "Holt," she gasped, her hands tightening on him as she tried to draw him closer.

He groaned once and thrust against her, all his muscles trembling. But instead of responding to her urging, he eased himself away from her. Smoothing one hand down her belly, he lingered just below her waist as she felt her skin jump and quiver with anticipation.

Flicking his tongue over her nipple again, he moved his hand lower and touched her at the same time. "Holt!" she cried as everything exploded around her. When he drew his hand through her hot slickness one more time, she felt herself trembling on the brink of convulsing around him.

In the next instant her control would disappear completely. The knowledge made her freeze, and slowly Holt pulled his hand away from her. "What's wrong?" he asked as his fingers skimmed over her belly.

Forcing herself to relax, she smoothed her hand down his back and over his hip again. "Nothing's wrong. I just don't want to go anywhere alone."

"I don't think you have to worry about that," he murmured, catching her hand and bringing it to his hard, hot flesh. He reached down to touch her again. "I want to give you as much pleasure as you're giving me."

Arousal coiled tightly inside her at his touch, making her feel completely helpless in his hands, and she moved her hips away from his fingers. "I need you, Holt. I need you now."

He hesitated, but when she stroked one finger down his silky length he groaned and slid between her legs. Slowly, he eased himself into her.

When he began to move, she clutched at his back as sensation spiraled upward and pulled her into him. Feeling herself winding tighter and tighter, she dug her nails into his back and felt herself moving with him.

"It's all right, Tory," he whispered. "Let go. Let it happen."

"I...I don't know if I can," she answered as her body began to quiver.

"Yes, you can," he murmured into her ear. The touch of his tongue on her earlobe made her shudder, and she felt herself losing control. Reaching between their bodies, Holt touched her one more time as he thrust into her, and she convulsed around him.

The world spun out of control as the shudders that racked her body seemed to go on and on. Holt's arms wrapped around her, and he groaned her name as he surged into her again and again, each time sending her spinning higher and higher. They clung together, trembling, for what seemed like forever before her body slowly returned to earth.

Holt shifted to the side, wrapping his arms around her and pulling her close, needing the touch of her body against his. Closing his eyes, he absorbed the tremors that periodically rippled through her body and felt her heart slowly quieting against his palm. Her floral fragrance drifted up to him, mixed with the musky, seductive scent of their lovemaking.

Something had happened when he had joined his body to hers, something he didn't want to think about. The sweetness of her unselfish giving, even when it had become obvious that she was far less experienced than he'd imagined, had stirred something deep inside him. Tory had moved him in a way he hadn't expected, and he wasn't quite sure what to do about it.

Except not to think about it. He inhaled again, her fragrance drifting up to him from the dark red cloud of hair that swirled around them. "Why didn't you tell me?" he finally murmured.

"Tell you what?" Her voice was muffled against his chest, but he could hear the tension in her words.

"That you weren't very…experienced."

"I wasn't a virgin." She tried to pull away from him, but he wouldn't let her go. Finally she gave up and lay still against him.

"You were frightened when I tried to give you pleasure." He reached out and stroked her back, its silky softness making him ache for her again. He was afraid he would never be able to get enough of this woman.

Leaning away from him, she looked him in the eye. Her face was flushed as she said, "It was the first time we'd made love. I was nervous. Weren't you?"

Reaching around, he cupped her breast again, feeling himself stir when she caught her breath. "At first I was. I got over it real fast, though." As his thumb slowly circled her nipple, he watched her eyes darken and her breathing quicken. She might be nervous, and she might be startled by her response, but she couldn't hide her desire from him. "Let's see if you've gotten over it."

He watched her as she reached up and pressed his hand to her breast. Blood surged through his veins and pooled in his groin, igniting a fire that only she could cool. Rolling her on top of him, he cupped both her breasts in his hands as he said, "This time you can be the one in control."

In answer she leaned down to kiss him, her long, fragrant hair sweeping over his chest as she touched her tongue to his lips.

The moon shone directly through the window as Tory slept next to him. She'd fallen asleep almost immediately after they'd finished making love, curled around him in a completely trusting way. He knew he should go downstairs, away from the distraction of lying next to her, but he couldn't bear the thought of leaving her.

And that frightened him more than almost anything else would have. He'd warned her he could make no promises, and she'd said she didn't expect any. But he found himself wanting to give her the words, to tell her he didn't want to leave her. Thank God she was asleep and couldn't tempt him to say things he knew he would regret in the sunlight.

Because he didn't have the right to say anything to her. All his rights had died in that garage with Barb and their dog. To be truthful, they had died even before that, when he had turned his back on Barb and her agony. No, he had forfeited any rights he might have to claim a future with Tory. Never again would he be able to hurt a woman the way he had hurt his wife.

He shifted in the bed and turned to tuck Tory closer to him. She moved against him, her leg slipping between his as she turned in her sleep. He kissed her mouth, unable to resist.

Her eyes drifted open, and she smiled at him. The warmth and caring he saw there were like a physical blow. "Go back to sleep, Tory."

She smiled again and snuggled closer to him. Her face was bathed in moonlight, turning her pale skin to cream and highlighting the few tiny freckles that dusted her nose. Opening her eyes again, she looked over his shoulder at the full moon framed in the window.

"Look at the moon," she whispered. "It's so beautiful."

He didn't turn. Watching her face, seeing her expressive green eyes soften as she gazed out the window, he felt a searing pain in his chest. He couldn't let this happen. He wouldn't be able to bear it when Tory was eventually hurt.

"The side we can see is beautiful, but don't let the beauty deceive you. There's a dark side of the moon that nobody ever sees."

She tore her gaze away from the window and looked at him. "How do you know the dark side isn't equally beautiful?" she asked softly.

"It isn't. Trust me, I know."

"I don't think you're being fair to yourself, Holt." She smiled at him again, then snuggled closer and closed her eyes. In another minute she was asleep.

He laid next to her, cradling her in his arms for the rest of the night, but he didn't sleep. He thought about her words, about the trust that had looked at him from her eyes, and cursed himself until the moon sank in the sky and the gray light of dawn filtered into the window.

When Tory woke up the next morning she was alone in the bed. Rolling over, wincing at the slight stiffness of long-unused muscles, she raised up on one elbow and looked at the other side of the bed.

Holt had been there. It was no dream. The sheets and comforter were twisted and rumpled, and the pillow still bore the indentation of his head. Memories swept over her of the night before, of the passion they'd shared, and she felt the flush creep up her cheeks. Maybe he'd been as unsure of himself as she was this morning. Maybe he'd already left her house.

Holt wouldn't have done that, she knew. He would stay until Teddy got here, and he would be back this evening, regardless of how he felt about what had happened last night. He wouldn't let his personal feelings get in the way of his job.

She froze on the bed, poised to swing out of it. That was exactly what he'd told her last night, when he'd told her about his wife. He hadn't let his personal feelings interfere with the job he had to do then, either.

Slowly she got out of bed, barely feeling the cold floor beneath her feet. Maybe she was wrong and he was right. Maybe there wasn't anything left inside Holt except a passion for justice. And wouldn't it be ironic if she'd fallen for a cop who was just as much a prisoner of his job as Ed Barber had been?

It wasn't true. It couldn't be true. She had seen too much inside Holt, too much pain and grief, too much caring for other people, to believe that he was nothing more than a man doing a job. His heart was still there. It was buried deep underneath a load of guilt and pain, but it was there. All she had to do was find it.

She threw on her clothes and hurried downstairs to find him drinking a cup of coffee and talking to Spike. He straightened abruptly when she walked into the kitchen, and suddenly, remembering the night before, she found herself tongue-tied, unable to say a word.

He solved the problem for her. Pulling her close, he kissed her hard, savoring her for a moment, then carefully set her away from him. "Good morning," he said. His voice was level, but his eyes showed the need he tried to hide.

Her heart began beating again. Holding on to the look in his eyes, she answered brightly, "Good morning." Glancing from him to Spike, she added mischievously, "What does Spike have to say for himself this morning?"

Scowling, he turned away to grab the bag of dog food from the counter. "He says he's hungry. I was just going to feed him."

"I guess I forgot about him last night, didn't I?"

Holt's eyes softened as he set the bag of dog food down. "I'd say we both did." He reached for her, as if he couldn't bear not to touch her. "I don't think Spike minds at all."

"Neither do I," she whispered as Holt nuzzled her neck. He was sweeping her away again, pulling her beneath a rising tide of desire, but this time she barely noticed as the control slipped away from her. Lost in the sensations rippling through her, she leaned against him as he tangled his hands in her hair.

He stiffened and moved away two seconds before she heard the unmistakable sound of Teddy's car pulling into the parking lot. "Teddy's here," he said unnecessarily.

She ran a shaking hand through her hair. "I guess I'd better get ready for work."

"I need to go, too." The regret that flared in his eyes made it easier to move away from him. She could feel his eyes on her as she searched for her shoes, kicked off sometime the night before and forgotten.

"We need to talk tonight, Tory."

His words fell into the silence between them like stones into still water. She met his gaze and nodded. "Yes. I guess we do."

He waited silently while she combed and braided her hair and applied a hint of color to her lips. Then he walked her out the door, making sure it was locked securely behind them.

"Do you want me to walk you over to the clinic?"

She shook her head. "You don't have to. Teddy's already there, so I'm sure everything's fine. See, he just turned on the lights in my office. Why don't you go ahead? I'll see you tonight."

"All right." His gaze searched her face, as if he could find the answers he needed there. "Tory…"

"What, Holt?"

Instead of answering, he pulled her to him for one last kiss. Passionate and deep, it answered one of her questions. He wouldn't be back tonight just because his job demanded it.

"I'll see you tonight."

"I'm not sure that will hold me until then," she whispered.

Pain flashed across his face. "God help me, neither am I." Without another word he turned and got into his truck. Before she was halfway to the clinic, he had pulled out onto the highway and roared away.

She unlocked the clinic door and carefully locked it again after she entered. The lights in the reception area and her office shone brightly, but Teddy was nowhere in sight. He must have gone into the back to begin walking the dogs.

She barely had time to sling her jacket over a chair and

slip on a lab coat before Teddy appeared in the door of her office. His face was as white as her coat, and his hands were shaking. His shocked eyes were huge and black.

"I think you better come in the back, Doc, right away."

Chapter 12

Fear washed over Tory as she looked at the shaking young man in front of her. "What's wrong, Teddy?" she asked, her voice filled with dread.

"Come and see." He turned and headed to the kennel, and Tory rose to follow him, her heart thundering in her chest.

She smelled it as soon as she stepped through the door. Fear filled the air with a sour, acrid scent. Teddy walked to the end of the first row of cages, then stopped. "It's back there." He pointed to the corner of the kennel.

She was very sure she wouldn't want to see whatever awaited her. Teddy looked at her as she passed him, his eyes wide and horror-struck in his pale face. Suddenly he bolted for the door, and as she listened to it swing on its hinges she noticed the unnatural quiet in the kennel room.

At this time of day the dogs should be barking and the cats should be calling for attention, all of them needing food and clean cages and a walk to relieve themselves. It felt like even her patients were holding their breaths, waiting for her to turn that final corner and discover...

She stopped abruptly in her tracks, bile rising in her throat. An animal was sprawled on the floor on its back, its front and rear legs bound together and a length of twine knotted around its neck. A pool of dark red crept across the concrete floor.

Tory backed away, unable to take her eyes off the horrifying sight. Just as she turned the corner, though, she stopped. Something wasn't right.

Slowly she approached the obscenity. Before she even reached it she realized that whatever laid on the floor of her kennel wasn't an animal. It wasn't anything that had ever been alive. Touching the gray mass with one toe, she realized that it was nothing more than a rolled-up blanket. The red liquid was merely paint.

The nausea receded, replaced by a growing fear. Whatever it was, someone had left it here, meaning for her to find it. Someone had been in her clinic during the night.

She stood and backed up as she stared at the tableau on the floor. Once she'd turned the corner, she ran out of the room, fear clawing at her with sharp fingers. As she shoved her way through the swinging door, she practically ran into Teddy, emerging shakily from the bathroom.

"Don't go back there again, Teddy."

He gave her a look of disbelief. "Don't worry, Doc, I won't." His Adam's apple bobbed a couple of times as he tried to swallow. "Is he...he's dead, isn't he?"

"It's not an animal, Teddy," she said gently. "It was supposed to look like one, but it's just a blanket and some red paint."

Teddy swallowed again, disbelief in his eyes. "Are you sure, Doc? It looked awful real to me."

"I'm sure." Grimly she reached for the telephone. In a matter of minutes she'd spoken to the police officer on duty and explained the situation. After assuring the officer that she wouldn't touch a thing, she hung up the phone and turned to Teddy.

"Did you notice anything out of place in the kennel?"

He shook his head, obviously trying clear his mind and

concentrate on the question. "I turned on all the lights up front first, just like you told me to do. Then I went into the back." He swallowed again, and his face paled. "The first thing I noticed was the quiet. Usually all the dogs start barking when I go back there in the morning. You know?"

She nodded. "Then what?"

Teddy's face blanched again, and he turned away. She barely had time to wonder why before he started talking again. "Then I felt the breeze. I knew I hadn't left a window open last night." He was oddly insistent, and Tory studied his face, puzzled.

"I know you're conscientious, Teddy," she said gently. "I never would have thought you'd left a window open."

"The window was broken," he hurried on. "Someone had punched it out and opened the lock. I was worried that one of the animals might have gotten out, so I checked all the cages." He stopped and paled again. "That's when I found it."

"It's all right, Teddy," she said again, studying the boy. The more he talked about what had happened, the more agitated he seemed. "All the animals are accounted for, aren't they?"

The boy nodded, his freckles standing out in stark relief on his white face. "They all seem okay."

"So no harm's been done other than the broken window." Tory forced herself to sound confident as she balled her hands in the pockets of her coat.

Teddy flushed, the red stain on his cheeks vivid against the dark fear still lingering in his eyes. "All the animals are fine," he mumbled.

Tory watched as Teddy's fingers dug at the seams of his blue jeans. "What's wrong, Teddy?" she asked quietly. "Is there something you're not telling me?"

Teddy stared at a point over her shoulder, his face a picture of misery. Finally he blurted out, "It could have been one of the animals in the clinic. Whoever left that there could have killed one of our patients."

"But they didn't," she said, wondering at his reaction.

"None of the animals were hurt. Someone broke into our clinic, but the window can be fixed." She tried to put the fear out of her mind, to still the terror that lingered. Something was wrong with Teddy, and she had to get to the bottom of it. Something more than being upset about what had happened that morning.

Before she could ask him anything more, gravel sprayed against the wooden front of the building as a car screeched to a halt in the parking lot. That would have to be the police, she thought with relief. She didn't dare hope it was Holt.

"Open the door, Tory." His voice boomed through the front door, and she scrambled to open it. Holt stepped into the room and reached for her, crushing her against him.

Wrapped in his arms, she felt the fear retreating. His solid chest was a barricade against the evil that had violated the other room, and she leaned into him, not caring that they had an audience.

He held her tightly for a moment, his cheek resting against her hair. Then he eased her away from him and held her shoulders. "Are you all right?" he asked, his voice urgent.

She nodded. "I'm fine."

He looked over her shoulder. "How about you, Teddy? Are you okay?"

"I'm fine, too, sir."

Holt's fingers gentled on her shoulders, caressing her arms for a moment, then he let her go. "Then let's go take a look."

"Do I have to go with you?" she asked in a small voice.

He looked over at her, and his eyes softened. "Not right now. You can wait out here. More police will be coming, and the evidence team. You stay here and let them in."

"What do you want me to do, Chief?" Teddy's voice was shaky, but he looked at Holt and straightened his shoulders.

Holt looked at him and nodded. "I'll need you to go

over your routine with me, but not right away. You stay up here with Dr. Falcon.''

The next couple of hours passed in a blur for Tory as a steady stream of policemen came and went in her clinic. She turned away all her patients except those who were sick or injured and had to be seen right away. Finally, as noon approached, the last of the police officers left and she was able to lock the door behind them and sag against it in relief.

Only she, Teddy and Holt were left in the clinic. The dirty bundle of gray blanket had been taken away for the evidence technicians to examine. She sat in her office, looking at patient records and wondering what they would find, while Holt and Teddy cleaned up the kennel room.

The swinging door creaked, and Holt walked into her office and threw himself into her extra chair. When she swiveled around to look at him, his face was set in a hard, determined line.

"He got in through a window. Broke a pane and opened the lock, just as slick as spit. No fingerprints, no footprints, nothing.''

"What did it look like to you, Holt?'' She swallowed again, hoping he wouldn't give words to her fears.

He didn't speak for a while. Finally he said, very quietly, "I think it was supposed to look like Spike did when we found him in the woods.''

"I thought the same thing.'' Her voice was a whisper that barely moved beyond the boundaries of her desk. Biting her lip, she looked out the window. "I didn't hear anything last night.'' The guilt and fear had been eating at her all morning.

From the look that flitted over his face, she suspected he'd been beating himself up over the same thing. "I didn't, either. But chances are there wouldn't have been much to hear. If he'd wanted us to hear him, he wouldn't have arranged his little surprise inside the clinic. I figure he wanted you to walk in on it this morning, just like you did.''

"I feel so helpless, Holt. Like I'm being stalked by a shadow," she whispered.

"Dammit, how do you think I feel?" he exploded. "This guy is like a ghost, coming and going and leaving no trail. I feel like I'm trying to catch a piece of mist with my bare hands."

"Why do you think he did this?" Her voice was low and scared as she searched Holt's face for answers.

"The same reason he killed the cat and left it on your porch. As a warning. And a taunt. To let you know that he can get to you any time he wants. To tell you he almost had you when we found Spike."

A fist squeezed her heart, spilling terror into her blood. "Maybe I should leave, like you told me to originally. Go back to Chicago and stay with a friend for a while."

Slowly he shook his head. "I'm not sure that would be a good idea now, Tory. This guy is too focused on you. I'm afraid if you left, he'd follow you. And in Chicago, he'd have a lot more chances to get to you."

"I could sneak away during the night, not tell anyone where I was going." Even as she spoke, she knew she didn't want to leave. She wanted to stay with Holt, to trust him to protect her.

He shrugged, his face a careful blank. "If that's what you want, I won't stop you."

"It's not really what I want," she whispered.

"What do you want, Tory?"

"I want this to be over," she cried. "I want him sitting in jail, not able to hurt any more women. I want him to stop tormenting you."

"He's not going to hurt me. He's trying to hurt you." He stood up suddenly, and the chair banged into the wall behind him. "Maybe you're right. Maybe it would be better if you left. Why don't you start getting your stuff together right now?"

She stayed in her chair, looking at him. Leaving would be the smartest thing to do. There was no doubt of it. But looking at the faint lines of pain etched around his mouth, she knew suddenly that she couldn't do it. She couldn't abandon him, leaving him here alone to battle his demons. She had more faith in him than that.

"I can't leave, Holt."

For a moment, she saw the relief in his eyes. It was followed by the self-disgust she should have expected.

"Why not?

Her explanation better make sense, or he would never buy it. "Because you're right," she said slowly, realizing that she meant it. "In Chicago there's too much activity, too many people. A lot can happen in the midst of all the chaos there. And besides, I have the best protection I could ask for right here." She looked at him steadily. "You."

"I don't want to fail you, Tory." His knuckles whitened on the chair arm, and suddenly they were talking about far more than catching a killer.

"You won't." She leaned forward. "I'm locked into my clinic all day, and locked into my house all night with you. Do you think I'd be any safer than that in Chicago?"

"Probably not." His answer was grudging. "But it would make me feel better."

"No, it wouldn't. You'd be worried every single minute."

"You're right." He paced the tiny office, anger and fear vibrating off him. "I want you next to me every single minute of the day. I don't want you out of my sight for even one second." He spun to face her. "I'd chain you to my side if I could. That's the only way I'll feel safe."

"You already spend practically all your free time with me now. What more could you do?"

"I could move in with you." His words dropped between them, echoing loudly in the suddenly quiet room.

He wanted to take the words back, she realized instantly. Not because they didn't mean anything, but because they meant too much. She could see it in his eyes, and she started breathing again.

"Maybe you should," she said softly.

"I can't, Tory. I spoke without thinking." His voice was flat. "What would everyone in Eagle Ridge say?"

"I don't care. I didn't care what people said for the first eighteen years I lived here, and I don't care now."

His gaze sharpened as he looked at her. "What's that supposed to mean?"

"Nothing." But it did, and she knew she would have to tell him.

His radio crackled, and he pressed the button and listened. Finally he stood up, watching her. "I have to go. We'll talk tonight."

"Yes." There were things she needed to tell him, things he deserved to know. Especially after last night.

He lifted his hands to her face and stared at her. "Keep your door closed. Remember, no one who doesn't have an appointment gets in here. And wait for me to walk you home."

"I will." His hands were warm and hard against her cheeks, and full of comfort. She wished she could stand here forever, feeling his touch on her.

Pressing a quick, hard kiss to her lips, he looked at her one more time then turned and left. She watched him drive out of the parking lot and tried to ignore the trees that laughed at her as they whispered her name. There was triumph in their voices, and satisfaction. Soon, they seemed to be saying. Soon.

The sky was leaden with dark, heavy clouds by the time Holt returned that evening. Tory and Teddy sat in the reception area waiting for him, neither of them bothering with the pretense of work. When they heard the crunch of tires in the parking lot, Teddy stood and grabbed his coat.

Holt had barely opened the door when Teddy shot out into the parking lot. "I'll see you tomorrow morning, Doc," he muttered without looking at her.

Holt raised his eyebrows as he watched Teddy leave. "He's in a hurry tonight."

"Can you blame him? I'm not too crazy about being

here myself right now," Tory retorted, standing up. "Let's go."

"Hold on. I want to take another look around." He walked into the kennel through the swinging door, and through its small window Tory could see the light flick on. After a moment, the light was turned off and Holt returned. "Teddy did everything I told him to do." He watched her carefully. "He seems like a good employee."

Tory bristled. "He *is* a good employee. I was lucky he wanted to work for me." As Holt just watched her, she frowned. "You don't suspect him as the murderer, do you?" His eyes didn't change, and her stomach churned. "That's absurd," she cried.

"Nothing's absurd, Tory. Nothing." He paused, then said slowly, "He has a key to the clinic, doesn't he?"

"Teddy would never do anything like that." Her response was instant, but as her words died she remembered his odd reaction that morning.

"We'll see, won't we?" Holt walked into her office and turned off the light, returning with her jacket in his hand. "Why don't we go?"

The wind howled through the trees as they walked toward her house. The tall pines chanted her name, hypnotizing her and drawing her gaze from her house. The sound wrapped around her, closing out everything but the need to go to the trees. She didn't realize she'd turned and started walking toward the woods until Holt grabbed her arm.

"What are you doing?" he asked, his voice rough with concern.

She looked at him, dazed. "What do you mean?"

"You were walking toward the forest. How come?"

Stopping, she closed her eyes and fought the terror. "I didn't realize. They're calling me again, Holt, calling my name. Can't you hear them?"

"I don't hear a thing but the wind." His words were cold and hard. With fear, she realized. For her. "Get in the house, Tory."

Practically dragging her up the steps, he unlocked the

front door, but then turned and stared into the forest surrounding them. The force of the wind was fierce, bending the tips of the trees and splaying the pine boughs. She stood next to him, refusing to look at the trees, tightening her grip on his hand. Finally he opened the door.

"I didn't see a thing."

"Did you expect to?"

"I hoped to." He walked into the kitchen and turned on the lights, then checked the back door. Satisfied, he checked the rest of the house and in a few minutes was back in the kitchen. She stood by the counter watching Spike eat, her stomach twisting into a tight, hard knot.

"Do you have to go to the clinic tonight?"

She shook her head. "I made everyone take their animals home today, so the clinic is empty."

"Good. Then neither of us has to go out." He looked at her, and his eyes softened. "We'll have time to talk."

"Yes." The knot in her stomach swelled, pressing on her lungs. She drew in a breath, struggling for air.

Holt turned away from her and filled the kettle on the stove, then began rummaging in her cabinets.

"What are you doing?" she managed to ask.

"Looking for tea." He opened another cabinet without turning.

"I can make you some," she said, moving toward him.

"It's not for me." He located the canister. "You look like you need something hot."

She did, she realized suddenly. She was chilled to her core, frozen inside and out. Watching as he poured the hot water over a herbal tea bag, she said, "Do you want some coffee?"

"Sure." He looked at her. "It's been a long day."

And it wasn't over yet. Her stomach twisted as she reached for the instant coffee and spooned some into a mug. As she was stirring it, he gently took the spoon out of her hand and set it on the counter.

"Let's go sit down."

Without a word she walked into the living room. Balancing her mug in one hand, she carefully lowered herself onto one end of the couch and sat stiffly, her back not touching the cushion behind her. Holt eased down next to her, close enough so she could feel the heat from his body. It warmed her far more than the tea she drank.

They had to talk, she knew. There were things Holt had a right to know, after last night. Swallowing hard, gathering her courage, she opened her mouth to begin, but he spoke first.

"There were some fibers on the blanket in your clinic that didn't come from the blanket or any of the animals in the clinic. It's not much, but it's something. At least we have some physical evidence." He shifted and turned to face her. "He's blown a couple of chances at you and he's getting reckless. Sooner or later he'll slip, and we'll catch him."

It took her a minute to realize that Holt was trying to reassure her. Setting her mug on the floor with a shaking hand, she tried to smile at him. "I know you will. I won't tell you I'm not scared, but I trust you to protect me. There's no place I'd feel safer than here with you." She swallowed and continued in a low voice, "That's not why I'm nervous tonight."

He took her hand. "Why, then?"

"Because I have to tell you things I would rather keep hidden."

His hand tightened around hers. "There's nothing you *have* to tell me."

"Then there's something I want to tell you."

Holding her hand, he studied her face. "You look like you're being led to your execution. Don't you know, Tory, that nothing you say could ever make me think less of you?"

Some of the ice inside her began to thaw. "Thank you for saying that. But maybe you'd better hear what I have to say first."

"Shoot." He settled on the couch, still holding her hand. She shifted her grip and curled her fingers around his.

"Last night..." She swallowed and reached for her mug, taking too big a gulp.

"Last night was wonderful," Holt said softly.

"Yes, it was." She set the mug down and turned to him, determined to get it out. "But I wasn't completely fair to you. I should have told you about this before...before we made love."

Pressing his fingers to the pulse thundering in her wrist, he slowly raised it to his mouth and brushed it with his lips. "Tell me now."

"It's difficult for me to surrender control to anyone else. In any part of my life."

"That's not always a fault."

"Last night it was."

"Last night we were both nervous." He leaned over and brushed her mouth with his. "It'll be better next time."

"That's just it," she whispered, her heart aching. "I don't know if it will."

He watched her for a moment. "Tell me why."

She tried to pull her hand away from his, but he held it tightly. Finally she let her hand rest quietly in his. "My father was an alcoholic who wasn't around much. My mother was, to put it delicately, not very discriminating in her choice of companions when he wasn't home." She looked him in the eye. "Everyone in Eagle Ridge knew all about it when I was growing up. We moved around town constantly, to wherever my mother could find two beds. Every day in school I knew everyone including the teachers was looking at me, knowing what I was."

"And what were you?" he asked softly.

"The daughter of a whore and a drunk. The kid everyone pitied when they weren't laughing at me."

"That's why you left town as soon as you could."

"I got a scholarship to college and never looked back. My mother died my freshman year, and after that there was no reason to come back to Eagle Ridge."

"What about your father?"

"No one saw him again after my mother died."

"What does that have to do with me or what happened last night?"

She turned away, unable to look at the understanding on his face. She was afraid she'd start to cry. "The day I left home at eighteen, I swore I would always be in control of every aspect of my life. I vowed I would never be that helpless again, that vulnerable to another person. I swore I would make a success of my life."

"And you did." His thumb caressed the inside of her wrist. "You're a successful veterinarian, and now you own your own practice."

"I also swore I would never come back here."

His thumb stopped and he looked at her. "Did you come back because of Barber?"

She nodded, amazed at his perception. "After that happened, after he attacked me, I fell apart completely. I realized how fragile the structure of my life really was. Because I'd been so determined to control everything, my life was completely rigid, and a few blows from his baton cracked it beyond repair."

"You could have gone anywhere to start over. Why did you come here?"

"Because this is where it all started. I thought if I could confront the demons I'd left behind in Eagle Ridge, I could rebuild my life. From the ground up." She smiled tremulously. "And seeing Bobby Duvall was the first step. When I realized I wasn't afraid of him any longer, I felt better than I have in months."

"I still don't understand what this has to do with last night."

Her smile dimmed. "I was afraid last night," she whispered. "I was afraid to lose control. That wasn't fair to you. And I don't know if I'll ever not be afraid."

Slowly he set his coffee mug down and reached for her. Pulling her close, he cradled her in his arms as he nuzzled her neck. "Nobody expects everything to be perfect the first time two people make love. It'll be easier next time." His arms tightened, then he leaned away from her. "And it's not as if I gave you everything I had, either. What I told you last night was the simple truth. I don't know if I can give you anything more.''

A ball of regret lodged in her chest. Last night she had seen what they might have had together. But the images had been blurry and indistinct, as if she looked through a layer of thick fabric and saw only shadows beyond it. Would either of them be able to reach out and tear the barrier aside?

Slowly he pulled her closer. "You're shaking," he murmured in her ear.

Swallowing hard, she tried to tell herself to move away from him, that it would be better in the long run. But she wanted to stay close. "It's not easy to tell those things to someone I...care about."

"It took a tremendous amount of courage," he agreed quietly. "You're not regretting that you told me, are you?"

"Of course not." But she spoke too quickly.

He looked at her, astonished. "You can't believe that what you told me is going to make any difference, can you?" When she didn't answer, he shook her lightly. "Nothing that happened to you when you were a child was in any way your fault. If anything, your story only makes me admire you more. There aren't many people who could create success out of a cesspool like the one you were raised in. You have nothing to be ashamed of."

Reaching out, she cupped his cheek with her hand. "I'm ashamed of being afraid last night. And I'm afraid I hurt you because of it."

"Then I guess you'll have to figure out a way to make it up to me, won't you?" His eyes darkened to the color of smoke, and his fingers slid down to her waist.

The fear was still there, its wings beating in her head and its foul breath a trace of heat on her skin, but it had retreated to a distant corner of her mind. Leaning into his hand, she let her fingers creep up his shirt and slowly push a button through its buttonhole, her knuckles brushing the springy hair underneath. "I'll see what I can come up with,'' she murmured, hardly recognizing the low, husky voice as her own.

He tensed as another button, then another was freed. "I'd say you're doing a pretty good job."

When the last button opened and his uniform shirt fell open, she laid her hands on his chest. His muscles were strong and hard under her hands, his skin smooth and hot. He sat still as a stone while she smoothed her hands over him, tracing the shape of his ribs and the outline of his muscles with the tips of her fingers.

When she touched the hard nubbins of his nipples, he shuddered and closed his eyes. Sucking in a deep breath, he suddenly reached for her and crushed her against him. His mouth found hers in a deep, searing kiss that seemed to go on forever. When it ended, she was shaking as hard as he was.

Without a word he stood and took her hand, leading her up the stairs, not stopping until they stood next to the bed. Smoothing his hands down her face, he stared at her for the space of one heartbeat. What he saw there seemed to satisfy him, because he bent his head to kiss her again.

Something exploded inside her the instant his lips touched hers. She was on fire, burning for him. Aching for him.

He was equally frantic. His hands trembled as he swept her clothes away and pushed them to the floor. She heard a faint ripping sound when she tried to open the button on his slacks. In seconds they were naked on the bed, their arms and legs tangled as they rolled over the comforter.

Holt's hands moved constantly, sweeping down her body, touching her everywhere, as if he could be satisfied by that sensation alone. His greedy mouth roamed over her face, down to her breast, nibbled on her thigh.

She throbbed and ached, burning out of control along with him. When he rose and thrust into her, she arched up to meet him, gripping him with her legs. In seconds they both flew over the edge, riding the crest together. She heard a voice and dimly realized that it was hers, sobbing his name.

She floated for a long time, her body sated and still quivering, before he shifted and she felt the weight of his sweat-slicked body crushing her into the mattress. He tried to slide next to her, but she held him more tightly. "No," she whispered. "I want to feel you against me."

He eased to the side then pulled her close, his hand tracing lazy patterns on her back. "Believe me, I'm not going anywhere." Searching for her mouth, he kissed her gently, lingering over her swollen lips.

She shuddered one more time, then gave in to the need and curled around him. The wings of fear fluttered once in her mind, but she brushed them away easily. Maybe Holt was right, she thought hazily as she drifted into sleep. Maybe everything would get easier.

Tory awakened to the quiet sound of a zipper closing. Opening her eyes, she saw Holt standing next to her bed, reaching for his shirt. As if he could feel her eyes on him, he turned to look at her.

"Hey, sleepyhead." He smiled, and the sight made her heart turn over in her chest. Holt didn't smile often.

"Hey, yourself." She struggled to sit up, flushing as she grabbed the sheet to cover herself. Holt's eyes darkened as he watched her. "Where are you going?"

"We got a call about a prowler at a house between here and town. I'm going to check it out." He must have seen the fear rise in her face, because he leaned down and brushed his mouth over hers. "I called Teddy and he's at the clinic. When you're dressed and ready to go, call him and he'll walk you over there. Okay?"

She nodded. "Okay." Swallowing hard, she watched him button his shirt. "Do you think this prowler could be the murderer?"

"It's possible," he said grimly. "The house wasn't far from here."

"Be careful," she said in a low voice.

Sliding onto the bed, he pulled her to him for a hard kiss. "Don't worry. I'll be back before you know it."

His hands lingered at her waist, then he stood and strode to the door. Pausing to look back at her, he shoved his hands into his pockets and let his gaze drift to Spike, who lay on the floor with his head on his paws. "Take care of her, buddy," he said gruffly, then he turned and clattered down the stairs. A moment later the front door closed.

She wouldn't think about being alone in the house. Throwing off the covers, she went into the bathroom and started the shower. Ten minutes later she emerged and headed for her bedroom again, closing the door against the chill.

Spike wagged his tail in greeting, thumping it against the floor, and she relaxed. She dressed quickly and was slipping her shoes on when she saw the hair stand up on Spike's back.

A low growl rumbled in his throat, and he slowly stood. At the same moment, she heard the third stair creak.

Panic washed over her, and she looked blindly for a weapon. Seeing none, she grabbed a chair and rammed it under the doorknob, then ran to the phone and dialed the police. Her heart thundered so loudly she could hardly hear her voice giving the message. When she hung up the phone she turned and looked at Spike. He stood at the door of her room, vibrating as he growled. Tory curled her fingers around the telephone and waited.

Chapter 13

He didn't like the smell of this prowler situation. The rough vinyl of the steering wheel ground into Holt's fingertips, and he pressed the accelerator a little harder. He didn't like it at all.

Nobody had reported a prowler for weeks. Hell, no one had seen or heard a thing on the nights of the three murders. So why was there a prowler now, at six o'clock in the morning, at the house closest to Tory's?

He lifted his foot from the gas pedal and glanced at the narrow road, scanning for a place to turn around. The next instant he clenched his teeth together and deliberately accelerated. He was almost there. It would only take a few minutes to look around and make sure the prowler was gone, then he could bolt to Tory's and let one of his officers do a more thorough job.

He was turning into the driveway of the house that had reported the prowler when his radio crackled to life. As soon as he heard the words *Dr. Falcon* and *prowler* he spun the steering wheel viciously to the side and gunned the engine. The Blazer shot onto the road, fishtailing wildly as Holt struggled to control both the truck and his fear.

He would be damned useless if he ran into the house terrified and panicked. That knowledge was the only thing that allowed him to block out his terror and suppress the images of Tory. But pictures of what the bastard would do to her if he didn't get there in time hovered at the edges of his mind, taunting him with his helplessness.

Skidding into her driveway, he was out of the truck before it had completely stopped as he ran toward her house, he searched frantically in his pocket for the key she had given him the evening before. Shoving it into the lock, he threw the door open and rushed inside.

The first thing he saw was the broken window, the curtain lifting lazily in the breeze. In spite of his vow to stay detached, he felt his stomach clench and tighten as fear hit him like a gut punch.

"Tory!" he yelled, frantically scanning the first floor then taking the stairs two at a time. "Are you here?"

"Holt?" Her voice was shaky and so low he could barely hear it, but it was coming from her bedroom. Thank God she was alive. Prayers he didn't even realize he knew tumbled from his lips.

As he reached the top of the stairs, he heard her fumbling with something inside her bedroom. He saw a flash of red on her door out of the corner of his eye, but then the door opened a crack and he shoved it completely open.

He let his gaze sweep over her once then he crushed her into his arms and held on tight. Her heart thundered against his chest, its beat matching his own. Drawing a deep, shaky breath, the first one he'd taken since he ran into the house, he tightened his arms around her and breathed in the scent of her.

"I'm so sorry. I shouldn't have left you alone," he murmured into the fragrant cloud of her hair.

He could feel her tremble in his arms. "Did you catch him?"

"I didn't see a thing. He was gone before I got here."

She leaned back in his arms, her face white with fear. "Was I imagining it, then? Maybe there wasn't anyone in the house."

"You weren't imagining it. There's a broken window downstairs." His voice was grim. "Tell me what happened."

She swallowed hard and bent to pet Spike. "I finished my shower and came in here. It was chilly, so I shut the door. I was almost dressed when Spike started to growl, then I heard the stair creak." She swallowed again and looked at him, terror blotting everything else from her eyes. "The third stair from the bottom squeaks. I've been meaning to fix it."

"Thank God you didn't. What happened then?"

"I rammed a chair under the doorknob and called the police. Then I waited."

He didn't want to think about how terrified she must have been, waiting in her room while a murderer climbed her stairs. Listening to him get closer and closer to her. He swallowed hard, trying to dislodge the sickness from his throat. "I'm so sorry, sweetheart. I never should have left you alone," he repeated.

Her face was white, but she looked at him steadily. "You did the right thing, Holt. Who would have guessed he'd be so clever?"

"I should have." Rage built inside him as he realized what a close call she'd had. "I should have been more suspicious. I swear I won't leave you alone again, Tory."

Her eyes were huge and so dark they looked almost black. "Where did he go, Holt? You were here only a few minutes after I called. How could he disappear so fast?" Her face was frozen with fear.

"I don't know, but we'll find out." He took her hand, the feel of her icy, stiff fingers stoking the rage inside him. "Believe me, we'll find him."

For a moment she clung to him, her cold hand curling around his like she'd never let go. Then she stood and reached for her shoes. "Maybe you'd better take a look around. Since he left in a hurry, maybe he got careless."

"I'll wait for you to come downstairs with me. I don't want you out of my—"

Shock hit him as he turned toward the hallway. Her door stood open, and painted on the side facing the hall was a large red X. The red paint dripped down the door, making it look like spatters of blood against the dark wood.

"Oh, my God." She spoke faintly behind him, and he immediately grabbed her arms.

"This is good, Tory," he said too quickly. "Maybe he got some paint on his hands and left a fingerprint somewhere. This gives us a chance."

She didn't look like she'd heard him. She stared at the door, her arms wrapped around her shoulders. "I heard him doing it," she whispered. "I heard something scratching at the door, but I thought he was trying to get in. I stood here and listened to him on the other side of my door."

"He won't get that close again, Tory, I swear it." Holt's fingers curled into the softness of her upper arms. She just kept staring at the door.

Finally she looked at him. "I need to get out of here. Can I go over to the clinic?"

"I'll walk you over there and make sure everything's all right. I want to talk to Teddy, anyway."

He was fairly sure Teddy wouldn't have heard anything, but it was time to have it out with Tory's kennel boy. Past time.

Teddy knew something. Holt was sure of it. He'd been afraid that if he pressured him the kid would clam up, but it was too late for niceties. Teddy would tell him what he knew, and he would tell him today.

Ten minutes later Holt had checked the clinic completely and satisfied himself that nothing was out of order. He heard Teddy whistling as he cleaned a cage. Holt stood by the door, waiting until the young man stepped around the corner and saw him.

"We need to talk, Teddy." Holt watched the kid pale

and felt a vicious stab of satisfaction. He'd been right. "Let's go outside. I don't think you want Dr. Falcon to hear what you have to say."

Tory had watched as Holt strode through the clinic grimly, then told her he had to go. Two of his officers would be arriving soon, he'd said, to look around her house and to keep an eye on things at the clinic. He'd told her he'd be back as soon as he could, kissed her goodbye and was gone.

That was four hours ago. A few clients had trickled in, all of them morbidly curious about the police car that sat in her parking lot, but she'd had more than enough time to sit in her office and let her fear eat away at her.

Holt had looked so grim, so implacable when he'd left. So closed in, as if every fiber of his being was focused on finding and catching the person who had been in her house that morning. Is that the way he'd looked to his wife when she was desperate for comfort? A weak person could crumble if faced with that single-mindedness. A woman who didn't have her own demons to wrestle could never understand that kind of need.

But she did. She understood it all too well. And instead of resenting Holt for shutting her out, she prayed endlessly that he would be safe, that his need to solve these crimes wouldn't drive him to recklessness.

Teddy appeared in the door of her office, a mop in one hand, his face pale. His gaze focused on the calendar on the wall behind her. "Is it okay if I mop the front now?"

"Go ahead. I don't expect any more clients this morning." Leaning back in her chair, she added, "You can leave for lunch today, Teddy. The police officer in the front of the clinic is going to be there all day."

Instead of thanking her, his face got even paler, if that was possible. "No, thanks, Doc. I think I'll just stay here today." He licked his lips and mumbled, "I brought my lunch with me."

"Teddy," she said gently, "are you worried about what happened this morning at my house?"

Reluctantly his eyes met hers. They were filled with misery. "I would never have forgiven myself if you got hurt," he whispered.

"Nobody's blaming you," she answered, puzzled.

To her surprise, his face flamed red. "I've got to mop. Before the mop dries," he said in a strangled voice as he turned and hurried away.

Tory listened to the furious swishing of the mop on the floor in the other room, unease stirring inside her. Did Holt somehow imply to Teddy that it was his fault someone had broken into her house?

No, he wouldn't have done that. Tory dismissed the idea instantly. Holt could never be unfair. Sighing, she stood and rolled her tight shoulders. Teddy was probably just as tense as she was, and just as nervous.

Avoiding the parts of the floor Teddy had already cleaned, she opened the front door and saw the two policemen conferring next to their car. When they saw her they both ran over.

"Is something wrong, Dr. Falcon?"

"No, everything's fine. I just wondered if you'd found anything at my house."

One of the policemen looked at the other, an unspoken message passing between them. "We're probably not supposed to say anything, but heck, it is your house. We found a partial fingerprint in red paint on the wall outside the broken window. It's smeared, but it's better than anything else we've gotten so far on this case."

Tory felt as if the day suddenly brightened. "Do you think you'll be able to identify it?"

"We've sent it to the state lab. It'll take about twenty-four hours to get an answer, and a match if it's on file anywhere."

"Thank goodness."

The two police officers nodded. "It's about time we caught a break on this case."

Tory shivered in the cool autumn air, and one of the officers noticed. "Hey, Doc, you'd better get back inside. It's cold out here."

"And Chief Adams would have our butts on a platter if he knew you were out in the open," the other officer added.

The two men glanced at each other. "In fact," the first one said, "why don't I spend the rest of the afternoon in the clinic with you?"

"That's not necessary," Tory said, but the young officer gave her an engaging grin.

"It's a lot warmer inside than sitting in a police car."

"All right," Tory answered, aware that she'd been manipulated but willing to overlook it. She didn't want either officer to get in trouble with Holt.

She saw them exchange another look and felt the fear unexpectedly flooding over her. *Don't be ridiculous,* she told herself, laying her hand over her churning stomach. *They work for Holt.* But she stood in the doorway of the clinic and barred their way in. "You'll understand if I call Chief Adams first?"

They both looked startled, then reluctantly impressed. "Go ahead. You're smart to be cautious," the first one said.

It only took a moment to dial the police station. Holt wasn't there, but she recognized the dispatcher's voice. Marge asked to speak to both of them, and in another moment she'd assured Tory they were indeed Eagle Ridge police officers.

The second officer disappeared in the direction of her house as the first policeman settled onto the bench in the waiting room. He sat there all afternoon, chatting with her clients and thumbing through a magazine. After the last client left, he tossed the magazine on the bench and stood up to stretch.

"You can take off now, kid," he said to Teddy.

Teddy shook his head. "Chief Adams told me to stay here until he gets back, and that's what I'm going to do." There was a stubborn set to his mouth.

The police officer looked annoyed, but shrugged. "Suit

yourself." He turned to Tory. "Want me to check the clinic for you?"

Tory heard a truck pulling into the parking lot and felt relief flooding through her. "Chief Adams is here now. He can take care of it."

A moment later she heard Holt knocking at the door. "It's me, Tory."

She hurried over to open the door. His face was hard and set as he looked at her. She longed to throw herself into his arms, but instead she closed the door quietly behind him. Holt looked at Teddy and tensed.

"What the hell are you doing in here?" His low voice vibrated with anger. For a moment she thought he was talking to Teddy, but then she realized he was looking at the police officer.

The officer shuffled his feet and gave his boss an uneasy look. "I figured it would be safer for her if I was inside with her."

"And who was supposed to protect her from you?"

The younger man looked bewildered. "What's that supposed to mean?"

"It means that this crime isn't solved yet, and it looks like our criminal has some police experience. Until it is solved, everyone on this police force is a suspect." Holt turned to look at her. "And what the hell were you thinking of to let him in here?"

"I called the police station to ask you first," she said defensively. "You weren't there, but Marge talked to him and assured me that he was one of your officers."

"Marge doesn't give the orders around here. I do." He swiveled to face the younger man, who was ramrod straight and red-faced. "In the future, you obey your orders. If I tell you to stay somewhere, you stay there."

"Yes, sir," the officer mumbled, and practically ran out the door.

Holt turned to Teddy and gave him a long, hard look. After what seemed like forever, he said, "You can go home now."

Tory was puzzled by the relief that swept over Teddy. He looked like he'd been holding his breath all afternoon and had finally let it out. She turned to Holt to ask him what was going on, but Holt took her hand and shook his head once. They stood quietly, listening, until Teddy left and the sound of his car trailed out of the parking lot.

"What is it, Holt?" she said.

"Let's go to your house." He walked into the kennel. In a few moments the lights went off and he was back. "Why don't you get your coat and purse?"

She tried to ignore the police car pulling out of her driveway as they headed for the house. It was easier than ignoring the sound of the trees. There was very little wind today, but they still whispered to her. "Soon," they crooned. "Soon."

In her house, she noticed that the broken window had been fixed and new locks installed on all the windows. Her blood chilled at the reminder of what had happened that morning. She was afraid to look up the stairs.

He must have read her mind. "It's okay. The paint's gone, and nothing else in your house was disturbed. I checked it myself."

"Do you really think one of your men could be the murderer?" she asked.

"I can't ignore the fact that whoever is doing this seems to know just how to avoid leaving any traces. It would be criminally careless if I didn't suspect them."

"But do you really think one of them is responsible?"

"I sure as hell hope not."

He spun around restlessly and began checking the house. She moved into the kitchen to feed Spike, watching Holt the whole time. Something was wrong.

When he finally came into the kitchen, she asked quietly, "What's wrong, Holt?"

He jerked around. "What makes you think something's wrong?"

"I can tell." She was almost frightened by her certainty, by the ease with which she was able to read him.

He drew in a deep breath. "You're right, something is wrong." He paused, shoving his hands into his pockets and whirling to look out the window. "I had a long talk with Teddy today."

"About what?" Her hands trembled with sudden fear, and the bag of dog food dropped to the floor with a quiet thud. A sick feeling churned in her stomach as she remembered Teddy's odd behavior the morning they'd found the blanket and paint in the kennel.

He turned to face her. "About what's been happening around here. He's been acting pretty damn peculiar lately, and today was the last straw. I couldn't wait any longer to find out what he knows."

"He couldn't know a thing," she whispered. "He's only a kid, Holt, not a murderer. It couldn't be Teddy." *Not Teddy,* she thought. *Dear God, not Teddy.*

"I don't think he's the murderer, Tory." His voice was gentle, and he reached out for her, steadying her with hands on her shoulders. "But he's not completely innocent, either."

"What do you mean?" The words burned on her tongue, pain mixing with the bitter taste of betrayal.

"If it makes you feel any better, he's been almost as terrified as you since this all began," Holt said.

"Why?" she whispered.

He took his hands off her shoulders and shoved them into his pockets. "It seems a group of his friends have been pressuring him to help them break into the clinic. He's been refusing, but he's been worried about it."

"The day I opened the clinic, when someone had broken the lock on the back door." She felt herself pale. "He was acting so strange. Almost guilty. I just assumed it was because he was nervous."

"He was nervous, all right." Holt's voice was grim. "Nervous because he thought he knew who had done it."

"Why didn't he say anything to me?"

Holt sighed. "He's eighteen years old, Tory. He didn't want to snitch on his friends."

She looked at Holt, horror growing inside her like some malignant thing. "He's only a kid," she said. "A teenager. What kind of friends does he have? And why would they want to break into a veterinary clinic?"

"You answered that yourself when you had that first break-in. Drugs, Tory. That's why someone would want to break into a veterinary clinic." At her incredulous look he sighed and turned to look out the window. "Just because this is a small town doesn't mean there aren't any big-city problems here. We have kids on drugs, just like Chicago. And those kids will commit crimes to get their drugs."

She stared at Holt, at the tension that stiffened his back and made his muscles rigid, and realized he was holding something back. "There's more to it than that, isn't there? There's something you're not telling me."

Slowly he turned to face her, regret in his eyes. "Yes, there's more to it than that. I wish to God I didn't have to tell you this, but I don't think it's just kids who are behind this."

"What do you mean?" She moved closer to him.

"I mean that someone put this idea into those kids' minds. Someone told them there were drugs in the clinic."

"Who?" she asked.

"Teddy didn't know," he said grimly. "But I have an idea."

"Do you…" She stopped and licked her lips. "Do you think it's connected to the murders?"

His face tightened. "I don't know. Murdering three women is a big jump from stealing drugs. I hope we'll find out tonight."

She felt like her feet had grown roots and burrowed into the floor, anchoring her there permanently. "What's going to happen tonight?" She could barely force the words out of her mouth.

He walked to the window and stared at the darkening sky. "Teddy has agreed to help us. He's going to tell his friends we're going to Pitcher for the evening," he said, naming a town thirty miles from Eagle Ridge. "We're not going anywhere, of course. I'm going to be waiting in the clinic for whoever shows up.''

"What do you mean, you're going to be at the clinic. Where am I going to be?''

He turned to face her. "You're going to be sitting in this house with one of my deputies right next to you. He'll have a gun and he won't hesitate to use it.''

Tory shook her head. "On whom? You said everyone with a police background was a suspect in these murders. How will you pick which one stays with me?''

"I'll figure out something. I'll leave two of them here if I have to.''

She shook her head again. "No. I want to be in the clinic with you.'' She swallowed hard and looked at him, hoping he didn't see the desperation in her eyes. "It's my business and my building. I want to be there.''

"You'll be safer here in the house,'' he said flatly.

"That's debatable, but I really don't care. I'm not about to let you go sit in that clinic by yourself.''

Understanding dawned in his eyes. "Are you worried about me?'' he asked, incredulous.

"Why is that so strange?'' she retorted, defensive. "Do you think I want you to get hurt?''

His eyes softened as he looked at her. "I'm not going to get hurt, Tory. And I don't want you to get hurt, either.''

"Then we'll stay in the clinic together,'' she said stubbornly. "That way we can make sure.''

He stared at her for a long time, then his lips curled into a reluctant smile. "You're like a dog with a bone, you know that? You won't give up.''

"That's right, Holt,'' she said softly. "I'm just like you.''

The smile faded from his lips as he watched her. He spun around abruptly to look out the window again. "All right, you can stay with me. But you'll do exactly what I tell you to do, when I tell you to do it.''

"You're in charge. I just want to be there.''

"All right.'' He sighed, and his face was unreadable

again. "Go get into some warmer clothes. We'll leave in
a few minutes."

Holt looked at Tory, sitting next to him in the front of
his car. She had been quiet since they'd left her house,
locking Spike inside and turning on the outside lights. He'd
expected her to pepper him with questions, but instead she
just stared out the window at the blackness of the forest
surrounding them.

"You okay?" he asked softly.

She looked at him. Even in the darkness of the car he
could see the fear in her enormous eyes. "I'm fine. I was
just thinking that I'm glad I'm here with you and not at
home by myself."

Suddenly he realized why she'd been so adamant about
coming with him. She'd been concerned about his safety,
but she didn't want to be left alone, even with another
police officer in the house. She trusted him to keep her safe.

Fear slammed into him like a train. What if he couldn't
keep her safe? What if something happened to her in spite
of his efforts?

Nothing would happen. It couldn't. Holt didn't want to
examine his feelings. He just knew he would rather die than
let Tory get hurt.

Abruptly he turned the wheel of the Blazer, hearing the
tires squeal as he skidded off the blacktop and onto the dirt
road.

"What's the matter?" Tory's voice, breathless with fear,
came from the seat next to him.

Loosening his fingers from their grip on the steering
wheel, he made a conscious effort to regain control of his
emotions. "Nothing's wrong. I almost missed my turn."

"Where are we going?"

He could hear her trying to control her fear, too, and he
wanted to reach out for her. But he needed both hands to
steer on the uneven, hard-packed dirt. "This is an old log-
ging road. It curls around and stops about a half mile behind your house. We'll park there and walk to the clinic."

He felt her tensing beside him. But instead of protesting, she said in a small voice, "Does everyone know about this road?"

"Most people in town probably do." He kept his voice casual, knowing what she was asking. "But it hasn't been used in a long time. After the last murder, it was one of the first places I checked. There hadn't been any vehicles on it. I'm still not sure how he got to that clearing near your house, but he didn't come this way."

"Thank you, Holt. It would be horrible to think he'd come the same way, bringing her with him."

"He didn't." The road stopped abruptly in front of him, ending in a solid wall of trees. "Here's where we get out and walk." His hand on the door of the truck, he hesitated, looking at her. "Are you going to be all right with this? Walking through the woods, I mean?"

Her face looked wan and pinched in the dim glow from the cargo light. "I wouldn't want to do it by myself, but I'll be fine as long as you're here with me." She tried to smile. "Your hand might be sore by the time we get there, though."

Once again fear washed over him. She trusted him so much. And he felt so inadequate to protect her. The murderer danced in front of him like a mirage, just out of reach. And the longer it took to get him, the closer he got to Tory.

"Let's get started," he said, getting out of the truck and slamming the door. He didn't want to give Tory time to think about walking through the dark woods. He switched on a flashlight and saw the first of the white rags he had tied around the trees earlier that day. Taking her hand, he led her into the trees.

Chapter 14

Tory took a deep breath and clutched Holt's hand more tightly as she let go of the truck and stepped between two trees. For a moment she felt as if she was walking blindfolded into the unknown. Her nerves tightened and thrummed with fear, then Holt moved his fingers over hers. Reassurance seemed to flow into her hand, and the fear receded slightly. Holt's flashlight swept in a golden arc in front of them, illuminating trees and branches in a random pattern. Outside its light, the darkness surrounding them was absolute.

"I tied white strips of cloth to the trees so we could find our way to the clinic without getting lost. All we have to do is follow them."

He made it sound so easy. Trying to keep her eyes on the flashlight and away from the blackness and the looming trees, she murmured, "I hope there are a lot of them."

Squeezing her hand, he said, "Don't worry, we won't get lost. It's only half a mile."

"A lot can happen in half a mile," she muttered. There

was a burst of sound over her head and she jumped sideways, brushing against one of the huge pine trees.

"It was an owl," Holt said, pulling her closer. "We startled him."

"Not as much as he startled me," she retorted, keeping her eyes fixed on the area outlined by the flashlight. She refused to think about what might lie in wait for them outside of that comforting yellow arc.

They walked silently for a few minutes, hearing the wind sighing through the pines, their footsteps muffled by the layers of pine needles under their feet. When a branch creaked above them, Holt glanced at her and asked softly, "How are you doing?"

She didn't even pretend not to understand what he was asking. "Better than I expected," she replied, surprised to find it was true. "These trees don't seem to bother me, at least not like the ones in front of the clinic."

His hand tightened on hers. "We're almost there. I can see the last of my markers, so I'm going to turn off the flashlight." He paused and pulled her to him, wrapping his arm around her shoulder. "Ready?"

Swallowing hard, she nodded. When he switched out the light, the blackness closed around her like a suffocating blanket, smothering all her senses. An ancient, primeval dread rose inside her, and the hair on the back of her neck prickled. She was in the forest, surrounded by darkness and the unknown.

Before she could bolt in the direction of the clinic, Holt swung her around in front of him. His face was a white blur in the darkness. "Wait, Tory. We have to approach the clinic carefully. I don't want to scare anyone away." His voice was a whispered murmur in the inky blackness that enveloped them.

Swallowing hard, she struggled to beat back the panic that threatened to engulf her. Finally she was able to say in a shaky voice, "I know. Just don't let go of me."

"Don't worry about that."

Was she mistaken, or was there an odd note in his voice,

one of hot possession? In the darkness she couldn't tell. Curling her fingers around his, she stood next to him, letting the warmth from his body seep into her soul. After a few minutes she stopped shaking and realized she was beginning to be able to see through the gloom.

"Getting better?" Holt asked.

She nodded, then realized he couldn't see her. "Yes, it is. I can see a little bit."

"Let's start walking, then. I want to be in the clinic soon." Without waiting for her to answer, he began to move. Tory edged forward, straining to see the ground in the darkness and feeling with her foot before she put her weight down.

"There's not much on the ground here besides pine needles, but if you stay right behind me you won't have to worry about tripping on anything." She could see the pale outline of Holt's face as he turned his head to talk to her, and she gripped his hand more tightly.

She followed him through the dark forest, occasionally stumbling over uneven ground. The owl hooted from a long way off, the mournful notes trailing away into the night. A flash of white startled her, then she realized it was the last of Holt's rags, tied around a tree next to her. It fluttered slightly in the breeze, and suddenly she felt much better.

There was nothing irrational about being frightened in a forest at night, she told herself. Any normal human being would be. Deep down, buried under layers of sophistication and polish, everyone was a little afraid of the dark. The fear rose out of the ancient, instinctive parts of the brain, recalling eons past when the dark was a very real danger for primitive hunters.

And the trees hadn't bothered her at all tonight.

Standing a little straighter, she looked over Holt's shoulder and studied the shadows for a hint of her clinic. As if he could read her mind, Holt murmured, "There it is, over on your right."

The low building seemed to blend into the trees that surrounded it, and for a moment Tory felt her stomach roll.

The clinic was completely dark and silent, and she didn't relish the idea of going inside after what had happened there.

But she had no choice. This was her clinic, and it had been her decision to stay with Holt tonight. Concentrating on the feel of Holt's hand wrapped around hers, she tried to ignore her fluttering stomach as the clinic got closer.

Holt stopped at the edge of the trees and turned to her. The pale light of the crescent moon illuminated his face, highlighting the sharp planes and angles. "I want to take a look around before we go inside. Are you all right here by yourself for a few minutes?"

Her first impulse was to say no, to beg him to take her with him. Swallowing hard, she nodded. "I'll be fine."

Even in the dim light she saw his face soften. Bending, he brushed a quick kiss across her lips. "You're really something, you know that?" He trailed his finger down her cheek and stared at her for a moment, then turned to look at the clinic.

"I don't think anyone is around, but I don't want you out of the trees until I make sure," he finally said. He led her into the woods about ten feet. "Stay here until I come for you. You can see the clinic, but no one there will be able to see you." His jaw tightened and he looked away. "If I don't come back fairly quickly, or if you hear something alarming, head toward the house. Stay hidden in the woods until you can get in your truck and drive away. Keep driving until you get to the state police station in Escanaba." He pressed the keys to her truck into her hand.

Fear pounded at her as she grabbed his hand. "What aren't you telling me, Holt?"

"Nothing," he said. "As far as I know, there isn't anyone around except us, and I won't find anything unusual when I check the clinic. I just want you to be prepared."

"You had to think awfully far in advance to bring the keys to my truck." Tension skittered through her veins as she stared at the clinic. It looked peaceful and serene in the pale moonlight, completely untainted by the evil that had invaded it.

"That's my job. Thinking ahead is what I'm supposed to do."

Pulling her close for the space of a heartbeat, he kissed her hard then stepped away. "I'll be right back, Tory."

He seemed to blend into the shadows cast by the trees as he moved toward the clinic. He was clearly outlined as he stepped out of the cover of the woods, then he disappeared into the shadows surrounding the building.

She barely allowed herself to breathe as she tilted her head to listen, straining to hear the sound of Holt's footsteps. The night was utterly silent. The owl had stopped calling, and for a moment even the wind stopped blowing. It was as if every creature of the night held its breath and waited along with her.

The moments stretched tighter and there was still no sign of Holt. She shifted from one foot to the other and sent up a constant stream of prayers for Holt's safety as she wondered frantically where he could be.

When the back door of the clinic eased open, she gasped and shrunk behind the tree. Then Holt stepped out and headed toward her, and she rushed to meet him.

"What were you doing in the clinic? Is everything all right?"

"Everything's fine." He took her hand and led her toward the building. "I just had to make sure there weren't going to be any nasty surprises inside for us."

He pulled her into the building and closed and locked the door behind them. Silence echoed off the walls of the kennel, the empty cages mocking her with her inability to control what happened in her own clinic.

"What do we do now?" she asked, forcing herself to use a normal voice when she wanted to whisper.

"Now we sit and wait. We may not get any company, but I have a feeling we'll have a visitor."

"Who do you suspect?"

He looked at her, his face grim and his mouth a hard

line. "I can't tell you that, Tory. It wouldn't be fair to the person I suspect, especially if I'm wrong. We'll find out one way or another tonight."

Shoving her hands into her pockets to hide their sudden trembling, she looked at the shadows in the kennel and swallowed. "What do you want me to do?"

Holt laid his hands on her shoulders and swung her to face him. "You amaze me."

She looked at him with astonishment.

"Most people would be scared as hell in this situation. They'd be whining and moaning and asking to go home. And all you do is ask me what you should do."

"Believe me, I moved beyond scared a long time ago. I even moved beyond petrified. Now I'm in basic survival mode. And I have you pegged as my best bet." She tried to sound flippant, wincing when her voice wavered on the last words.

His hands tightened on her shoulders as he drew her closer. "I won't let you out of my sight until the murderer is caught, Tory. I promise you."

She watched, mesmerized, as a flame appeared in his eyes. "I know," she whispered. "I know you'll protect me, Holt. I think I've known it all along."

He stared at her, then lowered his mouth to hers. He tasted of the night and the forest, dark and mysterious and potent with promise. Desire flared to life inside her, sweeping away her fear and making her forget why they were in the clinic.

For a moment they clung together, heat pouring from one to the other. Then Holt stepped back, his face glittering with passion and need and regret. His hands lingered on her arms before they fell away. "I can't allow myself to be distracted," he whispered. "I'm sorry."

"I know." She forced herself to move away from him, and wrapped her arms around herself to hold in the trembling. "Tell me what to do."

She could see him gather himself. Then the cop was

back, his eyes flat and assessing. The lover had disappeared completely.

"I want him to get far enough into the clinic that he won't be able to run once he knows we're here. There's no way he's going to slip through my fingers."

His voice was grim. "You think there's more going on here than just a break-in at my clinic, don't you?"

"It seems awfully coincidental that we have this break-in business going on at the same time as the murders." He slanted her an unreadable look. "Especially since you seem to be the target of both."

Tory felt herself begin to shake, and it wasn't from passion this time. "Then you think the person who is trying to break into the clinic is the murderer."

"It's a possibility, yes. But I still have to prove it."

"What happens if we catch someone tonight?" she whispered.

"He'll be treated like any other suspect," Holt answered grimly. "But you can be sure I'll check his fingerprints against the one we found on your wall."

He drew her behind the first row of cages. There were two chairs in the aisle, and he led her to one of them. "This is the boring part," he warned as they sat down. Tory edged her chair closer to his, but he didn't seem to notice. "We could sit here all night and come up empty, or he could walk in the door in a few minutes." He looked at her and his mouth softened. "So no talking from now on. And no anything else, either."

"All right." Her low voice echoed through the empty kennel, but she realized with amazement that the silence and emptiness didn't bother her anymore. She was in her clinic, and Holt was with her. Nothing else really mattered.

She reached for his hand, and as her fingers twined with his he turned and brought their joined hands to his mouth. His kiss only brushed her knuckles before he turned away, listening again, but the heat from his mouth swept over her, warming her heart.

Tory had no idea how long they sat in the kennel, silent

and watchful. After a while the noises from the outside were comforting in their familiarity. The owl was close to the building, and she found herself listening for his four spaced hoots. The murmuring of the insects and animals was a reassuring blanket of sound that rose and fell with the wind.

Every once in a while she glanced at Holt. His face was still and set, and he never looked at her. All his energy was focused on listening. If he hadn't been holding her hand, she was sure he would have forgotten she was with him.

She shifted restlessly in the chair, stiff from sitting for so long. Then Holt slowly straightened. Tory froze as he gently disengaged his hand from hers. In the darkness she could feel him gather himself, and she saw his right hand check his gun.

She hadn't heard a thing. Straining to listen, she leaned forward in her chair. Without turning his head, Holt leaned toward her.

"Someone's coming."

His words were no more than a puff of air that caressed her ear and then dissipated. As he leaned away from her, she realized the night outside had grown abruptly silent. The lack of sound was suddenly overwhelmingly frightening. She remembered her most recent dream, where the only sound in the woods had been the crunching of pine needles underfoot and the drag of a heavy burden over the ground.

Was the same shadowy figure making his silent way toward her clinic?

Holt turned to look at her, then leaned over and brushed her hair off her face. "Don't move. You'll be fine. He won't even have to know you're here."

He would know, she thought. He would be able to hear the pounding of her heart anywhere in the kennel. The sound was so loud it almost drowned out the quiet clicking of the lock on the door. Almost, but not quite.

She felt Holt gather himself again, then stand up. But instead of moving into the aisle, he crouched next to the last cage. His gun was drawn, held in a steady hand as he waited for the back door of the clinic to open.

She heard the lock gave way. It was followed by a rush of cold night air that streamed past her face as the door opened. A moment later it closed quietly, and footsteps approached her.

Before they reached her, the footsteps turned and headed down the main aisle of the kennel. He had no idea they were waiting for him. He was headed for the main part of the clinic, where anything valuable, including the drugs, was kept.

Just before the footsteps reached the door that led into the rest of the clinic, Holt stepped out from behind the cages. Tory saw the arc of light as he switched on his flashlight, then heard his grim voice saying, "Hold it right there."

There was dead silence from the other side of the cages, and just as Tory sprang out of her seat she heard a voice begin to swear.

The obscenities spewed forth in a continuous, ugly stream, and she froze in her tracks as she recognized the voice.

For a moment she stood motionless as the old fear swept through her, then she stepped forward, rounded the corner and stood behind Holt. Bobby Duvall squinted into the light, holding one arm over his eyes as he strained to see.

A black cloth sack dangled from his hand, and his meaty frame was completely covered in black clothes. A black knit cap covered his blond hair, and he'd used something to darken his face. Neither she nor Holt spoke while he cursed at Holt, and when he finally wound down Holt said in a mild voice, "A little early for Halloween, aren't you, Duvall?"

Bobby spat an obscenity at him, then clamped his mouth shut. For a moment the three of them stood staring at one another, then Holt shifted and said, "What are you doing here, Duvall?"

His voice had hardened, but Tory could hear the anger

in it. She waited for Bobby to answer, wondering what he would say. But instead of answering, he suddenly lunged for Holt, shoving him to the side. Holt staggered against a cage and recovered quickly, but Bobby was already beyond him.

Without even thinking, Tory stuck out her leg as Bobby rushed past her. He stumbled and fell heavily to the floor, and Holt was on top of him immediately. The flashlight rolled along the floor as Holt fumbled with his handcuffs, and Tory picked it up and held it on Bobby as Holt snapped the cuffs into place and hauled Duvall to his feet.

Holt told him his rights in an expressionless voice, then pushed him toward the back door. But as Bobby turned, he saw Tory standing in the shadows holding the flashlight. Tory saw the hatred fill his eyes.

"This is all your fault, Tory Falcon," he shouted.

Amazingly, all her fear had dissipated. The sight of all that rage on Bobby's face only made her sad. She reached behind her to turn on the lights, never taking her eyes off Bobby's face. "How do you figure that?" she asked.

"You set me up. You and him." He jerked his head in Holt's direction. "You've had it in for me for years."

"That's not the way I heard the story." Holt's voice was carefully expressionless, but Bobby turned on him.

"What do you know, city boy? You thought you could come up here with your city ways and show us all how it's done, but you haven't been too successful, have you?"

"Successful at what, Bobby?"

Bobby's lip curled in a sneer. "Solving those murders, that's what. How many women have died now, Chief?"

"You tell me, Bobby."

Bobby opened his mouth to answer, then suddenly clamped it shut. The three of them stared at each other for a moment, then Holt took Bobby's arm. "Down on the floor, legs spread. And you'd better not move, Duvall. I'm feeling real nervous tonight."

Bobby's eyes filled with hatred again, but he clumsily lay down on the floor. Holt picked up his radio and said a few terse words into it, and in a few minutes police cars filled the parking lot. In another few minutes Officer Jack Williams had bundled Bobby into his car and driven away.

Holt led Tory from the clinic as the other officers entered it. They didn't speak as they walked toward her house. Leaving her sitting on the couch, he walked into the kitchen and picked up the phone. For the next hour he made call after call, talking in a low voice and making notes. Finally he hung up the phone, walked into the living room and sat next to her on the couch.

"What's happening?" she asked, reaching for his hand. He took it and held on tight.

"Not much right now. His father's down at the police station raising hell, but Duvall's staying locked up."

"Do you think he's the murderer?"

A muscle danced in Holt's jaw. "I don't know. He used his police background to find out about my wife, and he's admitted sending you that anonymous note. He sure as hell has the knowledge to avoid leaving clues. God knows he has a motive for going after you. But I can't tie him to the murders. Yet."

"The fingerprint."

"Yeah, we got lucky. The fingerprint is in the state lab, along with a set of Bobby's. We'll see if they match."

Tory drew in a long, shaky breath, afraid to hope. "So the murderer could be sitting in jail right now."

"It's possible, but I'm not going to assume he is."

"Who else could it be?" she asked, turning to Holt for reassurance. "I can't think of anyone else in Eagle Ridge who would know that much about police work. Can you?"

"Bobby does seem like the logical suspect. But I'm not writing anyone off." He glanced at her, and her heart contracted at the worry in his eyes. "It makes me nervous when things are too tidy."

"That's just because you have a devious mind," she said, pulling him closer. Suddenly she couldn't handle any more talk about murderers or who had been in her house that morning or what Bobby Duvall had been up to. The stress of the evening had frozen her into a mass of fears, and she wanted to forget about it.

She gripped Holt's hand as he swiveled in his seat to watch her, and she slowly relaxed, letting him see what was in her eyes. She was alive and with Holt, and right now that was all that mattered. Unexpected desire roared through her body with the force of a flash fire. Shifting her hand in his, she twined their fingers and brushed his mouth with hers.

His eyes were hooded, and when he raised his head to look at her the frustrations of the day were gone, replaced by a different kind of tension. His eyes darkened and smoldered as he curled one hand around the back of her neck. "You think I'm devious? You haven't seen anything yet."

"I thought I'd seen quite a bit," she murmured.

He smiled at her then, a slow, intimate gaze that swept her body and left her throbbing. "The best is yet to come."

Pulling her close, he locked his mouth with hers. She tasted his anger and frustration and the pent-up energy of the day in the fierce pressure of his lips. His tongue swept into her mouth, branding her with his possession and sweeping her into a dark tunnel of passion.

If he hadn't wrapped his arm around her and locked her body to his, she would have slid to the floor. Desire pulsed through her, hot and heavy, and she tried to press closer to him. He groaned deep in his throat as she shifted her hips against him.

He slid both hands into her hair, pulling it out of its haphazard braid. Holding her face still, he plunged his tongue into her mouth then slowly retreated, time after time, until need twisted inside her like a knife.

Drawing a ragged breath, she reached for the buttons on his shirt, but he suddenly caught her hands in his. "No," he muttered, his eyes slowly focusing as he looked at her. "Not tonight." His breath shuddered out of his lungs. "I want to love you tonight."

Her hands stilled on his shirt as she looked at him and saw the need in his eyes. His need to give to her, to set the pace, to be in control. And that was something she could give him, she realized as she let her hands fall to her side. Fear rustled in a far corner of her mind, but she pushed it away. Tonight she would give him the gift of herself, the one thing he needed from her right now.

"I'm yours," she whispered. *Forever,* she wanted to add, but couldn't bring herself to say the word. Holt was right, it seemed. It would have to be one night at a time.

He stared at her for a long moment, his face taut and hard. Passion flared in his eyes at her words, but he didn't say anything. Slowly he touched one finger to her lips, the pad rough against the sensitive, swollen skin, then he took her hand and led her out of the room and up the stairs.

The door to her bedroom stood open, all traces of red paint gone. She barely spared it a glance. Tonight nothing existed but the two of them, standing so close she could feel the waves of desire pouring off his body. Moonlight spilled into the room as he cupped her face in his fingers, then slowly swept his hands down her body.

Aching to touch his skin, to feel his heat and power, she reached again for his shirt. "Not yet," he murmured, bringing her hands to his mouth and pressing his lips against her palms. "Not yet. I want to savor you first."

Reaching for her blouse, he unbuttoned it, letting his knuckles caress her bare skin. Once the last button was free, he didn't pull the blouse off. Instead, he reached out and unclasped the front hook of her bra, easing the lacy froth of material off her breasts.

Then he stood and looked at her. Following his gaze, she saw her breasts hidden in shadows by her blouse, their nipples barely visible. Heat gathered and pulsed deep within her. She wanted him with a desperate physical ache.

"Touch me, Holt. Please."

He met her eyes, and the hot intensity she saw there only made her ache more. "Like this?" he asked in a low, guttural voice. He used one finger to ease the blouse off a nipple, then brushed it one time with the pad of his finger.

Her eyes fluttered closed, and she didn't try to disguise

the shudder that rippled through her. Her body clenched as tight as a fist, her legs trembling as sensation poured through her. "Yes," she moaned. "Yes."

The soft cotton of her blouse scraped against both nipples as he pushed the material away from her breasts. He reached out and cupped her breasts in his hands, his thumbs rotating around the tight peaks.

She swayed toward him as wave after wave of need pulsed through her. Blindly she reached for him. "I need you, Holt."

His hands slid from her breasts to her shoulders, and her blouse and bra fell to the floor. She stood in front of him, naked from the waist up, as he fumbled with the waistband of her slacks. In a moment they, too, fell to the floor.

Then he picked her up and laid her on the bed, following her onto the sheets. She pulled at his shirt. "I want to touch you, too."

"Later." He pressed her into the mattress, his mouth hot and needy on hers. "You can touch me all you want later."

His lips trailed over her neck, then he found her ear. Sucking gently on the lobe, he found her breast with one hand and pulled lightly on her nipple at the same time.

She writhed underneath him. Need snaked through her veins like a rope of fire, sheening her body with sweat and making her ache unbearably. When he moved down her body and took her nipple in his mouth, she bucked and arched, trying to get closer to him.

He raised his head, his eyes black and wild. "Do you want me, Tory?" he asked.

"You know I do." She could barely manage to form the words.

"Then let me take you." He reached for her hands, capturing them in one of his and slowly raising them above her head. His gaze swept her body as she lay stretched out on the bed, completely vulnerable to him. Then he looked in her eyes, and when she saw the vulnerability mixed with hot passion in his, suddenly she understood.

Not only did he need to be the one in control tonight,

he needed her to surrender to him, completely and without reservations. He needed her to need him tonight.

She beat back the brush of fear and smiled at him, a slow, seductive smile full of promise. "Take me, Holt. Please."

His eyes closed, and a noise that sounded almost like a growl rumbled from his throat. Bending his head, he circled one nipple with his tongue, making lazy passes around it without actually touching it. With her hands stretched above her head, she felt exposed and completely at his mercy. But instead of making her afraid, it only heightened the sensations coursing through her.

Holt shifted to the side. Then, watching her, he slid one hand down until it rested between her thighs. When he eased one finger inside her, she tensed and clamped her legs together. Keeping his eyes on her face, he took one nipple in his mouth and tugged gently on it, moving his finger at the same time.

Sensations crashed over her, tension coiling in her belly until she was afraid she would explode. "Holt," she cried, her body arching involuntarily toward him.

"Let go, Tory," he said in a thick voice. "Don't fight it. Give in to it. I want to watch you when you climax for me."

This was the gift he needed from her tonight, she told herself as she fought the instinctive panic. She looked Holt and felt the fear retreating. This was Holt. She trusted him. She could allow him to have control because he wouldn't abuse that trust.

Gradually she relaxed the muscles of her legs, watching him the whole time. He moved his finger again, deep inside her, and she swallowed as the tremor rippled through her. "I want you, Holt." She kept her gaze fixed on his face. "I want to feel you inside me."

He trembled, and she knew that only his iron will kept him in control of his body. He watched her face as she felt herself trembling on the brink. Suddenly she convulsed, flying over the edge into space, and he let go of her arms and pulled her close.

He held her until her shudders eased, then stood and peeled off his clothes. In another moment he was inside her, his arms wrapped tightly around her. Incredibly, when he began to move she felt the tension building again.

Moments later he groaned her name as his arms tightened convulsively around her. At the same time the shudders of release began to rack her body again, and she wound her arms and legs around him and clutched him to her.

She floated for a long time, the sound of his heart beating against hers the only link to reality. Finally he stirred and raised himself on his elbows.

"Are you all right?" he asked softly.

She smiled at him and let her hands slide down his back. "More than all right. I'm wonderful."

"Are you sure?" She could hear the doubt in his voice. "I know you didn't want…"

She laid a finger on his mouth before he could finish. "It's all right." She brushed her mouth over his. "I trust you. Completely."

His eyes darkened as he stared at her. "I don't deserve a gift like that." His voice was so low she could barely hear him.

"Why not?" she asked, holding his gaze. "You've never shown me any reason not to trust you."

He shifted abruptly and rolled onto his back, staring at the ceiling. "I told you before I don't know how much I have to give. I still don't know, Tory."

She looked down at him. "I guess we'll find out sooner or later, won't we?"

"I don't know."

She looked at him for a long time. Finally she cuddled into his side. "I have time. I'm not going anywhere. I'm back in Eagle Ridge to stay."

"How can you be so nonchalant about this?" he demanded. "Why don't you tell me to get out of your life?"

"Is that what you want?"

"You know damn well it isn't. But handing me the gift of your trust when I can't give you anything in return doesn't seem like a very good bargain to me."

"That's the thing about gifts," she said, closing her eyes and wriggling closer to his warmth. "You can't always choose when you get them, and sometimes you can't give anything in return. That's why they're called gifts."

Slowly his arm came around her, and he pulled her close. "All I know is I would die if I lost you."

And as she fell asleep in his arms, she knew that was enough. For now.

Chapter 15

Moonlight filtered down through the trees, illuminating the scene in flickering light. A woman knelt on the ground. Her features were blurred and indistinct, but the terror that pulsed from her grew until it filled the small clearing. The figure in front of the woman stood in the shadows, the faint light glinting off the blade of the knife he held, highlighting the serrated edge.

The trees murmured with glee and anticipation, the rustlings of their branches the only sound in the still night. Horror and hopelessness shimmered off the woman kneeling on the ground. The figure in the shadows took a step forward, and everything dissolved to red.

Tory woke with a start, her heart pounding, and looked around frantically. Instead of the trees and moonlight she expected to see, she was in her bed. Holt was lying next to her, one arm curled around her waist.

"Holt! Wake up," she said desperately.

He was instantly alert. In one smooth motion he reached next to the bed and pulled his gun out of the holster. Pulling back the safety with an audible click, he aimed it at the door. "What is it?" he asked softly.

"Put down the gun. Please. There isn't anyone in the house, as far as I know."

He searched the shadows for a moment, then listened intently. Finally he clicked the safety into place and lowered the gun. She noticed he didn't put it on the floor.

"I had another dream, Holt. A different one this time." She grabbed his arm. "I think he's about to kill someone, but it hasn't happened yet."

"What did you see?" He stared at her, his face suddenly intent.

"A woman in a clearing, with someone else. Someone who had a knife in his hand. It had a wavy edge." She gestured with one hand, grasping him tightly with the other. "She was afraid, Holt. I could feel it. She knew he was going to kill her, and she was terrified."

"But she wasn't dead yet?"

"No."

He slid out of bed and reached for his clothes. "Could you tell where it was?"

Closing her eyes, she pictured the clearing in her mind. She'd been there before, she was sure of it. Suddenly she remembered. "The place you found Spike. There was a little clearing just off the road that I saw before you got there. That's where it was."

"You're sure?" he asked grimly.

"I'm positive."

He stood next to the bed, fully dressed, looking at her. "After the last murder, I have to take this seriously. If there's a chance to save a life, I have to go. Especially since no one knows what kind of knife he used, but you just described it perfectly."

"I understand, Holt." She ignored the tendrils of fear that crept around her chest. "If he's in the woods with some other poor woman, he won't be here looking for me. Please hurry and go. I don't want anyone else to die."

"I'll call the station from the truck and get someone out here with you."

"Fine. Just go now, before it's too late."

With one last look Holt clattered down the stairs and into the night. A few seconds later his truck roared onto the highway.

She sat in the bed, soaking up his warmth, until she could no longer hear his truck. When the night was silent once more, she slid out of bed and threw on a pair of jeans and an old flannel shirt, shivering in the cold house.

"Spike," she said softly, bending to wake the dog. He looked at her instantly, wagging his tail, and scrambled to his feet. He had healed quickly, the smooth pink scar circling his neck the only evidence left of the abuse he had suffered.

"Let's go downstairs and make some tea while we wait for Holt," she said, waiting for him to follow her. "And we'll turn up the thermostat at the same time," she added as she started down the stairs. An icy draft swirled around her feet as she headed into the darkness.

She reached the bottom of the stairs and turned on the light just as Spike began to growl. Fear roiled in the pit of her stomach as she froze, staring into the corners of the room. There was no one there.

But the window next to the front door was open. Her heart pounding and her pulse skidding in her veins, she stared at it, paralyzed. Surely Holt would have noticed an open window when he left, she told herself with sick fear. Someone must have opened it after he left. She had to get out of this house.

Spike was still growling, staring at the kitchen. Her palms slippery with sweat, Tory saw her keys on the table next to the front door and grabbed them, then fumbled with the lock on the front door. The new dead bolt needed a key to open it, and her hands shook so much she couldn't push the key into the hole.

Spike yelped once behind her, then he was silent, but she didn't have time to look. Drawing in a sobbing breath, she finally managed to unlock the door. She pulled it open, but before she could bolt outside something hard and sharp poked into her back.

"Don't be in such a hurry to leave, Dr. Falcon," a voice murmured in her ear.

The keys dug into her palm as her hands dropped to her sides. She knew that voice. It was the one that had woken her from sleep so many times in the past few months. It was the voice that echoed in all her nightmares.

"Barber," she managed to say. "What are you doing here?"

"I would think that was fairly obvious. Haven't you figured it out yet?"

"Figured out what?" She stood perfectly still, barely breathing.

"You know what's going on." His voice took on an angry edge. "Don't try to tell me you don't. You know all about the three women who were killed."

"I know about them, yes. What does that have to do with you or me?" She bit on her lip hard enough to draw blood. She couldn't sound frightened. That was just what he wanted.

"I killed them. With this knife. The same one I'm going to use on you."

Slowly she turned to face him. The police officer she had faced on a Chicago expressway was gone. In his place was a nondescript fisherman, someone who would blend into the woodwork in the Upper Peninsula. In his checked jacket, jeans, baseball cap and boots he looked like three-quarters of the men who lived in Eagle Ridge. Only his eyes revealed the madness inside him.

"Why, Ed?" she asked softly. Her only hope was getting him to talk, stalling him until Holt could return.

His face twisted. "Because you ruined me. Because of you, I was thrown off the police force. I lost my pension and my respect. And now I'm going to finish what I should have finished months ago. You're going to pay for what you've done to me."

"Why did you kill those other three women? They didn't do anything to you."

"They got in my way. The first one looked like you. It wasn't until she was dead that I realized I'd made a mistake. The postmaster wouldn't tell me where you were, so I had to kill her."

"What about the third woman?" she asked, edging toward the open door. If she could get out of the range of that knife, she could run to her car. Barber was a big man, his bulk evident under the jacket. She was sure she'd be faster than he was.

It was almost as if he'd read her mind. Grabbing one of her arms, he pulled her into the room. "Don't get any ideas, Dr. Falcon. You're not going anywhere until I'm ready to go."

He stumbled over Spike, lying unconscious on the floor, and pushed the dog to the side with his boot. "I ought to kill that worthless mutt," he muttered. "If he hadn't growled I would have had you last night."

"You must have kicked him in the head. He's already dead," Tory lied, her lip quivering as she looked at the dog. She couldn't look at Barber, couldn't let him see the truth in her eyes.

Barber tightened his hold on her arm and shoved at Spike with his foot again. Tory winced. "Leave him alone. He can't hurt you."

"You're awfully softhearted, aren't you, Dr. Falcon?" Barber turned his attention to Tory, laying the blade of his knife against her chest.

"Why did you kill that third woman? She didn't have anything to do with me."

Barber shifted the blade as he watched her. "Someone had to die that night. It was supposed to be you, but you wouldn't come out to the trees. I called you, but you wouldn't come. So it had to be someone else."

"What do you mean, you called me?" A chill crept over her, far colder than the evening breeze coming in through the open window.

Barber jerked his head up and stared toward the road. Without a word, he opened the front door and pulled her through it, the knife at her throat. Dragging her behind him, he slipped into the woods as an Eagle Ridge police car pulled into her parking lot.

The trees were silent tonight. She didn't hear them call her name, didn't hear them whisper to her. The only sound was the wind, sighing through the branches.

The moonlight dimmed suddenly, and she looked up to see clouds scudding across the surface of the moon, hiding it from view. Panic quivered inside her as Barber pulled her deeper into the woods, farther into the darkness. She stumbled and sagged against him, losing her footing on the slippery pine needles.

Finally he stopped, breathing heavily. She could no longer see the lights from her house, and despair threatened to wash over her. *Holt,* she cried in her mind. *Holt, I need you. Help me.*

But Holt wasn't there. And when he arrived at her house, all he would find was an unconscious dog and an open window. He'd know what had happened, but by then it would probably be too late.

I love you, she told him silently. *Whatever happens, I love you.*

Barber peered in the direction of her house, listening. To distract him, she asked again, "What do you mean, you called me?"

He looked at her, triumph bright in his eyes. "I've been watching you. From the very beginning. As soon as I found out where you were, I've been here in the woods. Remembering. And waiting for my chance. You heard me. I saw that you did. When you walk from your house to the clinic, I saw the way you looked at me. I knew you heard me."

"The trees," she whispered. "I heard the trees calling for me."

"That wasn't the trees, that was me." He sounded angry, and the knife flashed in his hands.

"I thought it was the trees, but it was really you, hiding

in them." She looked at him with horror. "How could you do that?"

He stared at her, and his eyes glittered. The madness shone out of them, as bright as the edge of his knife in the moonlight. "Your blood. I tasted your blood once, and the blood remembers." His low voice quivered in the night air. "Blood always seeks its source. Once I realized that, I knew I could call you to me."

That wasn't possible. She knew it. But the mind was a powerful force, and if his beliefs and emotions were strong enough, that might be enough to forge some sort of link between them. "That's why I was able to see the scene of the last murder in my mind," she whispered. Fear twisted her heart in her chest as she realized what that meant. "Tonight you deliberately made me think you were killing someone else so Holt would leave," she said, tremors racking her.

"I had to get rid of that cop." Barber's face twisted with hate. "He never left you alone." His face relaxed into a gleeful smile. "But he's not here now."

"He will be soon. He'll be back."

"It'll be too late." As he talked, Barber had been pulling her into the woods. Now he stepped into a clearing, dragging her behind him. Horror washed over her as she realized it was the clearing where the last murder victim had been found.

If she didn't do something now, she would be killed. He'd cut her throat with that knife, like he'd done to three other innocent women. *I'm coming, Tory. Just hold on. I'm coming.*

Holt! He was on his way. Letting her feet drag in the dirt, she watched Barber slow down. She had to keep him talking until she figured out a way to escape or Holt got here.

"How did you find me up here? No one in Chicago knows where I went," she said, trying to keep the tremors out of her voice, focusing on Holt.

He gave her a look of sly satisfaction. "I watched you,

of course. When you left Chicago, I followed you up here. It didn't take much to find out you were thinking of moving back."

She had thought she couldn't be more terrified. She was wrong. "You mean you waited up here for me, waited for me to move to Eagle Ridge?" she whispered.

"I blended right in," he answered smugly. "If you dress the part and buy bait regularly, nobody pays any attention to a fisherman. Especially around here."

She shifted, testing him, and he immediately dug the knife deeper into her throat. Licking her lips, she asked, desperation in her voice, "What are you going to do after you kill me? Holt found one of your fingerprints at my house, you know."

"You're lying." The ugly anger flashed in his eyes again. "I know better than to leave fingerprints."

"But you did last time you were there. In red paint, outside the window you broke. By tomorrow morning, your name and description will be all over the country. They'll be looking for you, Barber. And it won't be like after you attacked me. It won't be just a slap on the wrist and losing your job. You'll be arrested and tried and convicted. You'll spend the rest of your life in prison." She clenched her hands at her sides, trying to stop them from trembling. Wave after wave of suffocating fear washed over her, trying to drown her. She struggled to keep her head above the deadly waters, knowing her only chance of escape was to convince Barber he was doomed.

Apparently Barber believed her. His face twisted with rage, but the knife he held to her throat trembled. "You're lying, bitch."

She didn't know how she did it, but she managed to smile. "Wait and see."

He reached out and grabbed her, digging his fingers into her arm. "You can be sure I will. Too bad you won't be around to see it."

Tory watched, paralyzed with fear, as he drew the knife from her throat. She screamed at herself to run, to take off, but her feet wouldn't move. All her energy was concentrated on the knife Barber held. He shifted it in his palm. She had made a mistake, she realized. Instead of buying time, she had infuriated him enough that he was going to kill her now.

Gathering herself, she prepared to tear her arm out of his grasp. Just as he pulled her closer to him and raised the knife over his head, an animal growled in the woods. As the knife flashed down, a ball of gray fur launched itself at them, its lip raised in a snarl and its teeth showing white in the darkness. The cold steel of the knife sliced into her at the same time a gunshot echoed off the trees.

Holt drove through the black night, his eyes searching for the place they'd found the dog. Desperate urgency pounded through his veins. If he didn't get there in time, another woman would be killed.

He spotted the tire marks on the shoulder of the road and swerved to the side, pulling the truck to a stop. As he got out of the car, one of the Eagle Ridge squad cars screamed past him, heading out to Tory's house. It disappeared into the darkness as he turned to the forest. At least Tory wouldn't be alone while he searched the woods.

The clearing Tory had described was easy to find, but there was no sign it had been disturbed. It stood deserted and silent, as quiet as the rest of the forest. The murderer could have heard him coming, Holt thought uneasily, and moved deeper into the woods. He could be standing silent behind a tree, waiting for Holt to leave.

But he didn't feel the presence of anyone else in the forest. There were no vibrations of fear or terror or anger. There was no tension in the air. There was nothing but the trees, tall and majestic, guarding their secrets.

Holt took another step into the woods, then another. Shining his flashlight on the ground, he looked for signs of recent disturbance, footprints, scuff marks in the dirt. Nothing. Not a pine needle was out of place.

Suddenly he froze. Faintly, far in the distance, he thought

he heard Tory's voice calling his name. *Holt, Holt, I need you.* The words crept into his consciousness like a breeze caressing his hair, as insubstantial as a curl of smoke.

It was his imagination, he told himself firmly. Tory was safely in her house, guarded by Jack Williams. She had seen the murderer at this spot, and after the last murder he had to trust her vision. Or whatever the hell it was, he thought uneasily.

Help me. The words sprang unbidden into his mind, louder this time, more frantic. He heard fear in Tory's voice, a fear that chilled him. It wouldn't hurt to check with Williams, he thought as he walked toward his truck. If he knew Tory was fine, he could concentrate on his search of the woods.

As he reached the Blazer he heard her again. *I love you. Whatever happens, I love you.* The desperate finality of her words twisted his heart in his chest. Something was wrong. He knew it with an ice-cold certainty. He threw himself into the truck and twisted the key in the ignition, fear and panic beating a primitive rhythm in his veins. He had to get to her.

"I'm coming, Tory," he muttered under his breath as the truck skidded onto the asphalt and leaped forward. His headlights cut through the darkness as he raced down the road. "Just hold on. I'm coming."

He didn't bother calling Jack Williams on the radio. He didn't need to. He knew what he'd hear.

Tory was in trouble. He knew it as well as he knew his own name.

Her whispered *I love you* had ripped aside the shroud he'd wrapped around his emotions, bringing them painfully awake. In spite of his caution, in spite of his warnings to himself, he loved her. He didn't have a choice. It was a part of him. But instead of joy, all he could feel was fear.

Her terror filled his mind and shriveled his soul, pulsating inside him like an evil black hole, swallowing everything that came close to it. He couldn't think logically. It didn't matter that he knew Tory would never go outside by herself or open the door to anyone. Something had happened, and she was in trouble. And a tiny voice at the back of his mind told him he might never get the chance to tell her he loved her.

He swerved into her driveway to see Jack Williams standing next to his truck, speaking into his radio. A fresh wave of fear swept over him. Leaping out of the car, he ran to where Williams stood.

"What?" he panted.

"She's not in the house, sir." Williams's face was grim. "When I got here, the window was open, the front door was unlocked and the dog was lying on the floor looking kind of dazed."

"Did you search the house?"

"From top to bottom. No sign of her." Williams swallowed and looked away. "No sign of a struggle, either, except for the dog."

Holt pushed past the deputy and headed for the woods at a dead run. Tory was in there. He knew it, just as he knew she needed his help. As he ran, he realized he knew where she was. She was in the clearing.

As he ran, a gray flash caught up with him. Spike's short legs were a blur as he struggled to keep up. Holt forced himself to go faster.

I'm coming, Tory. I'm coming. The words filled his mind like a mantra as he ran. *Hold on, sweetheart. I'll be there in a moment.*

He drew his gun as he approached the clearing. Two dark figures were silhouetted in the faint light, struggling. As the larger figure raised his hand, the knife he held glinted in the moonlight. Holt took careful aim and fired just as Spike launched himself at the figure holding the knife.

Tory stumbled forward as Spike attacked with a primitive growl. Holt reached her before she hit the ground and cradled her in his arms.

"Tory! Are you all right? Did he hurt you?"

She nodded weakly. "I'm fine. Almost."

Dark red blood covered the left side of her body. Rage

and fear slammed into him with the force of a locomotive, making his head roar. "You're hurt." He was amazed at how calm he sounded.

"It's not as bad as it looks," she said, reaching out for him with her right hand. "You came. I called for you, and you came."

He twined his fingers with hers and squeezed. "I heard you calling me, Tory. I knew you were in trouble."

She smiled as she closed her eyes and leaned her head against the tree. "I knew you would," she whispered.

"We need to get you to the hospital. How badly are you hurt?" he asked, afraid to hear the answer.

"It's just my arm. I think if we can get a tourniquet on it, I'll be fine until we get there."

He eased her to the ground and tore a strip out of his shirt. Then he tied it around her arm, cursing himself when she winced. But the flow of blood seemed to slow as he watched her carefully.

"Let's go," he muttered, scooping her into his arms.

"Wait. I saw Spike go after him right after you shot him. You have to make sure he's all right."

"He can rot out here, as far as I'm concerned."

"You don't mean that, Holt. I know you don't."

"He almost killed you. Do you think I care what happens to him?"

"I think you care about justice. And letting him bleed to death in the woods wouldn't be justice."

"It would be for him. Isn't that what he did to three women?"

"That's not the sheriff talking, Holt. That's the man. I don't want you to have anything else to feel guilty about when this is over."

He looked at her arm and tightened his mouth, but said, "All right. I'll have to put you down."

"I'm fine, Holt. Just make sure Barber's all right."

His arm tightened around her. "It's Barber?"

She nodded weakly. "I'll tell you all about it. Just get Spike away from him."

Holt stood up, battling the murderous rage that was building inside him. But he turned and headed toward where he'd seen Spike savaging Barber. He found the dog sitting next to Barber's unconscious form. Blood oozed from a bullet wound in the man's shoulder and from dozens of wounds that had been inflicted by Spike's teeth.

Holt made sure Barber was still alive. He had a pulse, although it was thready. Glancing at him one last time, Holt bent down and framed the dog's face with his hands. "He'll survive, buddy. But you did a hell of a number on him. You're a good dog, Spike."

Spike wagged his tail, his murderous rage against Barber seemingly forgotten, and when Holt hurried to Tory, the dog followed him.

As Holt bent to pick her up, he heard someone crashing through the woods and saw the beam of a flashlight bouncing off the trees.

"Over here, Williams," he called, and the next moment Jack Williams stepped into sight.

"Is she all right?" he asked, his worried gaze on Tory.

"She's got a cut on her arm, but otherwise she says she's okay." He nodded to his right. "The murderer is over there. Her dog got hold of him."

Williams walked over to Barber and stopped abruptly. "My God," he said, a note of awe in his voice. "Remind me not to get on that mutt's bad side."

"I'm getting Tory to a hospital. Do you think you can handle him?"

"No problem. He's not going to be giving anyone any problems for a long time."

Nestling Tory against his chest, Holt tried not to jostle her as he headed out of the woods. "Do you think you could tell me what happened, or do you want to wait?"

Her eyes had been closed, but she opened them to look at him. "I want to tell you," she said. Swallowing once, she tightened her arms around his neck and whispered, "He killed all three of those women. He told me all about it."

Her eyes clung to his. "He planted that vision in my

head to get you out of the house. I'll tell you later how he did it. As soon as you left, he came in through a window. When I went downstairs he was waiting for me. I tried to get away, but he dragged me into the woods.

"He told me a lot of things. I was trying to stall him, and told him you'd found his fingerprint. I thought it would scare him, but instead it made him mad. He was just about to cut my throat when you shot him." She touched her left arm with her right hand. "That's why he missed and cut my arm instead of my throat. Then Spike got hold of him."

Rage turned Holt's vision red, and he knew if Barber was in front of him right now he wouldn't hesitate. He'd kill him without a second thought for the fear and terror he'd inflicted on Tory.

She held her gaze steady on his, but couldn't hide the glaze of pain. He cursed Barber again. "He won't hurt anyone again, Tory. It's all over."

"I knew you would save me," she whispered. "I called you, and you came."

He stepped over a log and into the clearing around her house. "We're not at the hospital yet," he muttered.

He eased her into his car and buckled her in. Leaning her head against the seat, she closed her eyes. When they turned onto the main road, she turned and looked at him. He could see her pain and the way she tried to hide it. "It's a long way to the hospital, Holt." She tried to make her voice light, and failed miserably. "Do you think maybe you could break a few speed limits on the way there?"

"You bet," he said, keeping the rage out of his voice and trying to sound reassuring as he turned on his siren and pressed his foot to the floor. "I'll break the sound barrier if that's what it takes."

Chapter 16

Tory sat up in the hospital bed, the sutured and bandaged cut on her arm throbbing painfully. She had refused to take any painkillers, wanting to be alert when Holt came to visit her.

And she knew he would. She'd heard the nurses talking about him. Apparently he had refused to leave her alone, even in the emergency room when they were examining her and suturing her arm. A smile curved her lips as she thought about the tone of the nurses' voices as they discussed Eagle Ridge's chief of police. Holt had apparently made quite an impression on the staff of the small community hospital.

One of those nurses bustled through the door, holding a tray with a tiny paper cup and a fresh bottle of water. "Are you ready to take your medication, dear?" she asked.

"What is it?" Tory replied.

The nurse's lips compressed slightly. "It's a painkiller for your arm. You don't have to sit there and suffer, you know."

"I just want to be alert for a while longer."

The nurse's expression softened as she set the tray down next to the bed. "I guess I'd feel the same way if I had a guy like that coming to see me."

"A guy like what?" Tory asked carefully. She'd been half-unconscious when they'd arrived at the hospital, and she wanted more information than she'd gleaned from the nurses' overheard conversations.

"He just about tore this place apart, you know." The nurse stood by her bed, finally letting a smile crack her lips. "He wouldn't leave until you were in this bed and he could see you weren't going to die." Her smile widened as she looked at Tory. "He had a few choice words to say to our supervisor when she told him to leave. Her ears are going to be burning for a while."

"Oh," was all Tory could say.

The nurse fluffed her pillow, then straightened. "He'll be back, honey, and he's not going to mind if you're a little groggy. Take those pills and ease some of your pain."

"Maybe later," Tory murmured, suddenly anxious for the nurse to leave.

The nurse eyed her sternly, then sighed. "It can wait ten minutes, no more," she said as she walked out the door.

Tory tugged the thin hospital gown over her shoulders and pulled it together behind her, struggling to straighten it with one hand. A voice from the doorway said, "Need some help with that?"

"Holt!" Her heart began to pound as she watched him walk toward her. He wore jeans and an old shirt, and the lines of weariness and worry weren't completely gone from his face. But the light in his eyes glowed steadily as he pulled up a chair and sat next to her bed.

"How are you feeling?" he said softly.

"I've had better days," she admitted. Reaching out, she took his hand. "But I'm lucky to be alive, so I don't care how much it hurts."

"The doctor said you'll regain full use of your arm, although you'll have to have physical therapy for a while. Apparently no vital nerves were severed."

"That's good," she said, not taking her eyes off his face. "Did Barber survive?"

"Barely, but he'll make it. And he'll stand trial as soon as he's mended enough." Some of the light went out of his eyes as he stared at her. "What the hell happened? What was going on between the two of you?"

"First tell me what happened with Bobby Duvall."

Holt's face darkened. "He's sitting in a jail cell in Eagle Ridge, and he's going to stay there for a while."

"Even though he wasn't the murderer?"

"He broke into your clinic, Tory. That's a crime."

"He didn't get a chance to steal anything."

"Are you defending him?" Holt's voice rose in disbelief.

"Of course not. But right now I mostly just feel sorry for him."

He stared at her, then shook his head. "He would have stolen everything in your clinic. And you feel sorry for him?"

"I can afford to feel sorry for him. His life is ruined. He'll never be a big shot in Eagle Ridge again, and that was the only thing that mattered to him."

"He told us he needed money to keep up his image in town. That's why he broke into your clinic. But how did you know that?" Holt continued to stare at her, surprise in his eyes.

"It was obvious," she said gently. "Especially once I moved back here. That's all a bully ever really wants. To be important, to be somebody. Bobby won't ever frighten me again. He's too pathetic for that."

"And Barber won't have the chance to frighten you again. The only way he's ever going to see the light of day is through the bars of a prison cell." His voice was rough with concern.

"I know. The cloud over my life is gone. I can't feel it anymore."

"What does that mean? What was going on, Tory?"

Shifting her fingers in his, she gripped his hand. "It all

started when he attacked me in Chicago." She took a deep breath. "Remember I told you he bit me? Well, apparently when he tasted my blood he thought it gave him some sort of power over me. He was so sure about it that it actually made him able to forge some sort of link with me. That's why I had those vivid dreams, the ones of the accident and later the ones where I saw the scenes in the woods. I guess when he started thinking about me, reliving what had happened, I started seeing it, too."

"What about the last one, when you saw the woman being murdered?"

"He did that on purpose to get rid of you. He knew that as long as you were with me, he couldn't do anything to me. So he did that to lure you away."

"And I bought it, hook, line and sinker."

His voice was filled with disgust, and she tightened her hand in his. "Neither of us could know that was what he was doing. Until he told me, I had no idea why I was having those visions."

"And what about the trees?" he asked.

She could feel her face getting paler. "That wasn't the trees, that was Barber. He was always there, in the woods, watching me. He was using his mental hold on me to try to lure me into the woods. I just interpreted it as the trees calling me."

Holt shifted in his chair. "What happens now? Is he going to creep into your mind for the rest of your life, whenever he wants to?"

"No." She spoke with absolute certainty, knowing that she was safe from Barber forever.

"How can you be so sure?"

"Because his power over my mind has been replaced with one much stronger and more potent." Smiling, she loosened her hand from his and touched his face. "You heard me calling to you, didn't you? That's why you came to the house and went into the woods. You knew I was in trouble."

"How did you know that?" He leaned forward and watched her intently.

"Because I heard you when you were looking for me. I heard you telling me to hold on, that you were coming, that you would find me." She grabbed his hand again and squeezed tightly. "You blocked him out completely. All I could hear was you." Watching him steadily, she said, "The power of love is a thousand times stronger than the power of evil."

He shifted in his chair again. "Tory..."

She touched his lips with her hand. "You don't have to say anything, Holt. I know you're not ready to hear this, and you might not ever be, but I need to tell you. I love you. That's what saved me last night. That's what gave me the strength not to despair, not to give up. That's why I could hear you so clearly." She watched him through the mist in her eyes. "I had to live so I could tell you that I loved you. You have a right to know."

He watched her for a long time, then he slowly picked up her hand and turned it in his. "Why do you think I heard you so clearly last night?" he whispered. "Why do you think you were able to hear me? It isn't one-sided, Tory." He paused, swallowing, then looked at her. "I love you, too."

The raw truth stared at her from his eyes. His love was there, steady and real. But it was shadowed by fear. And as she watched him, she suddenly understood. He loved her, and he was terrified. Terrified of failing her.

Slowly she leaned forward to take his hand in both of hers. Her stiff, painful arm shrieked in protest, but she ignored it when she felt the tremor ripple through him.

"There's nothing to be afraid of, Holt," she murmured.

"There's everything to be afraid of," he retorted. "What if I fail you like I failed Barb? I couldn't bear it if I hurt you like that."

"That's the chance we both have to take. There are no guarantees in life, no promises that everything will be happily ever after. We can't control everything that happens to us." Her fingers entwined with his, and she looked at him, her eyes swimming. "All we can do is take the hand we're dealt and shape it into the best hand for us."

She held his eyes with hers, determined to make him understand that the past couldn't control their lives. It was a lesson it had taken her too long to learn. "It's up to us to make what we want of life, Holt. Both of us have baggage from our past, but if we work hard enough and love each other enough, it doesn't matter. Nothing matters except how much we love each other."

He slid onto the bed and drew her into his arms. "If that's true, then we'll have a deliriously happy sixty years or so together. But that doesn't mean I'll ever stop being scared of failing you."

"You will fail me sometimes, Holt," she said gently. "And there'll be times when I'll fail you, too. Neither of us is perfect." She felt her lips curling into a smile. "It would be pretty boring if we were. But because I love you, I'll forgive you, and you'll forgive me. Whatever happens, we'll face it together. And as long as we do, nothing can separate us."

"I can't believe how lucky I am to have found you, Tory." His hands cupped her face and his thumbs brushed over her cheekbones.

"I'm the lucky one, Holt. You helped me face the demons that have ruled my life for too long." She touched his hands. "We faced down death together, Holt. And we won. Surely we're not going to let life defeat us."

His thumbs stilled as he stared at her, his gray eyes softening in the harsh hospital lighting. Then slowly he drew her into his arms. "Not a chance. I'm afraid you're stuck with me for as long as you're willing to put up with a cop."

"I don't think I could accept anything less than a life sentence," she murmured, laughter in her voice.

"Hey, that was supposed to be my line." He leaned back and gave her a mock frown.

"I was just trying to prompt you," she said. Joy bubbled

through her veins and swelled in her chest until it felt like it would burst.

"All right, Dr. Falcon," Holt said, sliding onto his knees next to the bed. "I pronounce myself guilty of loving you to distraction. Will you put me out of my misery and say you'll marry me?"

"Yes," she whispered, "yes, yes, yes."

Epilogue

The wind sighed through the trees as Tory stepped through the door of her clinic into the warm red light of the setting sun. Spike darted between her legs and disappeared into the woods as Tory pulled the door shut and leaned against it.

It had been a year since she'd come back to Eagle Ridge. A lot had changed in that year, she thought with satisfaction.

Spike barked in the distance, and Tory pushed herself away from the door and headed for the trees with a smile. He must have spotted a rabbit again, she thought as she stepped into the woods.

"Spike! Come back here," she called.

After a moment he came bounding to her, a grin on his face and his tail flagging in the air. "Come on, fella. We've got big plans for tonight."

The dog followed her to the house, but before she could unlock the door and go inside she heard the roar of a familiar car engine behind her.

Her husband jumped out of the Eagle Ridge police car and came striding toward her. Wrapping his arms around her, he gave her a thorough kiss. Then, holding her shoulders, he leaned away from her and looked her over with a frown.

"You're still supposed to be working. Is something wrong?"

Wrapped in the safety of his arms, she reached up and brushed his hair off his forehead. "I'm fine. I closed the office early because I had a surprise in mind, that's all. What are you doing home so early?"

Reassured, Holt slowly smiled. "I had something in mind, too."

She felt the answering grin tugging at her mouth and struggled to keep her face straight. "What a coincidence."

"Isn't it, though? Do you want to tell me what your surprise was?"

"You go first."

"Well," he began, "there's this little restaurant in Escanaba. The ambience isn't much, but it holds a special place in my memory. I thought you might want to visit it tonight."

Tory felt her mouth tremble as a sheen of tears filled her eyes. "That sounds wonderful. Do you think I could have an extra large order of fries to go with my burger?"

"You're crying. What's wrong?"

"Nothing's wrong." The tears spilled out of her eyes and ran down her cheeks.

"Tory, you're crying." Holt's voice was infinitely patient.

"Everything makes me cry lately."

He laid a hand over the gentle swell of her abdomen. "So this is the kid's fault?"

She threw herself into his arms. "No, it's your fault for being so romantic."

"I hardly call taking you to a fast-food restaurant romantic." But his arms tightened around her.

"It is when it's the place we went on our first date, the day you picked me up from the hospital. It is when it's the first anniversary of the night we met."

His hand skimmed down her back. "We could go somewhere nice in Escanaba," he said.

"Don't you dare even think that. There's no place I'd rather go tonight."

"What about your surprise?"

She wiped her eyes and smiled at him. "I was just going to vary my usual routine of falling asleep on the couch by fixing you dinner. I thought that would be a real shocker for you."

Concern clouded his eyes. "If you're too tired we can go another night."

Tory shook her head. "Tonight will be perfect. I'll just fall asleep in your lap on the way home."

"And I'll carry you into the house and up to bed."

Tory stretched and twined her arms around his neck. "I like the way your mind works, Mr. Adams."

"I like everything about you, Mrs. Adams."

Holt kissed her, then leaned back and looked at her, his face serious. "I wasn't sure if you would want to be reminded about the night we met."

"What happened in Eagle Ridge last year was horrible, but something wonderful came out of it. I love you, Holt."

"And I love you."

Tory melted into her husband's arms as the sun dipped closer to the horizon. Orange, purple and pink exploded across the sky, and the wind murmured through the woods. The scent of pine curled around them, and they smiled as they looked at the trees.

And the trees smiled back.

* * * * *

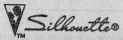

Take 4 bestselling love stories FREE

Plus get a FREE surprise gift!

Special Limited-time Offer

Mail to Silhouette Reader Service™

**3010 Walden Avenue
P.O. Box 1867
Buffalo, N.Y. 14240-1867**

YES! Please send me 4 free Silhouette Intimate Moments® novels and my free surprise gift. Then send me 6 brand-new novels every month, which I will receive months before they appear in bookstores. Bill me at the low price of $3.34 each plus 25¢ delivery and applicable sales tax, if any.* That's the complete price and a savings of over 10% off the cover prices—quite a bargain! I understand that accepting the books and gift places me under no obligation ever to buy any books. I can always return a shipment and cancel at any time. Even if I never buy another book from Silhouette, the 4 free books and the surprise gift are mine to keep forever.

245 BPA A3UW

Name	(PLEASE PRINT)	
Address	Apt. No.	
City	State	Zip

This offer is limited to one order per household and not valid to present Silhouette Intimate Moments® subscribers. *Terms and prices are subject to change without notice. Sales tax applicable in N.Y.

UMOM-696   ©1990 Harlequin Enterprises Limited

IN CELEBRATION OF MOTHER'S DAY, JOIN
SILHOUETTE THIS MAY AS WE BRING YOU

a funny thing
HAPPENED ON THE WAY TO THE
Delivery Room

THESE THREE STORIES, CELEBRATING THE
LIGHTER SIDE OF MOTHERHOOD, ARE
WRITTEN BY YOUR FAVORITE AUTHORS:

KASEY MICHAELS
KATHLEEN EAGLE
EMILIE RICHARDS

When three couples make the trip to the delivery
room, they get more than their own bundles of
joy…they get the promise of love!

Available this May,
wherever Silhouette books are sold.

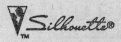

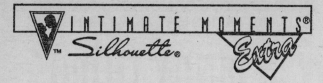

INTIMATE MOMENTS® ™ Silhouette® Extra

For an *EXTRA*-special treat, pick up

THE PERFECT COUPLE
by
Maura Seger

In April of 1997, Intimate Moments proudly features Maura Seger's *The Perfect Couple*, #775.

Everyone always said that Shane Dutton and Brenna O'Hare were the perfect couple. But they weren't convinced...not until a plane crash separated them, leaving Brenna at home to agonize and Shane to fight for his life in the frigid Alaskan tundra. Suddenly they began to realize just how perfect for each other they were. And they prayed...for a second chance.

In future months, look for titles with the EXTRA flash for more excitement, more romance—simply *more*....

INTIMATE MOMENTS® ™ Silhouette®

SILHOUETTE... Where Passion Lives

Order these Silhouette favorites today!
Now you can receive a discount by ordering two or more titles!

SD#05988	HUSBAND: OPTIONAL by Marie Ferrarella	$3.50 U.S. ☐ /$3.99 CAN. ☐
SD#76028	MIDNIGHT BRIDE by Barbara McCauley	$3.50 U.S. ☐ /$3.99 CAN. ☐
IM#07705	A COWBOY'S HEART by Doreen Roberts	$3.99 U.S. ☐ /$4.50 CAN. ☐
IM#07613	A QUESTION OF JUSTICE by Rachel Lee	$3.50 U.S. ☐ /$3.99 CAN. ☐
SSE#24018	FOR LOVE OF HER CHILD by Tracy Sinclair	$3.99 U.S. ☐ /$4.50CAN. ☐
SSE#24052	DADDY OF THE HOUSE by Diana Whitney	$3.99 U.S. ☐ /$4.50CAN. ☐
SR#19133	MAIL ORDER WIFE by Phyllis Halldorson	$3.25 U.S. ☐ /$3.75 CAN. ☐
SR#19158	DADDY ON THE RUN by Carla Cassidy	$3.25 U.S. ☐ /$3.75 CAN. ☐
YT#52014	HOW MUCH IS THAT COUPLE IN THE WINDOW? by Lori Herter	$3.50 U.S. ☐ /$3.99 CAN. ☐
YT#52015	IT HAPPENED ONE WEEK by JoAnn Ross	$3.50 U.S. ☐ /$3.99 CAN. ☐

(Limited quantities available on certain titles.)

TOTAL AMOUNT	$_____
DEDUCT: 10% DISCOUNT FOR 2+ BOOKS	$_____
POSTAGE & HANDLING ($1.00 for one book, 50¢ for each additional)	$_____
APPLICABLE TAXES*	$_____
TOTAL PAYABLE (check or money order—please do not send cash)	$_____

To order, complete this form and send it, along with a check or money order for the total above, payable to Silhouette Books, to: **In the U.S.:** 3010 Walden Avenue, P.O. Box 9077, Buffalo, NY 14269-9077; **In Canada:** P.O. Box 636, Fort Erie, Ontario, L2A 5X3.

Name:_____

Address:_____ City:_____

State/Prov.:_____ Zip/Postal Code:_____

*New York residents remit applicable sales taxes.
Canadian residents remit applicable GST and provincial taxes.

SBACK-SN4

▼ Silhouette ®

CONARD COUNTY

NIGHTHAWK
by Rachel Lee

Come back to Conard County in May 1997 with Rachel Lee's **NIGHTHAWK**, IM #781.

Craig Nighthawk was a loner. After being wrongly accused of a crime he hadn't committed, the reclusive Native American just wanted some peace and a chance to rebuild his ranch. But then he met Esther Jackson. She was on the run and stumbling badly, and of all the places on earth, this determined lady just happened to stop to catch her breath in his neck of the woods. What happened next was irresistible.

If you missed any of the other Conard County tales, here's your chance to have them sent to your door!

Silhouette Intimate Moments®

As seen on TV!
Free Gift Offer

With a Free Gift proof-of-purchase from any Silhouette® book,
you can receive a beautiful cubic zirconia pendant.

This gorgeous marquise-shaped stone is a genuine cubic
zirconia—accented by an 18" gold tone necklace.

(Approximate retail value $19.95)

Send for yours today...
compliments of ▼ *Silhouette*®

To receive your free gift, a cubic zirconia pendant, send us one original proof-of-
purchase, photocopies not accepted, from the back of any Silhouette Romance™,
Silhouette Desire®, Silhouette Special Edition®, Silhouette Intimate Moments®
or Silhouette Yours Truly™ title available in February, March and April at your favorite
retail outlet, together with the Free Gift Certificate, plus a check or money order for
$1.65 u.s./$2.15 can. (do not send cash) to cover postage and handling, payable
to Silhouette Free Gift Offer. We will send you the specified gift. Allow 6 to 8 weeks for
delivery. Offer good until April 30, 1997 or while quantities last. Offer valid in the
U.S. and Canada only.

Free Gift Certificate

Name: _____

Address: _____

City: _____ State/Province: _____ Zip/Postal Code: _____

Mail this certificate, one proof-of-purchase and a check or money order for postage
and handling to: SILHOUETTE FREE GIFT OFFER 1997. In the U.S.: 3010 Walden
Avenue, P.O. Box 9077, Buffalo NY 14269-9077. In Canada: P.O. Box 613, Fort Erie,
Ontario L2Z 5X3.

FREE GIFT OFFER
084-KFD

ONE PROOF-OF-PURCHASE

To collect your fabulous FREE GIFT, a cubic zirconia pendant, you must include this
original proof-of-purchase for each gift with the properly completed Free Gift Certificate.

084-KFD

COMING NEXT MONTH

#781 NIGHTHAWK—Rachel Lee
Conard County
After being wrongly accused of a crime he hadn't committed,
Craig Nighthawk just wanted to be left alone. Then he met
Esther Jackson, who was fighting her own battles but needed his
protection to make peace with her past...and ensure a future for them
both.

#782 IN MEMORY'S SHADOW—Linda Randall Wisdom
Single mom Keely Harper had returned to Echo Ridge to build a new
life. But when terrifying memories came flooding back, she sought
safety in the arms of town sheriff Sam Barkley. He knew the truth about
her past, and he was willing to go above and beyond the call of duty to
safeguard this troubled mother.

#783 EVERY WAKING MOMENT—Doreen Roberts
U.S. Marshal Blake Foster should have known better than to get
involved with prime murder suspect Gail Stevens. But now was too late
for regrets. Time was running out to prove her innocence—and his own
love—because Gail had fallen into the hands of the real killer....

#784 AND DADDY MAKES THREE—Kay David
Becoming a dad to the daughter he'd never known about meant that
Grayston Powers had to marry her guardian, Annie Burns, because
Annie wasn't about to abandon the child she considered her own. They
insisted it was a marriage in name only...but could they really deny the
passion between them?

#785 McCAIN'S MEMORIES—Maggie Simpson
Defense attorney Lauren Hamilton had a weakness for sexy bad boys,
and Jon McCain, her rugged amnesiac client, certainly fit the bill. She
needed him to remember something, *anything*, to help her clear his
name. Because her case—and her heart—hinged on the secrets of this
man without a memory....

#786 GABRIEL IS NO ANGEL—Wendy Haley
Rae Ann Boudreau would do *any*thing to serve a summons on a
deadbeat dad—even if it meant going undercover as a belly dancer.
Vice cop Gabriel MacLaren would do *any*thing to protect his star
snitch—but falling for the gorgeous process server who was threatening
his case hadn't been part of the plan....